THE MISSING

KIERSTEN MODGLIN

KIERSTEN
MODGLIN
love lies light

To my PawPaw Chet—
for teaching me to survive in the woods long before I was old
enough to have ever survived in the woods.

"Maybe there is a beast…
Maybe it's only us."

WILLIAM GOLDING

CHAPTER ONE

The sun was a liar. It sat high in the sky, shimmering with warmth and happiness. *Paradise*, it seemed to scream. *Welcome to paradise.* It gave no warning of what was to come.

I'd spent most of the morning lying on a lounge chair that was equally close to the beach and the cabana, where a man dressed all in white had been refilling my drinks as quickly as I could empty them.

I'd been fighting with my husband that morning, about work, as always. Because who brings their wife on a tropical vacation and plans to spend most of each day in the room at the resort, *so they don't get behind?*

Psychopaths, that's who.

So, I sat and I sipped drinks and read on my Kindle, and I tried to pretend that I wasn't bored out of my mind and all alone on a vacation that was supposed to be perfect.

I'd built it up in my head as perfect, anyway. But as soon as we'd arrived, I realized that wouldn't be the case.

As usual, my husband was too busy, too popular to fit me into his schedule.

The thing about sitting alone at the beach is that people either think you're very sad—and they give you that pitiful expression somewhere between a sorrow-filled frown and an encouraging smile whenever they walk past you—or they assume you're very lonely and try to sit next to you and strike up a conversation. I was in the mood for neither.

That's what I assumed was happening as the man jogged up the beach toward me. I tried to look away, to hope that he was headed in another direction, but he kept his body aimed straight for me, his smile growing as he drew nearer. He was tall and fit, with tanned skin that said he either lived in the area or worked outdoors a lot. He wore a pair of khaki pants and a lime green T-shirt, with dark sunglasses protecting his eyes from the sun. I looked up, shielding my own eyes and preparing to tell him that I was just waiting for my husband, *thankyouvery-much*, when his question interrupted me.

"Would you like a free boat ride?"

I furrowed my brow at him, so confused by the question that had come from nowhere. "Excuse me?"

"Boat," he said, his accent—I assumed Mexican? Cuban, maybe?— was thick, his finger outstretched, pointing toward the boat in the water. *Boat* was an under-statement. The thing was a small-sized yacht, blasting music while a few people danced on its upper deck. "Would you like a ride?"

I sat up straighter, laying the Kindle in my lap. "I'm

2

sorry, I don't understand… You want me to ride in your boat?"

He laughed, putting a hand to his chest. "Not *my* boat. I work on it. We have an extra spot…if you want…"

I looked around, waiting for him to laugh and say I was getting pranked. "Why?" Because I looked pathetic, sitting alone on the beach, most likely.

Sure enough, he gestured around me. "You are the only one out here by yourself, and we have an extra spot. Just one. My captain says to offer it to someone."

I eyed him. "Where are you going? The boat, I mean."

"Just around the coast and back." He pointed to the drink next to my chair. "Free booze, music, ahh, it'll be a lot of fun." He shimmied his shoulders, snapping his fingers as he danced to the music from the boat.

"Is it like a private event, or…"

"No, *Señorita*. We didn't get fully booked today, so sometimes the captain lets us invite a few extra people. We're just looking for one more." He glanced back toward the boat. "It's okay if you don't want to go… I can find someone else. I just thought you looked bored."

I stared at the Kindle in my hand and lifted the beverage to my lips, finishing the last of it. The people aboard the boat appeared normal.

No, correction, they looked like they were having fun. Something I desperately needed to do.

"Can I invite my husband?" I pointed behind me. *Not that he'd go…*

The man glanced toward the boat again, and I saw a group of crewmen dressed like him coming out onto the decks. "No, *Señorita*. I'm sorry. We have to leave now. It's okay... Maybe next time?" He waited.

I chewed my bottom lip, thinking for a moment. The waiter from the cabana approached me, a drink in his hand. What would that make it? My sixth for the day? I shook my head, handing him the empty glass. "No, thank you. I'm done for now. Charge the drinks to my room, and this is for you." I pulled the twenty-dollar bill from my phone case and handed it to him as a tip. "Can you do me a favor, though? If my husband comes looking for me, can you tell him I went on a boat ride? Tell him I'll be back in a few hours?"

"Yes, ma'am," the man said, tucking the cash into his pocket. "Thank you, ma'am."

With that, I turned to the grinning man, tucking my Kindle and phone into the oversized pocket of my bathing suit cover and following his lead toward the boat.

When we reached the dock, he gestured for me to walk across the metallic ramp and onto the yacht. I did so slowly, my footsteps heavy and loud, the alcohol and the heat beginning to wear on me. I hadn't noticed the buzz before, six drinks wasn't much compared to what I normally drank in an evening, but when you added that to the heat, apparently it hit harder.

As I neared the edge, feeling even unsteadier, two men appeared with their hands outstretched, to help me climb aboard.

"Welcome aboard, beautiful," one said. I stared at his thin mustache and dark eyes, offering a small smile. The man who had invited me jumped onto the deck with ease —no hand holding for him—and they immediately began untying the ropes that had been holding us to the dock onto the sides of the boat.

I walked forward.

"Drinks and music are upstairs, *Señorita*. Facilities downstairs," I heard the man call, and I nodded, waving a hand over my shoulder at him. "Make yourself comfortable."

As I walked across the deck, the sun seemed warmer on the boat, its rays beaming down on me. I looked back at the shore. I don't know why I did it. I knew he wouldn't be there, but somehow... Somehow I had hope that he'd have sensed me leaving. That he'd been keeping an eye on me from the window of our room and that, upon seeing me getting on a strange boat with strange people, he might've shown a little concern. I pictured him running across the beach, a hand in the air as he shouted for me, but it was just a mirage. Not even the good type of mirage. I knew this one was fake the entire time.

He would not run for me.

He would not notice that I'd left.

There was a good chance he wouldn't even know I'd been gone by the time I returned.

About that last part, at least, I was very wrong.

CHAPTER TWO

The boat cruised along the coastline, the wind whipping through my hair as the music blared and the drinks continued to flow. I was on my second glass of champagne—pacing myself, I thought—when the first of the boat's passengers approached me.

"This seat taken?" He gestured to the padded bench seat next to me, where I could sit with my back pressing into the railing, looking out over the ocean as we sailed.

I looked at it and back at him. He was young, probably mid-twenties, with wild and wispy black hair and long, pale limbs. He looked to be from Southeast Asia, and when he smiled, just part of his upper lip raised as he stared down at me with dark, kind eyes.

I shook my head slowly, allowing him to take the seat. When he did, he rested an arm on the metal railing behind us and looked out over the water. "Nothing like it, is there?"

I inhaled deeply, trying to pretend I was enjoying the

view, rather than obsessing over whether or not my husband had yet noticed my absence. "It's beautiful."

He looked back in my direction, his eyes meeting mine in a way that, if we were in a movie, he might've whispered, "No, *you're* beautiful." But, we weren't in a movie and I was twice his age, so instead, he just smirked at me and nodded.

"Where are you from?"

"You wouldn't have heard of it," I said simply.

"Try me." His grin widened.

"Leiper's Fork, Tennessee."

He stared at me for a moment, so long that I thought he might be going to say that he did, in fact, know my tiny little town. Instead, he grinned finally. "Is that near Nashville?" That was usually the question, because everyone only knew Tennessee because of Nashville or Gatlinburg.

"Sort of," I said, unable to hide the small smile on my lips. "You? Where are you from?"

"Here," he said. "Well, Florida. I grew up in Naples; moved to Key West when I graduated."

I didn't know if he meant high school or college.

"And, let me guess, you're a lifeguard now?" I gestured toward his plain, white T-shirt and red trunks. All he was missing was a dot of white zinc on his nose.

"Close," he teased. "I'm an offshore diver."

"How is that close?"

"Well"—he pulled one leg up under his lap—"instead of saving one life, I save thousands. Without me, this beautiful ocean you're enjoying would be filled with oil."

"You're solely responsible for that, then?" I quipped.

He studied me for a moment too long, and I worried

that he hadn't read my sarcasm, but then the smile returned. "Yep, it's all on me."

"Well, I guess thanks are in order, then." I tipped my drink toward him.

He sighed dramatically, placing his arms back around the railing. "All in a day's work."

I laughed, my face burning from his attention. It's not that I was attracted to him—I was a married woman, after all—but the combination of alcohol and attention I hadn't seen from a man, any man, in years had me feeling giddy and light. Like the fizz at the top of a champagne flute.

"So, what about you? What do you do?"

I thought for a moment. There was a time when I could've answered honestly, proudly. But those days were long gone. Instead of answering, I looked out at the water, realizing for the first time that I'd lost sight of the shoreline in the distance. I tried to shove down the sudden unease at being in the middle of the ocean surrounded by strangers.

What had started out as a stubborn, fleeting urge to get back at my husband had turned into something real. Here I was, in the middle of the sea, with no one I knew having a clue where I was. I pulled out my phone, planning to text my husband and let him know where I was, but I had no service. I groaned. Suddenly, I felt very foolish indeed. I swallowed, batting back tears as I felt them forming in my eyes.

"Is everything okay?" he asked, interrupting my thoughts. I glanced his way, having nearly forgotten he was there, still waiting on an answer as to what I did for a living.

"Sorry, I—I'm just realizing this was a stupid idea." I tucked my phone back into my pocket. The heat I felt on my face wasn't coming from the sun any longer, but rather the embarrassment and worry swelling inside of me.

"What was?" he asked, leaning toward me as the wind picked up.

I put my head in my hands, mortified that I was suddenly having a breakdown aboard the fancy vessel in front of this carefree, entirely too-handsome man. "I shouldn't be here right now."

He chuckled, as if I were making a joke. "Well, sorry, sweetheart. It's a little too late to decide that."

I furrowed my brow at him. "This was a stupid decision. I don't even know anyone on this boat, and I…" There was no point in continuing to rant. He was right. I was here, and I was staying until the boat ride ended.

He tipped his bottle of lager toward me. "Hell, I don't know anyone on here, either. That's half the fun of it, isn't it? Total freedom." He winked. "Live a little."

I scowled but didn't say anything else. It wasn't worth the argument. Besides, he was right. And even if he wasn't, there was nothing either of us could do about it. I'd have to wait until we returned to land, which, as the sun had begun to sink closer to the horizon, I had to believe would be soon.

At realizing I wasn't going to argue, he said, "What are you in such a hurry to get back to anyway?"

"My life, maybe?" I scowled, a bite to my words.

"What part of this isn't your life?" he asked, running a hand through his hair. "You're living it, aren't you?"

"Just forget it." I pulled my legs up onto the seat with me, wrapping my arms around my knees. I can't explain it. I don't know why the nagging feeling that something was going to go wrong had filled my insides with such vengeance, but as we watched the endless ocean, the gap between us and the shore growing larger and larger, my inner voice screamed that I'd made a terrible mistake.

Finally, the man gave up, walking away from me with a simple shrug. He made his way across the deck, toward the only other girl on our boat. She was younger and outgoing, her short, black curls flowing in the breeze as she danced to the music that I'd all but tuned out. He began dancing behind her until they were both laughing so hard they had to stop.

I couldn't help staring at them with envy. I'd been carefree once, too. What had happened to that girl?

Life.

That was the answer. Life and a mortgage and a husband and responsibilities. This was the first thing I'd allowed myself to do in so long that felt free and reckless. I struggled against the worry, trying to bring myself peace.

I stood from my seat, making my way across the deck and toward the bar and, as I did, the boat rocked with a big wave. I grabbed hold of the wall, just as everyone braced themselves. A bottle of beer slammed to the ground and rolled across the floor, spilling the wheat-yellow beverage as it went.

Just then, the engine stopped.

My heart sped up, my throat suddenly dry as I looked

at the bartender, and then around at the others. Everyone seemed just as confused as I felt.

"What the hell happened?" one of the men called. A dozen or so of the people from the deck—crew members, I realized, despite their casual clothing—disappeared below deck.

I stared at each of the remaining faces in silence, my breath loud in my ears as chills swept over my arms. Finally, my gaze fell back to the bartender just as a few members of the crew reappeared, following two men in uniforms that matched the man who'd invited me. Their stern expressions looked official.

"It's okay," one of them said, holding out his hands in a gesture of reassurance. "Nobody panic. We're having an issue with the engine. We can fix it, but we need to get to the nearest port in order to do it."

Relief cascaded over me, but it was watered down in an instant as he went on, "There's a port a few miles ahead. We're going to ask you to bear with us. Once we port, you'll have to disembark until we're able to get it fixed."

"So, you aren't taking us home?" the young Black woman with short hair asked, her voice shaky.

"Unfortunately, we're too far to make it back safely. We need to make it to the closest port."

"Which port is it?" the man who'd been talking to me earlier asked, obviously well-versed in the area.

"It's…" The man looked behind him at the other silent members of the crew. "It's not a public one. But it's our only option. Once we arrive, our crew will see you safely to shore as we work to get it fixed and get everyone back aboard. There'll be a beach there, room for you to get out and play. So, just think of this as an extra bit of fun." He winked, but there was a sense of trepidation about him that matched my own. Something was more wrong with the ship than they were telling us, I could tell. Were they going to be able to fix it? What would happen if they couldn't?

"How long will it take?" one of the other passengers asked, a thin man with a clean-cut pompadour and glasses.

"It shouldn't take more than a couple of hours," he said. "Maybe even less. We won't know for sure until we're able to assess the damage. Worse case, we'll call for another boat to pick you all up once we're there. We'll have you home before long, don't worry. For now, we ask that everyone stay away from the railings, come down to the lower deck, and take a seat. We want to keep you safe, first and foremost."

He nodded slowly, waiting for us to move toward him, and as we did, I saw the relief in his eyes. He was worried. They all were. Each of the crew members had the same sickly look on their face.

As they led us to the lower deck and we each took a seat on the padded benches around the edge, I pressed my back to the plastic wall behind me, taking deep breaths. Was this really all of us? It had seemed like so many people before, but I realized now that most of the passengers had been crew, caterers, and waiters. As it turned out, there were only five of us who were actually guests on the boat. Me and the Black woman with short, curly hair, the cocky Southeast Asian man who'd talked to me earlier, the skinny, glasses-wearing man who held a book tightly in his hands, and another young man with large biceps and wild and curly blond hair, who'd been joking around with the bartender for most of the ride, downing drinks quicker than even I had been. That man was staring at me then, apparently aware that I'd been studying him, and I looked away too quickly.

I pulled my phone from my pocket and checked the time. We'd been on the boat for more than four hours, though it felt simultaneously much longer and much shorter.

I glanced at the top corner, checking and confirming that I still had no service. Had he noticed I was gone yet? Did he even care?

I shoved the phone back into the pocket of my bathing suit cover and closed my eyes just as the engine fired up again. When I opened my eyes again, the crew had disappeared, and we were left alone.

They hadn't turned the music back on after it had been cut off with the engine dying, so we sat in agonizing silence, watching the waves as we rode over them carefully. What had once seemed beautiful and peaceful now carried an ominous tone.

Half an hour later, I saw the outline of a landmass forming in the distance and stood without thought. I lifted a hand to my eyes, trying to shield them from the bright sun directly behind the land as I tried to make it out.

I heard footsteps and glanced beside me just as the woman approached me. She gave a halfhearted smile and nodded her head toward the port. "Is that it?"

"I'm guessing so," I said. Up close, I realized she was even younger than I'd initially thought. If she was twenty-one, it'd be a shock to me. How had she ended up on the boat? Which one of the men was she traveling with?

Though it must've been longer, it seemed like only minutes had gone by when I could finally make out the shoreline and the lack of a port. The island, green with vast wilderness and untouched mountains, had a large stretch of beach, but no sign of civilization anywhere.

"That doesn't look like a port, does it?" the thin man with glasses said as he made his way to stand beside me. He squinted his eyes, staring out over the water as he voiced what I knew we were all thinking.

"No," I said simply. "It really doesn't."

"What's going on here?" the cocky man who'd been talking to me earlier asked loudly. We turned around to see him confronting one of the crew members as he walked out across the deck.

The man stared at him, not speaking, and so the one who was a passenger went on, growing angrier. "Where are you taking us? What's going on?" He gestured toward the island as we grew closer.

"Land," the man said, with a strong accent, as he wagged a finger toward land. "We make land."

"But where the fuck is that land? They said we were going to a port! There's no port here. Where are we even at?"

"I..." the man's face contorted as he tried to understand what he was being asked. "I...sorry. Little English." He smiled politely but shook his head. He used one hand to sail through the air, as if it were the boat, docking carefully next to the other hand. "You be safe."

"How do we know that? We need to speak to the captain. This isn't what I signed up for," he demanded, growing more agitated.

The crewman looked terrified as he forced a smile and took a step back. "I...sorry...Captain very busy."

"Like hell he is!" the man screamed, taking an aggressive step toward the trembling crewman.

Without thinking, I rushed forward, grabbing the passenger's arm to stop whatever was about to happen.

"Ease up, will you?" I demanded harshly. "He obviously doesn't understand what you're saying."

Taken out of the moment, he stared down at me, confusion weighing heavily on his expression before he jerked his arm from my grasp.

"Little Miss Terrified suddenly got some nerve, didn't she?" he snarled, the warmness from our earlier conversation gone.

"Just let him get back to work."

Without another word, he grumbled under his breath and walked away. The crewman scurried away from us just as quickly, and I turned back to the rest of the group. They'd been watching with intensity, and I couldn't help noticing a hint of shock and worry in their eyes.

A few minutes later, the engine had been shut off again, and we were floating on the tide to get near the shore. I walked back toward the railing, leaning out over it slightly. Once we'd come to nearly a complete stop, I watched as several members of the crew launched themselves over the railing, splashing into the chest-deep water as they began pulling out ropes from the sides of the boat.

What were they planning to tie us down to? There was nothing here…

"If I could just have you all direct your attention over here," a voice called from behind us, and we turned around. The crew member who'd told us about the problems earlier was standing behind us, looking very serious. "While they're getting us secured, I'm going to have you five guests go ahead and board the dinghy so we can get you to safety and get everything repaired as quickly as possible." He gestured toward the opposite side of the boat where I saw a ladder hanging over the edge.

One by one, we disembarked from the ship, climbing into the small, inflatable dinghy with barely enough room for the five of us, plus the man already on board.

I was third to climb down, the boat shaking and swaying under my feet and causing me to feel seasick and nervous all at once. I put my hand over my pocket, checking to be sure my phone and Kindle were still there.

The crewman sat in the back, one hand on the tiller, and instructed us on how to distribute our weight evenly, directing the first man on the left side, since he was on the right, and the next on the right, then me, on the left next to the man I'd spent my morning talking to.

We sat on the edges, our feet tucked under the inflatable sides, as we waited for the young woman to board. Once she was on, sitting next to me, we were ready to go, and I heard the small engine start up.

We were off in a flash, and this ride, were it not for the circumstances, was actually a little fun, despite the fact that I kept worrying I was going to fall overboard with each curve, turn, or wave.

He steered us around the boat silently, his gaze trained on the land up ahead, and within minutes, we'd reached the shore. He cut off the engine and stood, leaping over the side and onto the wet sand. He held out a hand, helping the young woman and me off the boat before the men stood. The thin one took his hand, wobbling out of the boat carefully, but apparently he had taken too long, as the other two men jumped out around him, causing the boat to shift and him to fall. His body launched forward, and though the driver tried to catch him, his face slammed into the side of the boat.

"Oh!" I cried, reaching for him as I tried to get him to stand up. His upper lip was bloody already, but he swiped it away.

"My bad, bro," the blond one said through his giggles.

"I'm alright," he said, his cheeks pink with embarrassment. He stepped overboard gently, and I glared at the men, not a hint of regret in either of their eyes. I couldn't wait to get away from them.

Once we were all safely on land, the man climbed back on the boat.

"You're leaving?" I asked.

"I have to help..." he said softly. "I...be back soon. Relax." He gestured toward the beach. "Have fun." With that, the engine started up and he was backing away. We watched him zip off toward the yacht, and I turned back to the group.

"Are you sure you're okay?" I asked the man with glasses.

He nodded, rubbing a finger over his swollen lip again. "I'm fine, thanks. Just a bump. I bleed easily."

I nodded. "So"—my gaze fell to the rest of the group— "what should we do?"

"I don't know," said the blond man. "But I need to take a leak." He walked away from us, hurrying across the beach toward the tree line. I looked to the girl, who appeared the most frightened of us all.

"How are you doing? Are you okay?"

"I'm fine," she said, but there was no confidence in her tone.

"Well, while the three of you sit around and cry, I'm going to take advantage of swimming in uncharted waters," the cocky man said, darting away from us and farther down the beach. He tore off his white T-shirt, leaving just the red lifeguard shorts, and yipped and yelled as he ran into the water. Once he was out far enough, he dove down underneath it, resurfacing with a loud and proud *whoop*.

"Well, this is going to be fun, isn't it?" The man with glasses laughed, still holding his lip to stop the bleeding.

"Apparently so..." My gaze fell on the girl, who'd hardly said a word, her eyes still wide with shock and worry. "Are you sure you're okay?"

"I'm not feeling super well," the girl said, touching her chest suddenly. "I'm lightheaded. Do you think I could lie down?"

"Of course," I said. "Let's move up to dry sand." I put an arm around her waist, and the man moved onto her other side, doing the same. Together, we led her farther up the beach and laid her down. "Here you go." I pressed a hand to her forehead. "You're trembling... Are you nauseous? Weak? Do you have any health conditions?"

"No," she said, blinking her eyes slowly. "It just hit me all of the sudden... Adrenaline, I guess. I'm feeling dizzy."

The man spoke up. "Have you eaten anything today? The heat could've caused you to become exhausted. Or your blood sugar could be dropping."

"Just snacks on the boat. Cheese and some of the fruit. I'll be fine, honestly, it's probably just the heat." She tried to sit up, but shook her head, practically dropping back onto the sand.

"Okay, well, don't try to overdo it. Just rest. I'm going to go and see if I can get someone's attention to bring you some water. You may be dehydrated."

"I can go," the man said, his hand brushing hair out of her face. "If you want to stay with her."

"Okay, sure, that'd be great," I said. "Just tell them we need some water. Maybe some crackers too, if they have any."

"Thank you," the girl whispered, meeting my eyes with embarrassed tears in her own. "I feel so stupid. I don't know where this came from."

"You don't need to feel stupid. We're all out here drinking in this heat. It's bound to happen. And being on the dinghy could've made you sea sick, too. There's a lot at play here." I patted her arm gently as the man stood.

Suddenly, he yelled. "Hey!"

I looked up at him, then followed his gaze. "What is it—"

My stomach dropped.

The men were no longer in the water.

The boat was drifting away from shore.

No.

I stood up next to him. *"Hey, wait!"* I called, waving my arms in the air. What was happening? Did they need the boat farther out to fix it? Why hadn't they told us that?

Noticing what was happening, the other two men rushed toward us, screaming and waving their hands, too. The cocky man, still sopping wet, jumped up and down, his hands in the air. The blond cupped his hands around his mouth, shouting after them.

"Don't forget us!"

"What are you doing?"

"We're still here!"

"Hey! Wait!"

We shouted and waved and hurried across the sand, our cries becoming more and more panicked. I kept waiting for someone to come out onto the deck and announce that everything was fine, that they just needed everyone on board to fix the issue, but it didn't happen.

Instead, as we neared the place where the sand changed from white to tan, dry to wet, I heard a sound that sent chills down my spine.

The boat's engine started up.

"No, please!" I shouted, feeling my knees grow weak underneath me.

My first thought was of my husband.

Then my parents.

What would they think?

Would they ever know what had happened?

Would they find us?

The boat sailed farther away, no bodies moving on the

decks to see that they'd left us. But they had to know, didn't they? How could they have possibly forgotten?

But, if they hadn't, could they really be doing it on purpose?

As I watched it sail into the horizon, growing smaller and smaller as it picked up speed, my gaze fell to the man I'd spoken to on the boat. He leapt into the water and was attempting to swim out after the boat, his head the only thing visible as he screamed after it. The rest of us stood on the shore, watching our worst nightmare unfold.

At least, we thought it was our worst nightmare.

Watching that boat sail away, knowing we were stranded on the island, was just the beginning.

We had no idea what was coming.

CHAPTER THREE

BEFORE

I stared at the clear ceiling of the lanai, watching as the clouds passed overhead, giving way to the bright sun and covering it back up moments later. I squeezed my eyes shut when it came into view, then feeling the warmth leave my skin, opened them back up. My hands were outstretched to my sides, drifting under the water's surface and back up, the pool water engulfing each of my fingers slowly like spider's webs. I was mesmerized by the addicting way it felt, only getting better when I slowed my movements down. So, I lifted them again, holding them out like a claw and dipping them back in the water at a snail's pace.

If someone were to look out the window of the house, they might think I was dead. I'd been floating for hours now, my fingers and toes pruney, and the only sign that I was actually alive was the fact that I kept moving my fingers in and out of the water. I never wanted to leave.

Suddenly, as if conjured there by mere thought, I

heard a voice. It was muffled, as my ears were underwater, but I knew what I'd heard.

"Ma'am," it came again.

My eyes drifted downward, making out the shape of a woman dressed in a white, thigh-length dress, her hands folded in front of her. Her dark hair was gathered around her shoulders.

I let my feet drift down until they hit the concrete pool bottom. When they did, I stood, staring at her. I shook the water from my ears. "Yes?"

"Ma'am, your guests have arrived."

I glanced at the clock on the wall next to the grilling area, surprised to see that it had been more than just a couple of hours, but closer to five, since I'd gotten into the pool. I ran a drenched palm over my face and cleared my throat.

"Thank you, Belinda. Could you get them set up in the sunroom and offer them refreshments while I get changed into something more appropriate?"

She hesitated only for a moment, then jumped into action and walked back into the house. I made my way out of the pool, wringing my thick, blonde hair dry over my shoulder and lifting the folded towel, all fresh and warm from the sun, and wrapping it around my waist with ease.

Then, I slid into my sandals and walked across the lanai, entering the house through the side entrance so I wasn't forced to face my guests while still in a bathing suit and all wet.

Once inside, I climbed the stairs silently. I could hear Belinda in the sunroom, offering them lemonade and caramelized onion and feta canapés as I walked across the second floor and into the master bedroom. I cleaned my face and lotioned my skin quickly, brushing on a bit of mascara and blush. The one thing I loved about summer was how the sun always managed to keep my skin flawless, which meant I could skip the foundation and powder I would've usually put on before meeting with a client.

Once I was done, I ran the blow-dryer over my hair, drying it as quickly as I could and pinning it out of my face. I put on bright red lipstick and changed into a solid white jumper and a pair of Tory Burch sandals, spritzed perfume on my wrist and topped off the ensemble with a simple, elegant diamond necklace.

Then, as if I hadn't just rushed through the entire process, I walked out of my bedroom and made my way down the grand staircase as if I had all the time in the world. I walked across the foyer and into the sunroom slowly, a bright smile already plastered on my face.

When I entered the room, Belinda set the pitcher of lemonade down, though she'd been refilling one of the guest's drinks and had not yet finished. She cleared her throat and gestured toward me.

"Ms. Sheridan," she said, my name a full sentence as the guests stood as well. "This is Lester and Tom Allen."

I smiled humbly and shook both of their hands, starting with the oldest one. "Please, sit," I said, and once they had, I did the same, tucking my hands under my legs to smooth the pants as I went.

I rested them on my lap when I was done.

"Thank you both for meeting with me at my home. I'm sorry I couldn't make it into the office today, and I'm also sorry I was late. I had a conference call that ran over. I hope this hasn't given you a bad impression of me."

"No, ma'am," Lester, the older one, said and I noticed a more-than-slight Southern drawl. "Thank you for meeting us, 'specially because we weren't sure you would. We know your secretary said your prices start out at much more than we can afford, but it's Tom's wedding, you see."

"My fiancée's from New York," Tom chimed in, as if that explained everything. "And she just loves your work."

"I was more than happy to meet with you. Like my assistant told you, my prices for weddings start at thirty-five thousand and go up from there. Now, keep in mind, I'm going to be able to get everything from catering to floral arrangements at a discount no one else in the industry can get you. Not to mention, my events aren't just events. They're pieces of your life. Pieces you don't get to redo. Pieces you'll have pictures and memories of for the rest of your life." I smiled patronizingly. "You can't put a price tag on that, now can you?"

The old man looked at his son, and I watched his Adam's apple bob.

"But, as my assistant also told you," I went on, "I like to do a few heavily discounted events throughout the year, just as a way of giving back. I'm required to do them off the books, which is another reason I've asked you to meet me here, rather than at the office. If people found out about this... Well, you know how it goes, you do someone a favor and twenty more show up looking for favors, too. Are you from here in Naples, Tom?"

"We're from Savannah," he told me. "Drove overnight to get here."

I smiled again, reaching forward and patting his hand. "I'm so glad you did. Now, tell me, would the event be in Savannah—beautiful city, by the way. Or would you prefer to travel? What would the guest list look like? Tell me exactly what you're looking for. Describe your dream wedding."

I leaned forward, reaching for the digital tablet on the coffee table and opening the folio to begin taking notes as they spoke.

"Well, Alyssa wants...decently small. Just a few close friends and family, her sorority sisters and co-workers. And a few of my buddies. We'd probably do it in Savannah or outside the city somewhere close 'cause a few of our relatives are older and don't travel well. We aren't picky about most of it. She wants coral and gold colors, we don't care if it's inside or outside, and we haven't set a date yet, so we're flexible on that, too. As far as food, I thought we could just do a potluck and BYOB to save money there. We don't want anything too fancy, you know? But...she's got this Pinterest board, and she's always talking to me about how much she loves your work. I thought, well, I thought maybe this could be my wedding gift to her. If I told her you were planning our wedding"—he looked at his dad, who was smiling fondly back at him—"she'd be over the moon."

"Is that why you haven't brought Alyssa today? Is this meant to be a surprise for her?"

He nodded slowly. "I didn't want to get her hopes up if it wasn't going to work out. Truth is, if I brought her here and we couldn't afford to do it, she'd be devastated. I know it's a long shot. I just couldn't do it to her…"

I watched him closely, his innocent blue eyes staring at me, pleading with me. I closed the folio after I'd written down the last of what he'd said and leaned forward. "She's going to be so happy."

His expression lit up. "You mean you'll do it?"

"I can't do it for free, but how does twenty thousand sound? I have a friend who owns some event space in Savannah. I can call in a favor and get that for free. And I know if you can get the guest list under one hundred people, I can get the catering—two food options and a cash bar—for under three thousand. We could plan it for December, so you'd have six months to save in case anything came in over budget, but I don't think that'll be the case. Flowers can be something simple. I think we could do it for just a few hundred for the bouquets, as long as she doesn't want the venue decorated with them, but even then, I think we'd be looking at around a thousand if I can get a few favors there, which I'm positive I can. It'll be tight, but if you can do the twenty thousand, I'm sure I can pull together an event that you two will remember for the rest of your lifetimes." I paused, letting it sink in, then added, "Alyssa is going to get the wedding of her dreams, Tom. You're going to give that to her. Your first gift as man and wife."

His face flushed red, and he looked at his dad. For just a moment, I was worried they'd say no. Then, at the last second, Lester patted his son on the shoulder, his lips pressed into a tight line and looked back at me. "We'll do it."

"Oh, excellent. I'm so excited to plan this event for you."

Tom's eyes clouded with tears. "Thank you, Dad. Thank you both." He nodded toward me.

My smile was genuine as I watched them, a moment of true appreciation and love for each other. "I'll just have to cancel your honeymoon to Cabo," the man said with a laugh, and Tom joined in, pulling his dad into an emotional hug.

When they were done, both looking slightly sheepish for the emotional outburst, Lester cleared his throat. "So, when do we pay you?"

I clasped my hands together in my lap. "Well, now, ideally. It's the only way I can officially get your event on my books. As I'm sure you understand, I get hundreds of requests like this a year, and I'm only really able to do three or four, the ones I feel truly deserve it... But until you've paid, I can't hold your spot, and I can't start calling in any favors."

The man nodded, albeit hesitantly. "Do you prefer a check or card?"

"Neither," I said firmly. "It will have to be in cash. I'll give you a receipt, of course, but I no longer accept checks and, because I'm not in the office, I'm not able to accept cards. Like I mentioned, this event will be off my books anyway, because I'll end up losing money on the deal in all actuality. And I'm afraid I don't deal with the online payment systems, PayPal and the like. I'm old school."

The men exchanged a worried glance, and I quickly added, "Of course, if you'd rather not... It's not a problem for me. Don't feel like you've wasted my time. But I do have another appointment this afternoon. Would you like an autograph for Alyssa anyway?"

"No, no," Lester said quickly. "I'll just need to run by my bank. I don't have that much cash on me."

"I can get some out, too," Tom said, speaking to Lester.

"Will that be okay? If we leave to do that, will you still be here when we come back?"

I tapped the Apple Watch on my wrist and sighed. "I can be here for the next hour, but I have an appointment after that. How long do you think you'll be?"

"That's all the time we need," he said, standing up abruptly. "Our bank has a branch here in town. Let us just run over there, and we'll be back."

"Thank you again, Ms. Sheridan." Tom shook my hand, a genuine appreciation in his panic-filled eyes. It was likely more money than either of them had in their bank accounts. Likely more money than they'd ever spent on any one thing, but for his fiancée, he was willing to do it. To let his father fall further into debt. To mortgage his own future for a moment of happiness. It was why I did this. Why I'd built a career doing what I did.

After the front door had closed, and I heard the truck's loud engine pulling from the driveway, I stood, walking toward the kitchen.

Belinda was there, cleaning up the last of the dishes from the hors d'oeuvres she'd prepared. When she heard me coming, she turned off the water and glanced over her shoulder. "Did they decide to do it?"

"I think so," I said. "I never know once they leave. Sometimes they come back, sometimes they don't."

"How much are you charging them?" she asked.

29

"Twenty thousand," I said. "Five to split between you and your sister."

She nodded thoughtfully. "They didn't look like they had that much."

A sly smile played on my lips. "I very much doubt that they do. Love makes people do crazy things." Without another word, she turned the water back on and resumed her work. "I'm going to go up and get ready. Listen for the door."

A few minutes later, I was upstairs, packing my things into my suitcase. I unclipped my hair and ran my straightener through it. It was blonde now, but I was thinking I'd go dark next. Or maybe red. Extensions might be nice. I'd chopped it off months ago, and it didn't seem to be in any hurry to grow back, resting comfortably just above my shoulders.

I glanced at the clock. Nearly an hour had passed, and they hadn't returned. Had it been a waste of time? Were they going to back out on me, after all?

Once my hair was straight, I put the straightener in my bag too, loading up the toothbrush and toothpaste and looking around the room.

What else?

As I packed the last of my things up, I heard the familiar rumble that told me the truck was back. I couldn't stop my brow from raising instinctively. *Hm.*

Within a few moments, as I waited silently with bated breath, I heard the *thump, thump, thump* of a knock on the door.

Then, I heard footsteps climbing the stairs, and finally, Belinda pushed the door open gently. There was a pink to her olive cheeks that hadn't been there before. "They're here, ma'am."

I smiled at her with an *I told you so* sort of grin, and sauntered past, my shoes clicking against the hardwood as I made my way down the staircase. They were there, in the foyer, Tom looking nervously at his dad, who was sweating profusely.

"Gentlemen, you made it." I clasped my hands together in front of my waist. "I was beginning to get worried."

"Sorry it took so long. The man at the bank had to do some sort of report for…a withdrawal of this size."

"Of course. I understand completely." My eyes traveled to the overstuffed envelope of cash in Lester's hands. "Were you able to get it, then?"

"We were. Twenty thousand. It's all in hundreds," Lester said, holding the envelope out with trembling hands.

I took it from him carefully. "You don't mind if I count it?"

"Of course," Tom said quickly, and I turned away from them, walking back toward the thin table in the foyer and pulling out the two strapped bundles of cash. I thumbed through them quickly. Two hundred bills, all pristine and crisp, as if they'd come straight from the Federal Reserve. I inhaled the scent and slipped them back into the envelope.

"Everything looks to be in order."

"Do we need to sign anything?" Tom asked, eyeing me.

I straightened my shoulders. "Oh, certainly. I'll email the contract over to you, but I'll need both of your signatures, yours and Alyssa's. We'll probably need to meet once or twice in person, but most of the work can be done via video chat or phone. Once you get home and break the news to the bride, you can have her reach out to my assistant with any specific requests she may have—keep the budget in mind, of course—and as soon as you send the contract back to me, I'll be able to get to work."

"She's going to be so excited," Tom said, his eyes glimmering with hope. Life hadn't yet crushed it out of him.

"You said there'd be a receipt?" Lester asked, calming his son's excitement.

"Of course," I said, pressing my lips together and giving him a condescending look, as if the request were unnecessary, impractical. I walked back across the room and opened the drawer of the table, pulling out a small receipt book.

I scribbled the amount on the first carbon copy. Twenty thousand.

"Whose name do you want on here?"

"His," Lester said, jutting a thumb toward his son. "Tom. *Thomas* Clancy."

"Hm," I said, jotting it down. "Like the author."

Lester smiled, his tanned skin wrinkling with suppressed delight. "My wife's favorite."

I scribbled a signature on the receipt and wrote *Tom and Alyssa's Wedding* at the top, underlined it twice, then tore the top copy off and walked across the room with it in my outstretched hand. "Here you go."

Tom looked down at it carefully, then looked back at me. "Thank you so much, Ms. Sheridan. I really can't thank you enough."

"No thanks necessary. It's my pleasure. I look forward

to working with you." I rested my hand on his bicep, noticing how muscled and firm it felt despite his relatively small stature. "My secretary has your email, correct?"

"Yes, ma'am. That's right."

"Excellent. I'll have her send over a copy of the contract first thing tomorrow, then. Once you and Alyssa sign it, you can just send it back to me, and we'll get to work. How does that sound?"

"Great. Thank you. Thank you so much." He pressed his hands together in front of him as if in prayer. His face pinkened as he took a step back, practically radiating with glee. Within seconds, they had both turned away from me and were on their way out the door with little more than a wave over their heads.

I stood in silence, listening as the truck started up and the sound traveled farther down the street, taking my guests with it. I heard the sound of my suitcase being rolled carefully down the stairs, one step at a time, and when I turned around, Belinda had made it to the bottom step with my suitcase and purse.

"Everything ready?" I asked.

"Yes. I've got to grab the bag of trash when we head out, but the dishes and laundry are done and I've double-checked each room. Everything's in order."

"Perfect," I mused, opening the envelope and pulling out five thousand dollars. I handed the cash over to her. "Please thank your sister for me."

"Always a pleasure doing business with you," she said, a sly smile on her lips as she counted the money then slipped it into her bra.

With that, I tucked the remainder of the cash into my pocket, lifted my bags, and carried them toward the door, slipping outside and shutting it behind us. I opened my phone and clicked on the travel app, tapping the button for the garage to open and the button to check out.

As it asked me to rate my stay, I tapped the envelope resting in my pocket and grinned, then clicked *five stars*.

Would definitely stay again.

With that, Ms. Sheridan of 52 Wimbledon Way disappeared.

Just like all the others.

CHAPTER FOUR

I n the beginning, it wasn't supposed to be something I
did regularly. It started in college, when a girlfriend
mused about how easy it would be to fake an identity
while traveling. Fake phone, preloaded debit card, fake ID,
and *voilà!* You were a new person.

Wanting to test the theory, we decided to try it out by
renting a place in Miami, convincing a group of naïve and
miserably plain girls to come back to our house with us.
We convinced them that we were beauty moguls, who
were starting a makeup and fashion empire.

They'd melted into our hands when we offered to
show them how to do their makeup and to give them
designer dresses for just a hundred dollars each. There
were five of them, so we made two hundred and fifty
dollars each by applying some makeup to their pudgy
faces and giving them dresses we'd picked up at a local
thrift shop. They weren't new, and some of them weren't
even a perfect fit, but we convinced them it was vintage
and trendy, and they went on their way none the wiser.

We left that night with money in our pockets, checked out, and heard nothing else about it. From there, the cons grew larger, the targets bigger, the profits as large as the one I'd made today, and sometimes even larger.

When my friend got married, she told me she wanted out of the game. She wasn't interested in continuing the cons. Her husband made enough money, and she wanted to grow up. To be established. These days, the cons were rare, but I'd kept up the tradition. I was married now, too. My husband made plenty enough for us to survive and, if I wanted to, I could've gotten an unexciting job like the women I knew from our neighborhood or gone to six a.m. Pilates classes—perhaps I could work in a florist shop like Darla or at the local library like Kate, I could be a substitute teacher like Anna or a nanny like Paige—but the truth was, none of that was exciting enough for me. I needed more. I needed adrenaline rushes and huge payoffs.

Over the years, I'd done everything from convincing lonely seniors that I was their only surviving granddaughter to telling board members I could make them a buttload of cash if they'd just invest in my startup. Nearly every time, they bought. Not only that, they bought hard.

Men were easy. Wave a bit of blonde hair and a low-cut shirt in front of them, and most would pull out their pocketbooks before you'd finished talking. And, once they'd figured out that you'd lied to them, they almost never turned you in. Not when it was a couple thousand here or there compared to the millions in their accounts.

No, they didn't want to seem foolish in front of their friends.

Or embarrass themselves in front of their wives.

That was why Lester and Tom hadn't asked more questions.

Why none of them did.

Because they couldn't be outsmarted by a woman. What would that mean for their inflated man-brains?

I pushed open the front door, stepping inside the house and dropping my bags at the sight of my husband.

"You're back!" he said, his eyes lighting up with genuine excitement. I'd never grow tired of seeing that happiness on his face. I moved forward, wrapping him in a hug and inhaling his scent. "You look beautiful. How was Maui?"

I rolled my eyes with delight and pulled back just a bit, keeping my arms wrapped around his neck, my hands cradling his skull. "Amazing. How was it here? I missed you."

He kissed my lips. "Oh, same as usual here. We had the board meeting yesterday, and Leo came down for it."

"How did that go?" I asked, eyes wide. When my husband's boss came down, it usually didn't mean he had good news.

"Fine," he said, waving me off. "He just popped in. I want to hear about you. Did they love you? Are they going to stock the products?"

I grinned, nodding slowly as I allowed the smile to spread across my lips. "Yes, *and* I've got big news." I squealed. My lovely, oblivious husband believed I analyzed investments for the ultrarich, connecting them with startups and products I believed could make them a ton of money, the most current being a skincare line that was being handcrafted in Hawaii. He didn't need to know the truth about what I did. A bit of mystery was good for the marriage, I liked to think.

"What's that?" He patted my bottom, finally releasing me and moving to pick up my bags.

"This deal was the last on my books for a while, which means we finally have the time to go on our trip. If you have the time, that is."

His brows raised. "Really?"

"Yep, I'm officially done until the fall." I pressed my lips to his as he passed by me, then turned to follow him up the stairs. "When do you think we'll be able to go?"

He sighed. "Soon. Maybe next month. I'll have to call Kyle, Matt, and Dan to see when they plan to take off. Roman will just work from the resort."

I nodded. "I already talked to Eve. She said they've been waiting for us to say we're ready for months now, and Amber and Matt will probably work while we're there too, so the only one we'll have to worry about is Josie and Dan, but they should've been preparing to take off."

"Yeah, they're who I was thinking of... I know he had a rough year last year, so I'm hoping they'll be able to come up with the money."

"You know Dan. He always finds a way," I said, shrugging off the suggestion that he'd pass up the opportunity for our annual trip.

"Yeah, I'm sure you're right. Last Dan mentioned it, he said he was trying to close six million in April to get the rest of their portion saved up. I never heard if he had. I'm sure he'll just liquidate something if it really comes down to it."

I felt my stomach clench at the possibility of not going. Money had never been an issue with our group before. If, for some reason, anyone didn't have the money put aside, it would mean we'd have to wait even longer to go. I wasn't sure I could take it. I needed to get out of this town. Out of this house. I needed to go.

Noticing my silence, he stopped walking, turning around in the middle of the staircase and looking at me. "It's going to be okay. You know that, right?"

"I know," I said, not bothering to hide my disappointment. "I was just excited to go."

He set the bags down carefully and took me in his arms. "I'll tell you what, even if they can't go, me and you... We'll go away for a few days. I may have to work while we're there, but we can spend our evenings relaxing and having a drink by the water. Just like our honeymoon, right?"

I smiled at him, unable to suppress the tears I felt forming. "You mean it?"

"Of course. You've worked so hard to close these latest deals and plan our trip. You deserve a rest."

My eyes widened. "You really think we could make two trips this year work? What about the firm?"

"I can and will work from anywhere, and I'll delegate as much as possible." He kissed my nose.

"Are you sure?"

He squeezed me tight. "Anything for you, my darling wife."

I grinned, resting my forehead against his lips. I wasn't

worried. My husband had always taken care of me, and I didn't, for a second, doubt that he'd do the same now. After a moment, he let his arms drop from my waist and led me into the bedroom where he dropped my bags on the bed and pulled me in for a long kiss.

I loved the way he tasted of the cinnamon candies he loved so much, the way he kissed me, the way he held me. I pressed myself into him, reaching behind my neck and grabbing at the tie that held my jumper up and tugging it loose. As I felt it come undone, he tensed, breaking our lips apart. He smiled at me sadly.

"I'm sorry." He slid his phone from his pocket. I was relieved to realize it wasn't—as I'd thought—my undressing that made him tense, but rather his phone going off, though I hadn't felt it vibrating. As he glanced at the screen, I knew the disappointment on his face. "I have to take this, babe. I'm sorry." With that, he kissed my head and walked out of the room. "You've got Barrett," I heard him call from the hallway.

I tied the straps back around my neck with a sigh and opened my suitcase, beginning to unpack and sort through what would need to go where. What sort of homecoming was this? I'd hoped to be able to spend time with him upon my arrival, rather than him having to go straight to work. I knew how busy he was, and I wasn't a clingy wife—we both had our businesses to attend to—but I couldn't hide the disappointment. I missed him.

Once the bag was emptied, I carried my makeup and hair products into the bathroom and put them away carefully, waiting for Barrett to reappear so we could resume what had been so rudely interrupted. He hadn't seen me in five days; I was desperate to be with him again.

Sure enough, after a few moments, I heard the door open again and heard him call my name.

"In here!"

His footsteps tapped across the hardwood floors, and he reappeared in front of me. I knew from the moment I saw his eyes that the news wasn't going to be good.

"I have to go into work," he said.

"What?" I demanded, standing up from where I'd been on the floor, sorting through the various hair oils beneath my sink.

"I'm sorry. It shouldn't take long. Maybe an hour at most. I just have to sign a few things."

"And it can't wait til tomorrow? Or be done electronically?"

"I'm afraid not," he said. "Trust me, if there was a way to make it work so I didn't have to leave you, I would do that." He reached for my hand, and I placed it in his, standing up and resting my chin on his shoulder. I didn't want him to leave. I just wanted to be with him.

"I miss you."

"I miss you, too." He kissed the side of my head. "I promise I won't be gone long. And when I get home, I'll draw you a bath, and you can tell me all about your trip. How does that sound?"

I nodded, but it was halfhearted. "Fine."

He placed a finger under my chin, pushing out his bottom lip. "Come on now. No pouting allowed."

I rolled my eyes at him playfully.

"Hey, while I'm in, I'll tell my secretary to clear my

schedule for the week after next, okay? I'll convince the others to take the time off, and we'll head out. What do you say?"

"Really? You mean it?" My eyes lit up.

"You're not the only one who can negotiate around here," he confirmed, kissing my nose. "Okay, I've got to go. I'll see you in an hour." He grabbed my bottom with a fiery stare, his gaze raking over me. "Don't take a bath without me."

With that, he released me and rushed from the room, already back on the phone. "Ryan, I want you to get Billy Higgins on the phone…"

I heard his voice grow fainter as he descended the stairs and made his way across the first floor and outside. When I heard the front door shut, the house practically quaking with its force, I sighed.

I'd already begun planning the trip in my head, sorting through destinations and travel plans. I could already feel the sun on my face, hear the ocean, feel the wind blowing through my hair. I needed the trip more than I realized. If Barrett couldn't convince the husbands, I'd have to put in a call to the wives.

I nudged the cabinets closed with my foot and walked back into the bedroom, grabbing the envelope of cash from my purse. Then, I lifted the edge of the mattress and removed the small silver key from its hiding place.

Next, I walked across the room and toward the small sofa that sat a few feet in front of our bed, directly in front of the television. I leaned it forward and flipped it over. On the bottom was the space Barrett had hollowed out to place our small, metal cash box inside of. I removed the tape securing it in place and used the key to open it, staring down at all of the cash. Saved up over time and kept out of our accounts. Cash from bonuses he'd made at work. Cash from cons I'd pulled. It was exhilarating. Looking at numbers on the screen of our banking app was one thing but this...this was different. Cold, hard cash I could smell, touch, hell...roll around in it if that's what I wanted to do.

If I counted it, which I often did, I knew it would all be there.

And now, with the fifteen thousand I was adding, it would be complete.

Our annual splurge.

A sort of slush fund for our vacation each year.

One million dollars.

The trip of a lifetime.

The chance of our lives.

HER SCENT OVERWHELMED ME, her bare skin pressed to every inch of mine.

"Why do you have to leave?" she begged, trailing a finger across my bare stomach and underneath the covers. I felt her fingers wrap around me, making me rethink my decision. Maybe I could stay. Maybe I could tell my wife I'd had to work even later than planned.

Instead, I looked over at her, the beauty beside me, and smirked. "I have to get back home, you know that."

"Barrett," she whined, in a way I couldn't help finding sexy.

"Please. Stay with me." She pressed her lips to mine, and I tasted myself on them.

I closed my eyes, wanting desperately to find a way to stay, but I couldn't. For a brief moment, I lost my senses, but regained them just as quickly. *"I can't keep her waiting much longer. She almost came by the office last time and found out I wasn't there. We were too close to getting caught."*

She tucked her cheek against her shoulder, staring up at me with doe-like eyes. *"Would it be that bad if we were caught? That would mean we could be together. Your wife would finally know the truth about everything..."* Her hand hadn't left the place she'd put it moments ago, and I felt myself hardening under her grip. *"About us."*

"It would, Jessica. It would be the worst thing. If my wife knew about you, about us, she'd ruin me. She'd get half of everything—my company, my fortune, I'd have to sell the house and split the profits. I can't let that happen."

"So this is all there is for us?" She was heartbroken, and I couldn't blame her. Given the chance, I would've walked away from my wife and chosen Jessica years ago. But I didn't have the choice. We'd been young, dumb, and in love when we'd gotten married, and I'd felt sure a prenup would come across wrong. Now, I was paying for that. It wasn't like we were happy anymore. She knew it. I knew it. But she was sticking around for the same reason I let her. A divorce would be devastating, financially, to the both of us.

I reached down, forcing her to loosen her grip. *"I will tell her about everything. I promise you I will, but I need time to figure out how to do it. These things are delicate."*

She stared at me as if she didn't believe me, but she didn't argue. It was what I liked about her most of all. She never *argued. Didn't nag. She'd have questions. Requests. But never arguments. I was in complete control with her.*

Unlike my wife who needed to have control over every aspect of our lives.

"*I hate having to sneak around,*" *she said, rubbing her cheek against where she lay on my bicep.*

"*I do too,*" *I admitted.*

"*When do you think it'll end?*"

"*I wish I knew...*"

"*I love you, Barrett,*" *she whispered uncertainly.* "*I love you so much. I'm terrified you're lying to me. That you're never going to leave her.*"

I rolled over, running a thumb across her cheek. "*Hey...*" *I whispered, willing her to look at me.* "*I love you, too. You know that, don't you? I'm crazy about you. I always have been. From the moment you walked into my office. Sitting across from you every day, sitting across from you and being unable to touch you, was torture. And now, having you not there is even worse.*"

"*So tell your wife and spare yourself some torture. It's your company. You're rich. Hire the best lawyer and take it all back from her.*"

"*You don't understand how this works. I can't just take it all back. We're married, and there's no prenup. Her name is on everything, too. I have to be careful with the way I approach it.*"

She blinked, studying me. "*You're scared of her.*"

"*I'm not scared of her,*" *I argued.* "*I'm scared of losing the life that I've built. Because if she knew about you, she'd take everything. More than that, I'm scared for you.*"

"*Scared for me? Why? Is she dangerous?*" *she asked, furrowing her brow.*

"*Not physically, maybe, but she is powerful. I wouldn't put anything past her. I just need you to be patient with me, okay? This will have to be enough for now," I said, but she didn't respond right away.*

"I'm not afraid of her," she said finally, then pressed herself up so she was resting on her elbow. "I mean it, Barrett. If you want...I could help you get rid of her."

I swallowed, because there was no hint of a joke in her eyes.

"What do you mean?"

Once she'd told me, I almost regretted asking.

Almost.

CHAPTER FIVE

W hen Barrett got home from work, I was, as he'd requested, unshowered. I had taken off my clothes and dressed only in a silk robe. I'd been lounging on the bed, watching a reality show and drinking a margarita when he walked into the room. His body was heavy with stress, his shoulders slumped, but when he saw me, he straightened. His eyes trailed the length of my body, and the right side of his mouth turned up.

"Welcome home," I said, batting my eyelashes at him as if I didn't know what the fuss was all about, though I recognized the hunger in his eyes. I placed my drink on the nightstand. "How'd it go?"

"Fine," he said, kicking off his shoes and walking toward me. He grabbed my hand and tugged me toward him. I obliged, shimmying myself onto my knees and crawling across the bed. I sat in front of him on my knees near the edge of the bed and grinned, toying with the string on my robe.

"I waited for you," I said. "Like you told me."

The scarlet of his cheeks deepened, and his eyes filled with hunger. "I see that…"

I placed a hand carefully on his chest, leaning forward to kiss him. The kiss was soft at first, then filled with urgency and passion. My husband's desire was insatiable, as was my own. It was why we'd fit so well together for so long. We'd never grown tired and boring like most couples. A week apart, a week without sex, was enough to drive us to insanity.

He gripped my shoulders and tore the robe from them, taking in the sight of my bare body as if he were trying to decide which side of a steak to cut into first. I was a feast for him, the whole meal. But he'd savor it. Like always. There was no need to rush anything.

He reached for my legs, pulling them out from under me carefully and running his palms up my calves, then thighs, and finally resting them on my hips. He gave a tug, letting me fall backward so my legs were spread in front of him, my hair splayed across the comforter. I was his for the taking.

His hand traveled from my hip to the space between my legs, teasing me as I felt his gentle touch, never breaking eye contact. I let out a moan of ecstasy as I felt his fingers slide inside of me, and, at that, he lowered his mouth to meet them.

I closed my eyes, lost in the moment of pure pleasure, allowing my husband to take care of me in every way.

AN HOUR LATER, we wore satisfied grins as we lounged under the bubbles in our Jacuzzi tub. My legs draped across his, and he gripped my calf, resting his head against the back of the tub.

"So, they're wanting us to move to Oklahoma? Really?"

He nodded slowly. "They need someone to move to Oklahoma for six months. Ideally, for them, it'd be me, just because I have experience getting the other branches open and up and running, but I don't think they'll force it. I told them I wanted to talk to you."

I eyed him, one brow raised. "What's even in Oklahoma?"

"Um, cowboys, maybe?" He chuckled. "Cows…"

"What if you say no?"

"They'll find someone else," he told me, but there was hesitancy in his tone.

"What happens if you say yes?"

"It would be like a six-month paid vacation. The company would pay for our flights and accommodations while there. We'd get meal stipends and per diem on top of my salary. Then, once the six months are up, we'd come back home and return to normal."

"A six-month vacation?" I toyed with the idea. "Did they tell you where we'd be staying?"

"I'd imagine either a hotel or a short-term rental, but we haven't discussed the specifics. I wanted to talk to you first."

"But…you want to take it." It wasn't a question. I knew the look on his face. His discussing it with me was merely a formality.

"I want…to do a good job. To get the bonus that'll come along with it. To get a free vacation."

"A vacation to Oklahoma," I remind him. "It's not exactly a sought-after destination."

"Hey, if it was Key West, I'm sure Leo would be going himself. I agree Oklahoma isn't exactly on my bucket list, but it's a chance to see another part of the world, stretch our legs a bit. And there are cities in Oklahoma. And an airport. If you need to get out for work, you'll be able to. And…it's only six months."

I tucked my chin into my chest. The truth was, there was nothing holding me there. Barrett was my life. I had friends, ladies I met for yoga or ran errands with, and then there was Eve, Amber, and Josie—the wives of my husband's friends, women who were nice enough, who I could spend an occasional night out with, but we had nothing longstanding. Except for our yearly vacations.

I didn't work much outside of the house anymore, aside from the occasional trip to play out a con. I spent my days making our home beautiful, reading the books I loved, lounging by the pool, and working out. It wasn't that I didn't have a purpose, but that Barrett had become my purpose. For so long, I'd wanted to be with him, and now that I had him, I was determined to make it work.

As the years had passed, though, his work had become more and more demanding, and I'd become less and less of a priority. In Oklahoma, he'd be just as busy, but he'd have no friends to spend hours at a bar with, no true office to stay hours late at. Perhaps in Oklahoma, cramped in a hotel room or small apartment, he'd begin to remember again just how much he enjoyed being with me.

"Hey, we don't have to make a decision tonight. I told Leo that you needed time to get unpacked and settled in. I just have to let him know something by the end of next week."

"When would we leave?"

"It would be in the fall," he said. "After we get back from our trip. I've already told them that's nonnegotiable. They begin training the new team the month after next, and we'd fly out pretty soon after."

I sucked in a breath, trying to decide if I was truly considering going, or if I felt like I had no choice. "Okay, well, I'll think about it and let you know where I stand in a few days. I'm still feeling a bit jet-lagged." On cue, I released a yawn.

He squeezed the ball of my foot gently, pressing his thumb into it with a smile. "Take your time, beautiful. And, hey, it's not all bad. I forgot to tell you that I called Dan on the way to the office, and he said they'd move some things around so we can all go. So, Oklahoma or not, we're almost ready for the trip."

My eyes lit up, and I adjusted myself so I was sitting straighter. "Seriously?" I squealed.

"Yep. He started a text chain, and they're saying we can go either next week or the week after. What do you think? I told them it would have to be soon, before we'd need to leave for Oklahoma." He added quickly, "If we do, I mean."

I ignored the blatant assumption because I was entirely too happy to allow any negativity into my headspace. "Next week!" I announced, launching forward so that water splashed everywhere, though neither of us cared because we were too busy laughing and kissing. Too busy in love. "Next week. Can we go next week?"

"I think we can. I have a few things to do at work, so I'll have to work virtually, but if you're okay with that, I'll tell everyone to get the flights booked."

I pressed my lips to his, breathing in his scent. The truth was, of course, I didn't want him to work. I wanted him to enjoy his time with me. To relax. To live in the moment. But that wasn't my husband. Work would always be his mistress and, as long as he didn't have another mistress, I'd learned to be okay with it.

As okay with it as I could be.

"Book 'em, baby. Let's go." His eyes darkened with unexpected desire, and he kissed me harder, his arms snaking around me as my heart thundered in my chest. It was as if I could already feel the sun on my skin.

THREE DAYS LATER, after the flights had been scheduled and the plans had been confirmed, I was repacking our suitcases, working through loads of laundry and the dry cleaning I'd picked up that morning.

When I stuck my hand down inside of the front of Barrett's bag, my fingers connected with something unfamiliar. *What is this?*

I could've sworn I'd unpacked his bag completely the last time we returned from a trip. I latched onto the thin, folded paper and pulled it from his bag, my stomach tightening with worry.

As I unfolded it, a strange sense of foreboding came over me. On one side, there was a hand drawn heart.

On the other, a single sentence:

I can kill your wife for you.

CHAPTER SIX

THE ISLAND

By the time the sun had set that first night, we were all varying degrees of exhausted, dehydrated, and terrified. For a while, I think we all believed the boat might turn around, or that they'd come back with a new boat and had simply forgotten to mention that they were leaving and would return, but as the sky lit up with pinks and oranges of the setting sun, finally dimming to a pale gray dusk, there was no longer any denying what had happened.

We'd been left.

Abandoned.

And we had no idea why.

We'd tried using our phones over and over, but quickly gave in to the fact that none of us had any service, and, at someone's advisement—I couldn't even remember who at that point, it was all such a blur—we had agreed to keep our phones off, to conserve their batteries on the off chance we found an area with service.

That was about all we'd agreed upon.

Having no one to turn our anger toward, we first turned on each other, scattering to different points of the stretch of sand to vent our frustrations. Noah, the cocky, almost-lifeguard man I'd spoken to on the boat for some time, had spent quite a bit of time in the water, until the current became so strong he couldn't swim it. The other man, the blond one who'd urinated on the trees upon our arrival was called James, and he hadn't spoken much to any of us. He just drifted back toward the edge of the trees to be alone. I'd seen him gathering sticks at one point, though I wasn't sure if he was planning to build shelter, a fire, or beat us with them.

Ava was the young woman who'd nearly passed out, overcome by sudden dizziness upon our arrival, and Harry was the thin man with glasses who'd stayed close to me when I was trying to keep her conscious. But now that she was awake and calm, even they'd spread out, each of us keeping our distance from the others.

I think, even then, even in the early days when we had no idea what was going on, all of us sensed that we may not be able to trust each other like we wanted to. Because, with no one else there to doubt, we were left with no choice but to doubt each other.

As the gray sky turned to almost total darkness, the only light coming from the reflection of the moon on the stormy sea, we found our way back to each other, almost all at once.

"What are we supposed to do?" The question came

from Noah, the not-really lifeguard, and he made no effort to hide the fear and uncertainty in his tone.

"We need to find shelter for the night," Harry—*glasses*—said, taking the lead of the group. "At least at the edge of the forest, so we're somewhat hidden from the elements. Tomorrow, we'll have to look for supplies to construct a fire and figure out a way to desalinate some water or find a stream of some sort. We'll need a real shelter, too."

The rest of the group must've been staring at him in the strange way that I was, because his gaze danced between each of us and, ultimately, landed on me. "Don't stare at me like I have three heads. It's basic stuff. I read a lot of survival books."

I didn't nod, but he didn't wait for me to. It all felt strange. Thinking about tomorrow and any sort of future on the island was...impossible. We had to wake up from this nightmare. It couldn't be real. It couldn't be long term.

He glanced up at the sky. "We're lucky it's a clear night, so we have some moonlight to work under. If we can find a space between some trees where we can all sort of huddle together, take shifts where some of us stay awake, that's our safest option right now."

"But why are we here?" Ava demanded, voicing each of our biggest concerns. "Why did they leave us? We can't just move on without answers. When will they come back for us?"

I was glad she'd not asked *will* they, but *when* will they.

None of us could stomach the thought of an *if*.

"I don't have an answer to that," Harry said matter-of-factly. "But what I can say is that the tide will end up pretty high up on the shore tonight. We need to move farther up the beach, and we need to do that now."

Almost on cue, the ocean roared and the wind picked up, whipping our hair wildly.

"I found a space," James spoke up, surprising us all. "There's a big rock with a sort of ledge thing over near the edge of the trees. It's not very big, but the five of us could huddle underneath it for the night. I've been moving sticks and limbs there for a while, so they'll be dried out if we need them for firewood." His chest puffed slightly with pride, but enough that I noticed.

"It's not where you peed, is it?" Ava asked, her upper lip curled in disgust.

"No." He scowled.

"Fine, great. Let's go," Noah said, turning to face the woods and allowing James to lead us. It was about a twenty-minute walk from where we were, the journey made entirely in silence, and Ava had lingered back, purposefully walking next to me. I felt her eyes trailing to me every few minutes, as if seeking comfort, but I had none to give her.

I was an empty shell of anger and fear, still processing all that had happened.

When we arrived at the place James had mentioned, I saw a large moss-covered boulder that was elongated on one end, making for about three feet of covered space where we could sit in the shadows, or stay dry from the rain should any come our way.

"Okay, great, so..." Harry walked under the rock, appraising the cramped space. "One of us should stay awake at all times, and we can split up into shifts so everyone gets to sleep. Any volunteers for the first shift?"

My hand shot up. I'd always struggled with insomnia, but even as exhausted as I was, I had zero desire to let my guard down and fall asleep among these strangers.

"We should have two people, at least. To make sure we can trust everyone," Noah said, eyeing me. Despite his distrust, he wasn't volunteering to be the second person staying awake.

Harry stared at him, conceding with a nod. "Fair enough. Any thoughts on who the second person should be?"

"Well it can't be me," James grumbled. "I've spent the day lugging wood while you all collected puka shells and painted each other's nails."

I rolled my eyes, already irritated by James entirely. However long we were going to be here, I was sure it would seem like much longer if he didn't cool it.

"I'll do it," Ava said, her voice feeble, her hand in the air.

"It can't be the two girls," James argued quickly, as if he were a young boy suggesting we had cooties.

"Why the hell not?" I demanded, squaring my shoulders to his. I'd had about enough of him.

Noah put a hand between us, easing the tension. "Unless you're volunteering, James, it'll be the women who stay up for the first shift."

James grumbled but said no more, so Noah nodded toward us. "Okay, ladies. If you hear anything, you wake us up. If you see any lights in the distance, hear any animals... Anything. Otherwise, give it until you feel like it's been a few hours and then wake Harry and me up. We'll take the next shift... Since James needs his beauty rest." He grinned at me playfully, then turned around and dropped to his bottom underneath the rock.

"Are you sure you're okay?" Harry asked, not truly directed at either of us. When we nodded, he joined the men under the rock, each of their bodies separated by a few inches of space.

"Should we separate and sit on opposite sides?" Ava asked, almost hesitantly.

I wrapped an arm around her, shaking my head. "No, we'll be fine here. Together. The wind's getting chilly anyway."

We sank down on the ground just in front of the rock, watching the leaves rustle in the wind.

"Someone will come back for us," she said softly, and I realized I didn't know how much time had passed with us sitting in utter silence. "Right?"

I looked at her, her eyes doe-like and innocent. I reached for her hand and squeezed it gently. "Of course, they will."

The moonlight glimmered off the tears in her eyes, but I pretended not to notice. "How old are you, Ava?" I asked after a moment.

"Eighteen," she told me softly, her voice quivering.

"Eighteen..." I expelled a breath. Less than half my age. I guessed the others on the trip were closer to my age than hers, except Harry, who may also be in his mid-to-late thirties. It made me feel like I needed to be the parent, to keep them all protected, but I had no experience to teach me how to parent. This was all new to me, and I had no desire to lead the group. How on earth had she even ended up on the trip? "You're just a baby. What were you even doing on that boat?"

She leaned forward, putting her head in her hands. "I'm supposed to be on vacation with my parents and their friends. I was mad at my mom because she's being totally unreasonable about college. I wanted to change schools from my first choice because my boyfriend's going to one at home. She wants me to get out and see the world, and I just don't want to leave him..." She whimpered, swiping a tear from her cheek. "Anyway, I was mad, so I'd gone down to the beach alone, and this man approached me. He asked if I wanted to go for a ride on the boat; said they had an extra seat and it was free." She twisted one of her kinky curls around her finger. "I know it was stupid, but he thought I was twenty-one, and I just played along. I didn't think there would be any harm done. My parents are going to kill me..."

I reached out again, gripping her hand. "I'm sure they're just worried sick about you, sweetheart."

She bit her lip, looking unconvinced. "I just want to go home." With that, she leaned her head on her knees and began sobbing quietly, leaving me alone with my thoughts as I mindlessly rubbed her back.

According to Ava, the same thing that had happened to me, had also happened to her. Someone had offered her a ride on the boat for free, claiming they had just one extra seat...

I'd begun to suspect this when we were all introducing ourselves earlier and I realized no one that had been on the boat knew each other, but I didn't want to believe it. Because if they'd invited each of us on the boat, it would mean their actions were at least somewhat calculated. I wouldn't tell Ava my biggest fear, which was that we were being trafficked somehow, that we were having to wait for the person or people who had bought us to arrive.

Of course, my mind had always wandered to the darkest crevices of possibility. While most people try to see the positive, without my conscious effort—when faced with a situation—my mind has always gone down the rabbit hole of deception and despair.

So, I sat with my thoughts, wondering how we were going to get ourselves out of the mess we were currently in. Wondering how much time we had.

The rule of threes I knew: we could survive three minutes without oxygen, three hours without shelter from harsh weather, three days without water, three weeks without food. Which meant water and somewhere to hide would need to be our top priorities. Maybe after weapons. Could we somehow fashion the sticks James had collected into spears? I doubted it. We might be able to find sharp rocks or shells, but our time and resources were limited, which I assumed they knew, as they'd dropped us off without anything.

Which made me think they had to be coming for us soon.

If we'd been trafficked or kidnapped for ransom, they'd want us alive, wouldn't they? Would they ask my husband to give some sort of ransom money? Had we all come from wealthy families who could do the same?

"What about you?" I heard Ava ask, though I was so

deep in thought it took me a moment to realize she was talking to me.

"Hm?" I looked over at her, the moonlight reflecting on her still-damp cheeks.

"Who's out there looking for you?"

I thought about my husband. By then, he had to have realized I was missing. Even if he'd never come looking for me, when I hadn't returned that night, he'd have begun to worry. Right? I had to believe he had. I knew how easy it was for him to get lost in his work, distracted, almost buried by it, but surely... Yes, I forced the nagging worry from my mind. He wouldn't leave me stranded. He would notice my absence. He wasn't heartless, even if he was busy. If his wife didn't come home, he would notice.

I made myself believe it with increasing ferocity. He'd probably called my cell a few dozen times by then. Had he called the police? Sent out a search party? Was my face plastered across news channels? I knew it was likely that they'd made him wait a few hours, maybe even a few days before they considered me officially missing, before they'd take any action...

Would that be too late? Would we be long gone? Swept away to some far corner of the world?

Surely someone had to have seen the boat I left on. I'd told the waiter where I was going. If anyone asked him, he would've told them. Then they'd send out search crews looking for the ship. We couldn't be too far offshore, after all. It'd been less than half a day's journey from the time we left to the time we arrived here. If the Coast Guard—or whoever did the searching—took the time, they'd find us. As long as they acted quickly.

"Sorry," I answered her finally, noticing her worried stare. "My husband. My husband's looking for me."

She nodded slowly. "Was he vacationing with you? Why didn't he come on the boat?"

"Because they told me there was only one seat. Same as they told you." I left out the part about him being too busy to even come out of our suite. It didn't matter anymore. I loved my husband, I missed him, and I needed him to find me.

Her eyes widened at the realization that we'd been told the same thing about a single remaining seat. "Really?"

"Mhm."

"But what does that mean? Why would they have told us both the same thing?"

"I don't know, Ava. I really don't know about any of it…"

"If they wanted to hurt us, why would they have left us?"

I didn't answer; just shook my head and drew in my lips. I wanted to comfort her, but I had no answers that would've made her feel any better. Nothing about what had happened made sense.

"When we change shifts, we need to ask the others if they were invited onto the boat, too. I can't remember exactly, but I'm positive when the man invited me, he said that others had chartered the boat and they just had a free spot available. If that's not the case, if the five of us were each invited, it means they wanted us specifically. If that's the case, we need to find out what we have in common."

"What do you mean?" She hugged her knees tighter.

"There has to be a reason they targeted each of us. If

we have something in common, and we can narrow down what that is, maybe we can determine what's going on."

I knew it was a long shot. Money was the most obvious thing we could have in common. If we were being trafficked, though, it was likely completely random, but I needed to give her hope, if for no other reason than if at least one of us still held on to hope, it meant it wasn't entirely lost.

"You think someone planned this? Someone…picked us out?" she asked, apparently horrified at the thought. "You think this was done on purpose?"

"I just don't know what to think," I said. "We'll figure out more in the morning, okay?"

She nodded but didn't say anything else, and I worried I'd been short with her, but the truth was, I was exhausted. And terrified. And the longer I sat, the more both emotions began to wear on me.

I wanted to go home. I wanted to see my husband and talk to my friends and relax in a bed. Instead, I was sitting on a forest bed of branches and rocks and sand digging into my bare legs, and shivering from lack of suitable clothing to protect me from the raging winds, surrounded by complete strangers with no idea who I could trust.

And, if I could trust them all, it meant there was someone out there we couldn't trust. Someone who'd put us here for a reason we didn't yet know.

As I sat contemplating those concerns, the fact that I had no idea who it could be made me shrink in fear. Something very bad was happening…but what?

CHAPTER SEVEN

"Hey!" the harsh voice called, and I felt a hand shoving me. My back screamed in pain with the movement, like knives scraping into my flesh. When I opened my eyes, I was staring up at Noah's body looming over me. The sunlight peeked through the trees behind him.

"Shit!" I sat up, realizing I'd fallen asleep. My back was etched with the pattern of the ground beneath me, and I lifted a hand to wipe the dirt and debris off to the best of my ability.

"You fell asleep," Noah said, gesturing toward a sheepish-looking Ava. "Both of you. Why didn't you wake us up if you knew you weren't going to be able to stay awake any longer?" The anger was etched into his wrinkles and the stern way he was standing, his feet planted in the soil firmly. "You could've gotten us killed. We made the plan for a reason."

"Ease up, Noah," I warned. "We didn't plan to fall asleep. We all had a long day yesterday, and it must've taken it out of me more than I realized. Everyone's fine, aren't they?" I glanced around. James was standing behind Noah, and a weary Harry was still sitting underneath the rock, rubbing the backs of his legs.

"No thanks to you," he seethed.

"Okay, well, they still are. Turning on each other isn't going to solve anything right now, so instead of yelling at me, why don't we form a plan for what we're going to do today."

He folded his arms across his chest, looking prepared to argue, but Harry spoke up. "She's right. We need to form a plan. We need some sort of SOS signal on the beach, where planes could see it if they flew overhead, and we need to build a fire. Plus, we need to search for food and start looking for, or building, a more permanent shelter."

"What do we need a fire for right now? It's not like it's cold," James said.

Harry stood from underneath the rock and approached the group. He counted the reasons on his fingers. "Because we're going to need somewhere to cook our food, if we're able to find any, because fire keeps predators away but could attract help should any arrive, and because we're going to use it to desalinate our water."

"De-*what* it?" James asked, his brow furrowed as if Harry were speaking a foreign language.

"Make it drinkable," he explained.

"Do you actually know how to do that?" I asked him, impressed. Funnily enough, I'd looked it up several times, always wanting to know how to do it should the need ever present itself, but I'd never absorbed anything I'd read. I knew we needed to do something with condensation and sand...

"Yeah, I do," Harry said firmly, not bothering to explain. "So, we need to split up. We don't have a lot of time. The afternoon heat will be hard on us all, so we need to do most of our work in the mornings and evenings. James, do you think you can build a fire for us? I'll need two. A bigger one for a smoke signal and to keep predators away, and a smaller one for cooking and desalinating the water."

"Yeah, I think I can build a fire." James scoffed, appearing insulted, and walked toward the pile of sticks, branches, and logs he'd built last night. He picked up four of the largest ones, turning to walk back out toward the beach.

"What are you doing? Shouldn't you build them here?" Noah asked.

"There's too much brush here," James said without looking back. "With the wind, it'll start a fire. I'm going to find a spot in the sand."

"He's right," Harry agreed.

"I don't need your confirmation. No one appointed you captain here," James called spitefully over his shoulder.

Harry looked crestfallen, his cheeks pale with embarrassment, but I jumped in quickly. "Okay, that's taken care of. What else do we need to do?"

He appeared grateful, pressing his lips together as he thought aloud. "Someone needs to go hunting for food." Then, he seemed to think better of what he'd said. "Maybe just gathering for today. If we could find some fruit, particularly coconuts or pineapples, that would help keep us from dehydrating. We'll have to fashion some spears before we can actually hunt, but that's a project for tomorrow."

"What about this?" Noah asked, pulling a knife—its blade engaged—from his pocket.

In unison, Ava, Harry, and I gasped. "Why the hell do you have that thing?" I asked.

He smirked. "Just be glad I do. I'd like to see you try to open a coconut with a seashell or rock instead of this. We'd all dehydrate before you managed to get an ounce."

"Well, just put it away," I whined, putting up a hand to shield myself from it.

"I don't think I will. I'm going to go find us some dinner."

"You're going to gather fruit?" Harry asked skeptically.

"Nah, I'm talking about real dinner. There's gotta be some wild animals out here." He pointed the knife directly at me. "What do you prefer, boar or rabbit?" Then he pointed the knife at Ava. "Or maybe rattlesnake."

To my surprise, Ava's grin spread. "I'd like to see you kill anything besides a rabbit with that measly thing. You're not even holding it right." She reached for it, managing to swipe it from his grasp with minimal effort. "Besides, if we only have one, we're much better off using it to sharpen the ends of sticks. If this breaks or dulls too quickly, we're toast."

He ripped the knife back from her, his fingertips carefully gripping the blade. "Well, it's my knife, so I think I'll do what I want with it."

"Hang on now," I interjected. "That's very possibly the

only thing we have to find food for any of us. Ava seems to know what she's talking about. We need to listen to her."

"I *do* know what I'm talking about," she said. "My dad and I go hunting and camping all the time. If that knife hits a bone in something like a boar or a goat, it'll break. We can use it to fashion other spears that we can use for fishing and hunting, and it'll give us a much better range. And we can sharpen it on rocks or sea glass when it gets dull."

"Well, if you were going to be picky about its uses, I guess you all should've brought a knife of your own, shouldn't you?" he replied, folding it back up and sliding it into his pocket as he walked away, a gleeful grin on his lips.

"Where are you going?" Harry called. "We need your help!"

"I'm going to find food," he said. "You can thank me later."

"We shouldn't separate! It's too dangerous!" I yelled after him, but it was no use. He was gone. Huffing a breath of frustration, I turned back toward Harry and Ava.

"I guess it's up to us," Ava said sadly, a haunted look in her eyes.

"Then I think while James is building a fire, the three of us should build an SOS signal. It won't take long, and once it's done, we can search for shelter and maybe even some sort of stream with fresh water."

"Okay... How are we going to make the signal?" I asked.

"Let's get some of these sticks and logs that James didn't use, and we'll lay them out on the sand…" He went on instructing, and Ava and I followed his lead, carrying the logs to a clear spot of sand far enough away from the water that they wouldn't get washed away, yet not so close to the tree line that they might be covered up. We wanted a plane to see us. It was one of our only chances of escaping.

As we worked, we discussed theories about what had happened.

Ava had thought her parents might be trying to punish her by sending her to the island, but she had her doubts about why they'd include the rest of us.

Harry thought they may have gone back for help, but neither of us could understand why they wouldn't have told us that.

I told them my theory—that we had been kidnapped and that we may be trafficked or held for ransom. No one argued with the possibility, though we did agree it seemed far-fetched.

"I don't have a lot of money," Harry said. "I can't imagine why they'd choose me."

"My parents are well-off," Ava confirmed. At least I'd found a connection with one of them, but if Harry wasn't, the ransom made less sense.

As we worked, I watched James several feet away from us, still digging a hole around the fire pit he'd constructed. We hadn't seen Noah since he'd disappeared, and though that made me worry about him, I kept reminding myself that he'd chosen to go out on his own.

If he was in danger, it was his own fault.

"Hey, Harry, did you charter the boat or were you invited to ride on it?" I asked, remembering my question from the night before.

He wouldn't meet my eye, busying himself with straightening the logs. "They let me ride for free. I guess you guys didn't fill it up all the way or something."

"That's what they told us, too," Ava and I said at the same time. I watched the truth wash over Harry's expression, more worry seeping into it.

"We were chosen, then. For something. There's no way that's a coincidence..." He trailed off, shaking his head. For a while, we worked in silence, each left to our own thoughts.

When we'd finished, we stepped back, admiring our handiwork. The three letters were several feet thick, made up of sticks, logs, and stones.

SOS

"Do you think that'll work?" Ava asked, her fists pressed into her hips.

"It has to," Harry said, wiping sweat from his brow. He glanced up at the sky, squinting as he looked toward the sun. "If a plane flies overhead, even if they couldn't read it, they'd be able to see that something was here. The thickness of the letters, plus the contrast of the dark objects on the white sand..."

"What about at night?" Ava asked, chewing her bottom lip. She brushed a bit of her hair from her eyes.

"That's why we'll have to keep the fire going," he said.

"How often do you think planes fly over here? I

haven't seen one yet," I pointed out, looking at the sky too. It was true; I hadn't seen nor heard a single plane in the sky since we'd arrived.

"It depends on where exactly we are. We'd been sailing for less than a day, less than half a day most likely. We couldn't have gone more than two hundred miles, so we're looking at an island off the coast of...the Bahamas or Cuba, most likely. But..." He was thinking aloud again, not really talking to either of us as he mumbled and stammered along. "When we traveled and the sun had begun to set, I don't remember it being behind us. I'm nearly positive it was to our right, so we were heading south. That narrows it down to either Cuba or a part of the Keys that remains uninhabited. There are some private islands around here, but most are owned by billionaires. I can't see why this one would be sitting empty."

"Unless it's not empty," Ava whispered, causing me to look at her.

"What do you mean?"

"What if it's not empty, after all? What if there are others here?"

"You mean others who've been kidnapped?" Harry asked. "Or our kidnappers?"

"Either. Neither. Just...maybe there are others who live here. We haven't seen every part of the island. Maybe the other side has houses or people...maybe even a town."

Harry looked at me and one eyebrow shot up as if to say, *she's got a point.*

"But if there are other people on the island, do you think they know we're here?" I asked.

"They can't," Ava said quickly. "Right?"

"If they did, why would they just leave us out here to fend for ourselves?" I agreed, touching her arm gently. Harry looked toward the horizon.

"If there are others, we'll need to figure out where they might be. Even if there aren't, I think trying to get somewhere higher, somewhere where we can get a better sense of the island would be helpful. We can find out if there are structures, waterfalls, mountains, places for shelter, places to find food. As it stands, we don't know anything about this space. If it's big or small, even. If we can find a stream, or a waterfall, we'll find fresh water, but also plants and animals for food, too."

"How do you know so much about this?" I asked, narrowing my gaze quizzically at him. "Not just about the waterfalls, but about how far we traveled and what direction? And about what we should be doing? You said you read a lot of survival books. Are you some type of... adventurer?" I said the word, well aware of how bizarre it sounded. It wasn't as if that were an actual job title, was it?

He gave me a patronizing grin, but there was nothing cold in his gaze. In fact, he almost seemed embarrassed. "No," he said, shoving his glasses up over the hump on his nose. "Not at all. I just read a lot. I like to know things."

"What's the capital of Mumbai?" Ava challenged, crossing her arms.

"What are you talking about?" Harry asked.

"You really expect us to believe that you just happen to know all the things that will help save us here? How do we know you're not involved in it all?" She jutted a finger in his direction.

I looked at her, then at him. Despite the truth in her words, I did trust Harry. But was I wrong to trust? It did strike me as odd that he knew so much about our surroundings and next steps.

He looked at me, his brow furrowed as he waited for me to come to his rescue, but when I didn't, he sighed. "It's a trick question. Nothing is the capital of Mumbai. Mumbai is actually the capital of Maharashtra. It's also India's biggest city. And a lovely one. My husband and I went a few years ago." He tucked a hand in his pocket, waiting for us to respond. When I looked at Ava, her jaw was slack.

"Well?" I prompted. "Is he right?"

"How should I know?" she asked. "I was just throwing out a random question."

"You didn't even know the answer?" I scoffed, shaking my head.

"Well, what was I supposed to ask him? The capital of freakin'...Kentucky? I wanted to give him something everyone doesn't know."

"What *is* the capital of Kentucky?" Harry challenged her with a laugh, his head cocked to the side.

"Lexington," she said. "*No*, Louisville."

"Frankfort," he corrected. "Now, if we're done with that... Can we move on?"

I nodded, unofficially having been made the middleman in their argument. "So, where should we go?"

Harry looked up to where James was still working diligently on the fire, knocking over pieces of wood and struggling to keep them standing as he went.

"We should start a desalination system because we're

all going to start dehydrating soon, and then we should go and search for water, because no matter how quickly we're able to produce clean water, without pots or pans or bottles to store anything, it'll never be enough." With a grim expression, he turned away from us and began walking back in the direction we'd come from, back toward the rock that had provided us with shelter the night before.

When we arrived, we stopped, Harry's arms held back to keep us from moving forward.

"What is it—" Ava started to ask, but cut herself off when she saw what we were both staring at.

A small piece of bright orange paper lay folded on the forest ground, a heavy stone on its corner to keep it from moving. Harry looked at me, and I looked at Ava.

"Should we open it?" he asked.

I nodded, moving forward just an inch. "Maybe it's from Noah. Maybe he came back and couldn't find us. Maybe he found food and is telling us where to come." Even as I said it, I knew it was untrue. Noah didn't have paper, or the pencil that someone had used to scribble the message we were now all staring at, the paper laying open in my hands. No, I doubted very much that this message had come from Noah. But, if not him, then who?

I read the message twice before looking at the others, the words refusing to make sense in my muddled mind. It couldn't be true. It just couldn't. I glanced back down, forcing myself to read it again.

Kill your friends, save yourself.
Only one of you will leave alive.

CHAPTER EIGHT

W e didn't know how to react to the note. If you asked each of us, you might get different answers about why we did it, but the truth was, we only hid it because we were trying to figure out what to do with the new information.

Had one of the other members of our group planted it? James or Noah were the only ones who'd been away from the three of us, but we'd kept an eye on James most of the time and, for all we knew, Noah still hadn't returned from doing whatever the hell he was doing.

So, what then? Where did that leave us?

We had to believe someone else was on the island. Someone who, at the very least, knew what had happened, and at the worst, had constructed the whole thing. But why? What did they want with us?

Harry believed we should tell them all. He said everyone should have the information we did, that it was only fair. Ava and I thought differently. We'd seen both Noah and James acting foolish and pigheaded since we'd arrived, and that was without the knowledge that we were potentially meant to be fending for ourselves and taking each other out one by one in some sort of *Hunger Games*-esque challenge, so I was worried things would only get worse if they knew what the note said.

Our side of the argument won out when I pointed out that Noah was the only one with a weapon.

So, as the weight of our newfound information sat heavily on us, Harry tucked the note into his pocket and we made our way back out to the shore, where James finally had both a small and large fire going.

"This work?" he asked when he saw us heading his direction across the sand.

Harry bent down and studied both fires closely before standing back up. "You did a really good job, actually." There was a sincerity in his tone that seemed to catch James off guard.

"No big deal. I was in Boy Scouts as a kid," he said, shrugging with his hands in his pockets. "It's one of the only things I remember."

"Well, you've done really well. We'll want to set up a sort of ramp with different logs, so that when one burns out, the next one replaces it and keeps the fire going constantly, but we can do that later." He sighed, rubbing his hands together. "Now, this isn't going to be a fool-proof process, but if we can find the largest seashells with a big base to hold water and then some palm leaves, I can try to construct something to hold condensation from the sea water we'll gather."

"Will that work?" Ava asked.

"In theory?" Harry said, obviously unsure. "Maybe. But

it's not guaranteed. It's why we need to look for an actual water source…and soon." He glanced toward me, then at my shoulder. "You're already starting to get sunburned."

I followed his gaze toward the red patches on my shoulders. I'd be willing to bet my face looked the same. "I burn easily," I told him. "No big deal."

"Out here it is," he said. "We don't have aloe or salve to treat the burns, so they could easily get infected. Not to mention that they'll make you dehydrate quicker. You need to stand in the shade whenever possible." He directed me toward the shade with the wave of his finger. "Anyone else starting to burn?"

Ava checked her own dark shoulders and shook her head. "I'm good."

James did the same, shoving back the sleeves of his white T-shirt quickly before confirming that I, with my pale skin and freckles, was the only one who had managed to burn in just a few hours on the beach.

"Well, she's also the only one wearing hardly any clothes," James said, his eyes trailing down the length of my body in a way that made my stomach tighten. I wrapped the sarong around myself tighter, keeping my arms folded.

"Well, it's not exactly like I was packing for a trip here, was I?" I demanded.

"Hey, you won't hear me complaining," he said, his hands up in the air innocently, though the devilish look in his eye didn't evaporate.

"Anyway," Harry interrupted firmly, "we need to get to work. The sun's already higher in the sky, and once it reaches its highest point, it's going to be miserable out here." He looked back toward me, where I now stood several feet away. "If we're going to look for fresh water and others on the island, we should get this done in just a few minutes and then head out. The good news is, most of our search will be covered by the trees, so you won't burn anymore for today."

"So what are we looking for?" Ava asked, glancing out toward the ocean. "Seashells?" She started walking toward the sand without further prompting.

"Yeah"—Harry joined her—"the biggest ones we can find. We want something that can hold quite a bit of water since we don't have any pans or bottles of our own."

"Are you sure you don't want me to help?" I asked, feeling useless standing there watching as the three of them searched the shore.

"You can look for leaves," Harry called back after a moment. "The biggest, cleanest palm leaves you can find. Just stay in the shade."

I huffed, turning away from them and beginning to search the tree line for any such leaves. Moments after I'd gathered a few under my arms, I heard a rustle in the jungle ahead of me. I froze, trying to decide where the movement had come from. Had I imagined it?

I stood completely still, quieting even my breathing as I watched the trees blowing in the breeze. The visibility in the jungle wasn't great. In fact, someone could disappear just a few feet in front of you, the trees close together as they were, and leaves, vines, and other greenery growing up in every direction. Whoever, or whatever, was moving could be just a few feet in front of me.

Could they see me?

I could hear the others talking behind me, several yards away with no idea what was happening. If I called out or bolted, it was possible I could be grabbed or attacked without them even realizing it had happened. I refused to look behind me, determined to keep my eyes peeled for any sort of movement.

"Hello?" I called cautiously. "Is someone there?"

A branch cracked, and I jumped just as Noah appeared in front of me, a cocky grin on his face. "Boo."

"Jesus, you scared me." I placed a hand to my chest, my heart thundering under my palm.

He cackled, eyeing the leaves in my hands suspiciously. "What are you doing?" He nodded his head toward the others on the shore. "Better question, what are they doing?"

I couldn't focus on his question, because at that moment, all I could see was what was waiting in his arms. Five large, green coconuts sat nestled between his forearms and his chest. When he noticed my stares and slack jaw, he jutted out his chest a bit more.

"You like my nuts, hm?"

I groaned, annoyed by the joke, but my throat was suddenly too dry to argue. "Where did you find these?"

"Wouldn't you like to know?" His brow shot up playfully, his dark eyes teasing me.

"Noah, this is serious. Did you find more?" I turned to face the group, my hands over my head. "Guys! Hey! Look!" The wind carried my voice away, so they didn't hear my calls.

"Hey, I didn't say I was sharing," he said, and though I listened for the joke in his tone, I wasn't sure it was there.

I crossed my arms. "You don't have a choice. We'll all dehydrate if we don't get something to drink."

"I thought Captain Lotta-Brains was whipping up a water machine in his underground bunker."

He could be infuriating sometimes. The cavalier way he acted, even when we were literally facing dehydration and death, made it impossible to deal with him. But, he was also the only one on the island who'd managed to find a source of hydration so far.

"You know, you could try being nice to us. We're all in this together."

"Calm down, Efron," he teased, dropping the coconuts to the ground with a thud. He bent down, lifting one. "There are plenty more where these came from. Obviously, I'm going to share. I'm not trying to kill you all."

My throat tightened at his words. Why had he chosen to say that? That he wasn't *trying to kill us*? Why did he use those exact words? I tried to push the thought from my head, convince myself that I was just being paranoid... But was I?

"What's going on?" I heard Harry's voice calling from behind us. As I looked over my shoulder, I realized they had seen what was going on and were rushing toward us, seashells in hand.

"You found coconuts?" Harry asked, pure joy in his voice as he reached for one. Ava fell to her knees next to me, letting out a tearful laugh with utter relief. Noah knelt down in front of her, reaching for one of the coconuts and pulling out his knife.

"I guess you're going to tell me this isn't the right way

to do it?" He eyed Harry suspiciously, placing the tip of the knife to its shell.

"You could do it like that," he said, his tone unfazed. "But it won't work half as well as this." He scooped one up and shuffled a few feet from us, lifting it over his head and slamming it down onto a rock's sharp edge with one fell swoop. The coconut split open slightly, clear liquid spilling from its insides. Triumphant cries were heard from all around as he put his lips to the opening, gulping it down quickly. My mouth grew drier at the sight, and I felt my hands reaching for my own coconut without warning. When he had drained it all, he held it up, peering at the hole as he swiped the back of his hand over his lips. Then, he slammed the coconut into the rock again and again until it smashed—not in half like I'd been expecting, but into several pieces, its white, milky insides on full display.

As he gathered the pieces, everyone else scooped up their own fruit and headed toward the rock, waiting to mimic what he'd done. One by one, we cracked the coconuts open. James got his on the first try like Harry. Ava and I each took three different hits to get the liquid to begin leaking, and Ava's hardly came out even then, but that didn't stop her from attempting to drain the liquid as quickly as she could. For a moment, we were all silent, languishing in the delight of the lukewarm and sickly sweet libation.

Noah sat still, the only one who hadn't made his way to the rock, still attempting to cut it open with his knife, an unrelenting stubbornness in his jaw that said he wouldn't give up.

"You know, it's crazy. I've never even liked coconut juice. But right now, I can't think of anything better," Ava said, euphoria in her tone as she flopped back on the sand where she sat, one arm behind her head. She placed one of the pieces of coconut in her mouth, sucking on the fleshy meat of the fruit. Watching her, I did the same, wanting to get every bit of nourishment I could from it.

Finally, Harry scoffed. "Come on, Noah, don't be ridiculous. Just open yours like everyone else. You're only going to dull your blade if you don't manage to break it or slice your hand open."

"Yeah," Ava agreed, propping herself up with one hand. "And if you do that, we can't use your knife to get the rest of the meat out. That's the best part."

"Who said you could use my knife anyway?" he asked, though he swiped the blade on the side of his swim trunks and stood up, finally making his way toward the rock.

No one bothered to argue. At that point, I think we were all too unbelievably joyful to think about it. Instead, we rested on the sand, laughing and smiling to ourselves in pure delight. I heard Noah crack his coconut over the rock a few times and then his thirsty swallows.

Once he'd joined us back in our unintentional circle, James sat up once again. "So, where did you get these?"

"Yeah, where did you go today? Were there more?" Harry added.

"Plenty more," Noah said, expelling a belch.

"Where at?" James asked again.

"Not far from here." We waited for him to say more, but he remained silent.

"Are you seriously not going to tell us?" Harry asked pointedly. "We need to know."

"Why do you need to know? It can be my job to go and get them every day from wherever they are." He paused and gave a lopsided grin. "As long as you keep me happy."

Harry wasn't amused. "We're going to need more than this. A lot more. It would make more sense to move closer to wherever they were. Was there somewhere we could shelter nearby? You were gone for several hours; you could've walked miles in that time. Did you mark your trail? Do you know how to find your way back?"

"Calm down there, Indiana," he said, Southern drawl on full display. "I know how to get there, yeah. And there were plenty more, but I'm not taking you there. For all I know, that's the only reason you're keeping me alive."

From behind me, James snorted. "Yeah, 'cause we're all about to start killing each other."

Noah's eyes darted to James, then back to me, and they widened. At that moment, I knew he'd seen the note. Or else, he'd been the one to plant it...

"You didn't tell him?" he asked, his eyes narrowing. He clicked his tongue, obviously pleased. "I underestimated you..."

"Tell him what?" I feigned ignorance.

Noah sat up farther, squaring up his shoulders. "The note is gone, so I'm assuming you found it."

"You put it there?" Ava demanded angrily.

"Put what where? What are you guys talking about?" James asked, looking between us all.

When no one spoke immediately, Noah smirked,

leaning forward over his legs. "Do you want to tell him, or should I?"

"Why would you do that, Noah? Is this all some sort of joke? Do you think it's funny?" Harry spoke up, his voice quivering with anger.

"What are you talking about? Of course, I didn't put it there. I came back at one point to tell you all I'd found the coconuts, but when I saw the note, I left again. I gave it a little while, until you'd had enough time to find it yourselves, and then came back. I was testing you, to see how honest we were going to be with each other." He ran a hand through his hair casually. "I guess now I have my answer."

"Will someone tell me what's going on?" James demanded.

"There was a note left next to our camp." Harry pulled it from his pocket, shoving it toward James. We watched as he processed the words, then looked up, his eyes wide.

"What does this mean?"

"What do you think?" Noah asked, standing up.

"Why didn't you tell us when you found it if you weren't the one who left it?" Ava asked pointedly.

"I told you why. Because I was testing you," he said simply, stretching his arms up over his head. "Why didn't *you* tell *me* about it? Hm? You weren't planning to tell anyone else, were you? If I hadn't said anything, you three would've just kept it as your dirty little secret, wouldn't you? You weren't planning to breathe a word of it. Maybe you were even planning to act on it."

"What? *Kill each other?*" I groaned. "Get real, Noah."

"We were still processing it. We didn't know whether to show everyone or just throw it away," Ava argued.

"And we obviously got no say in the matter," Noah spat.

"Well, you'd already seen it, so I don't—"

Noah interrupted Harry's argument. "Yeah, but you didn't know that at the time."

I needed to find a way to calm the rising tension. But as Noah raised his voice more and more, it seemed to be impossible. "Look, we didn't see a point in telling everyone," I said, interrupting Harry as he started to speak again. "We weren't going to act on it. We didn't see any reason to pit everyone against each other."

"But who left it? If not any of us, that has to mean there's someone else on this island," James said, his brow furrowed. "And if that's the case, what if what they said is true? What if they'll only let one of us off the island?" Something in his eyes darkened, sending a bolt of fear through my chest. I didn't trust James with this knowledge. That was the truth. He was hot tempered and naïve, and I expected him to act impulsively.

"That's ridiculous," I said, too quickly. "If someone else is on the island, they're obviously just messing with us. They can't seriously want us to...to...*kill* each other. It's insane. We wouldn't dare..." I trailed off. It was too unbearable to think about.

"No," Harry agreed with me. "No. They can't. And even if they did, you're right, we would never do it."

"You'd really rather be stuck in this place forever than even consider the possibility that they could be serious?" Noah scoffed.

"Yes," Harry and I said at the same time, and I continued, "because it takes more than just considering the possibility. If it's real, if getting off this island means we'd have to kill each other...that's just not an option." As I said the words, my throat grew dry. I hadn't thought about it like that until that moment. Was I really willing to give everything up? To never return home? To never see my husband, my parents again? To die on this island...

"Yeah, I agree. This all feels like a setup anyway," Ava said, then her face lit up. "Oh, you know what? Maybe we're on a reality TV show."

James laughed, and Noah looked around, as if searching for the cameras. "Alright, guys... Bring out Ashton Kutcher." He wiggled his head around a bit, dancing in place gleefully, but I noted the sarcasm in his tone.

"It's not the worst guess," I said, suddenly feeling the need to defend Ava. "None of us has any idea what's going on here. Ava could be right."

"Look, none of this matters," Harry said, shaking his head as if forcing the thought from it. He pointed to the note in James's hand. "All that matters is that we won't be doing what that note says. We can't turn against each other. We're in this together, and we have to remember that." He looked toward the sky overhead. "We were going to look for water, but if we know where the coconuts are, I think it makes the most sense to find shelter near them for the day. We can rest, rehydrate, and then start exploring the island a bit more tomorrow."

"But..." Ava said hesitantly. "Should we leave the beach? I mean, what if someone sees our SOS signal, and they come looking for us? How will they find us?"

The question hung in the air as we realized she was

right. We couldn't leave the beach, not if we wanted to hold on to the hope that we'd be rescued, and we desperately did.

"She's right," I said. "We have to stay close by."

"I agree," James said. "But we should go get more to drink. That wasn't enough."

"Yes, and we should start building some sort of shelter here. There's a fallen tree over there"—Harry pointed as he spoke—"so I think if we can drag it over here and rest it against the boulder we slept under last night, we can lay other branches, brush, and leaves on the sides to give us more protection and keep us more concealed. It'll give us more space, too. So we can all fit inside at night, but we can still keep an eye on the shore and the fire both."

"Fine, you guys do that, and I'll go get more coconuts," Noah said, jutting a thumb over his shoulder.

"No, you're not going back alone," Harry said.

He ran his tongue over his teeth. "And who's going to stop me?"

"You need help," I interjected before the argument could catch fire. "You're going to need to bring a ton back, and you'll need help carrying them."

His thick, black brow raised slightly, the scar just above it wrinkling. "Are you volunteering?"

My stomach tightened at the thought, but I quickly weighed the alternatives. Harry was the only one who had a vision for the shelter, which only left James and Ava. I didn't trust Noah and James together even more than I didn't trust them separately, especially after the note's revelation, and I definitely didn't trust him with Ava. That left me.

"Yes—" I said.

At the same time Harry said, "No, I can go with him. You don't have to."

"No, you said it yourself… I shouldn't be in the sun. The forest is the best chance for me to stay in the shade. Besides that, I don't have a clue how to build a shelter. We need you to do that."

He twisted his mouth in contemplation. "I don't know… I can build the shelter later." His panic-filled eyes said what he couldn't articulate into words in front of the present company—that he didn't trust Noah not to hurt me. But there was no other option.

"Oh, Jesus, people. Come on. I don't have all day. The coconut train is leaving. If you're on it, you'd better keep up." With that, Noah turned away from us and stalked into the woods.

I looked at Harry and Ava, nodding affirmatively and hoping I looked surer than I felt. "I'll be back soon."

With that, I jogged across the sand to catch up with my companion, refusing to look behind me.

I'd be back. I'd see them again.

I had to believe that, or I was sure my legs would've given out then.

CHAPTER NINE

Noah walked through the jungle faster than I'd been expecting. Zigging and zagging between trees and boulders, making no effort to slow down in order for me to keep up. Even so, I was.

I'd managed to keep pace with him, practically running most of the way.

"Thank you for letting me come. I know you didn't want to show us the place."

He looked at me out of the corner of his eye, slowing only slightly at the sound of my panting. "Who says I'm taking you to the right place?"

My skin chilled, but before I could react, he let out a laugh.

"Relax. Jeez. You really are paranoid, aren't you? You and the dream team back there." The lump in my throat grew larger as I watched his hand trail down his side, toward the outline of the knife in his pocket.

"We just want everyone to get off the island in one

piece, Noah. That's it. And the only way we can do that is by working together."

His mouth upturned slightly, and he whispered, seemingly to himself, *"Matibay ang walis, palibhasa'y magkabigkis."*

I stared up at him. "What does that mean?"

His dark eyes softened as he looked over at me. "It's a Filipino proverb. My lola, *my grandmother*, used to say it. It means *a broom is sturdy because it is tightly bound.*"

"What does—"

"People are stronger when they stand together," he interrupted. "That's basically what it means."

"Oh," I said, feeling relief. "Yes, well, I agree with your *lola* then. Did you grow up in the Philippines?"

"Nah," he said, "my grandparents moved here before they had my dad. I've never even been there, but my parents made sure I was fluent so I could speak to them well."

"That's really nice." I could finally catch my breath, as his pace had slowed considerably.

"They both died a few years ago," he added, his tone grim. "My grandparents."

"Oh." His words caught me off guard. "Noah, I'm so sorry."

He gave a stiff nod but didn't respond. "You know what other phrase I remember her saying all the time?"

"What's that?"

He stopped abruptly, turning to face me. *"Huwag kang magtiwala sa di mo kilala."* I waited for him to explain, watching something deep in his eyes darken. "Don't trust strangers."

My breath caught, and he registered the panic on my face before snickering. "Relax, Ace, if I wanted to kill you, I already would've." His eyes slid down the length of my exposed body, and I wrapped the thin sarong around me with a shiver. "For now, you're more useful to me alive."

"Why do you do that?" I asked when he turned to walk away and I quickly regained my composure.

"Do what?"

"Why do you choose to be such an ass? You were kind to me on the boat...kind*er*. We're all just trying to survive here. Why are you purposefully making it more difficult?"

"I'm not trying to make anything more difficult, I'm just not interested in making friends like the rest of you. I'm trying to get the hell out of here."

"And what do you think the rest of us are doing?"

"Well, it looks a lot like you're preparing for sleepaway camp, as if our parents are coming back next week to pick us up. As if none of this is real. You aren't taking this seriously enough. Any of you. We can't make friends here. We can't build a shelter and pretend we just have to weather the storm. We have to figure out what's going on."

"No one's pretending this is anything less than incredibly dangerous, Noah. We know this is real and we know we have to find a way off the island, but the only way to do that is to work together. Making enemies out of each other will only make it worse."

"But we're already enemies, don't you see that?" he asked, no anger in his voice, just curiosity. "You saw the note... We're going to have to kill each other eventually. Or let nature do the dirty work. Either way, I have no interest in getting close to anyone because I fully intend to make sure I'm the one getting off of this island."

"It doesn't have to be that way," I said softly. "We would never hurt you, Noah."

He rolled his eyes. "Please. That's a lie, and we both know it. You would if it meant you were going to die otherwise, as you should. It's every man—*wo*man, I guess—for themselves out here."

"I don't believe that. People are generally good if you give them a chance."

"Believe whatever you want," he said, "but I'm going to do the same. And, I hate to break it to you, but our beliefs starkly contradict each other."

"Well, I want us all to make it home. I know we have family waiting for us..." I tried to appeal to his humanity, if there was even a shred of it to be found. "Who's waiting for you?"

His shoulders tensed. "Look, what do you not get about the fact that I don't want to be best buds?"

"I do get that. What I don't get is why that means we have to be enemies instead. I, for one, think we don't have to be either."

He was quiet for a moment, and I resisted the urge to look over at him, letting him process what I'd said and hoping somehow, I'd managed to get through to him.

"Look, you already have Too Tall and Princess Knives-A-Lot to help you with whatever friendship complex you seem to have. Can we just...not talk? We're almost there anyway. Keep up." With that, he picked up his pace, and I was forced to run to stay with him, my breathlessness keeping me from talking any more.

"Slow...down..." I begged, my chest growing tight as I tried to move faster when he disappeared behind a tree.

"Keep up," I heard his voice in the distance. He sounded so far away. Suddenly, black dots began to fill my vision, and I stopped in my tracks, trying to make sense of what was happening. My lungs burned for the air I couldn't seem to suck in fast enough. I clutched my chest, trying to ease the pain as I felt my knees go weak.

"Noah..." I said, or tried to... I couldn't tell. I felt my legs give way, and seconds later, my body connected with the ground with a loud thud. Darkness found me all at once.

CHAPTER TEN

When I came to, I saw tree branches stretching upward, the small sliver of blue sky and clouds peeking through. As the memory of what had happened came back to me slowly, I tried to sit up, to decide where I was and what direction I'd come from. Had he left me? Would I find my way back?

As I moved, a sharp pain tore through my skull, making me gasp.

"Whoa, hold on..." I heard a voice—Noah's voice—say, though I couldn't make out where he was. Had he hurt me somehow? Had he made this happen?

I tried to push up farther, but my head began to spin and my vision blurred, so I gave in and allowed myself to collapse once more. "What happened—"

I felt a hand on my arm, and when I turned my head slightly, I saw him sitting next to me. His chest was bare, his face solemn as he stared down at me, sliding one hand under my head. "You're dehydrated," he said. "Here, drink this..." He lifted a coconut to my lips, and I had no choice but to drink on command, allowing him to pour small amounts of the lukewarm liquid into my mouth, swallowing as quickly as I could. After a few drinks, he stopped. "Don't try to sit up just yet. I think you may have hit your head when you collapsed."

I moved a hand to my chest, remembering the pain, and realized there was some sort of fabric covering me. *Noah's T-shirt.*

I grasped some of the fabric between my fingers as it sank in and, as it must've registered on my face, he cleared his throat. "Don't read too much into it," he said firmly. "Your skin's burning badly, and I need your help carrying these back." He gestured toward the pile of coconuts next to my feet, at least ten of them, but I couldn't keep my head up long enough to count. Suddenly, the sound I was hearing hit me, and I realized what I'd just seen. "Water?" I asked, looking up once more.

"There's a waterfall," he confirmed, almost hesitantly. My mouth became dry at the thought. "Here, have some more." He lifted my head again—I'd almost forgotten his hand was still resting under my neck—and placed the coconut to my lips.

I sucked the liquid down obediently, the warm, sweet water suddenly heavy on my tongue. "Can we drink the water?" I asked when I'd swallowed the latest gulp.

He shook his head, looking to his right, where I knew the waterfall must be. "I don't know," he admitted. "I have no idea if it's safe." He rolled his eyes, the wrinkle between them deepening. His next sentence was hesitant, as if it physically pained him to say the words. "Harry would know."

I couldn't hide the grin that grew, almost forcefully, on my lips. Upon seeing it, he scowled.

"What?"

"It's just…that's the first time I've heard you call any of us by our actual names and not a nickname."

His gaze narrowed at me, the dark brown of his eyes locking on mine. "Yeah, well my throat's too dry to call him Captain Smarty Pants every time." With that, he lifted the coconut to his own lips and drained the remaining liquid.

I tried to sit up again, wanting desperately to see the water I could hear splashing over the falls ahead. I took it slow, relieved not to feel my head spinning as soon as I'd moved. The black dots in my vision didn't return. I pushed farther, sitting up slowly, and felt his hand on my back as he laid the coconut down. He studied me.

"You good?"

I nodded, inhaling deeply at the sight of the waterfall ahead. It was smaller than I'd been expecting, the water cascading over the top of the cliff coming in three small streams rather than a large powerful gush. The forest wrapped itself like a cocoon around the waterfall, leaving just a few feet of bare ground encircling the body of water on every side. Red flowers bloomed near the water closest to the fall, and the trees drooped over the small lake, making a sort of dome over the top.

I tried to catch my breath as I stared at the crystal-clear blue water just feet from me, my body physically aching to touch it.

"Did you know this was here?" I managed to squeak out.

His reply was a stiff nod.

"You knew we were all dehydrating, and you didn't say anything about the fact that you'd found a lake?"

"Calm down, Officer," he said, looking toward the water. "I planned to tell you all, but when I came back, I saw the note. That changed my mind. And, it's not like I let you dehydrate. I brought back coconuts so everyone could get a drink. I was just trying to decide what I wanted to do about this place..."

"That's why you didn't want to bring us back here... Why you insisted we stay near the beach..." The realization hit me with a sudden weight, and anger bubbled in my belly. "You were actually considering letting us die? Keeping this place to yourself?"

"You mean you weren't?" he demanded defiantly. "Not even a little bit?"

"No!" I said quickly. "No, not even a little bit. There's no way I would've kept this place from anyone."

He pressed his lips together. "Well, pardon the hell out of me for not being Mother Theresa. What am I keeping from them, really? We don't even know if it'd be safe to drink."

"But Harry will know. You're right about that," I said. "And besides, even if we can't drink it straight, surely we can boil it. We can use it to bathe, to clean wounds. They have to know about this place."

He shrugged. "Well, it's your secret now. I can't keep you from telling it, I guess, but all I'll say is that you need to think about who you trust here. You may be an angel, but not everyone here is. We could keep this place to ourselves. Bring back coconuts daily, sure, but never let them anywhere near here."

"You're not going to stop me from telling them?" I stared at him, trying to determine whether or not he was joking.

"Would I have just saved your life if I planned to kill you to keep this a secret? I could've just left you on the forest floor when you collapsed. I could've dropped you in the lake and let you drown while you were unconscious. Instead, I carried you here and nursed you back to health. Does that sound like someone planning to hurt you?"

Something about the way he said the words made me think he'd actively weighed those options before deciding what to do. "You carried me?"

"Well, you didn't fly."

I felt warmth spread through my stomach. "Why would you do that? What happened to every man for himself?"

He groaned, standing up and refusing to meet my eye. "Yeah, well, don't make me regret it. Come on, we need to get these coconuts back to the beach before The Professor and Warrior Princess come looking for us."

I started to stand, taking it slow, but losing my balance anyway. His hand shot out, catching me before I could fall and bringing me to his side. "Easy does it..." he whispered.

A smile spread to my lips again, and it didn't go unnoticed. "What?" he asked, steadying me before taking his shirt from my arms and lifting it above my head. "Here, let's get this on you before you burn even more."

"You'd better be careful, Noah," I said as he slid the white T-shirt over my body. "Someone might actually think you're a good guy or something."

He smirked again, his cool eyes meeting mine. I watched his gaze fall to my lips, the moment frozen between us so quickly I forgot to breathe. He leaned in, and I felt my heart flutter. I should've stopped it, but I was exhausted, dehydrated, and delirious. I felt powerless to do or say anything as his lips inched toward mine. My eyes closed, waiting for the connection.

"Maybe that's exactly what I want them to think." I felt his breath on my lips, suddenly chilled by his words. When I opened my eyes, he'd backed up again, his lips upturned with amusement.

My face burned with outright embarrassment as I bent to grab the coconuts from the ground, unable to say a word about what had happened. To my relief, Noah didn't either. Instead, we loaded our arms with the coconuts, and I waited for him to lead the way back to camp.

Most of the way, we didn't speak, and I didn't bother trying to keep up with him as my legs burned from the snail's pace I seemed barely able to maintain. When we'd been walking so long I was half sure he'd changed his mind about leaving me on the forest floor and was just waiting for me to collapse again, I began hearing the roar of the ocean waves and feeling the warm, salty breeze that could only come from being near the shore.

Noah turned to me, one brow raised, his voice low. "Tell them what I showed you if you want, I won't stop you, but hear me out first: if anyone does decide they want to take the rest of us out, that place is ours. Yours and mine. It's safe. We have shelter there, water, food. I'm not proposing we let anyone dehydrate, but what I'm saying is that we keep our secret for a while until we get our bearings. Until we figure out who's on whose side here. We don't really know these people. We don't know that we can trust them."

"I don't know if I can trust you either."

"Fair enough," he said with the bow of his head, "but I did show you the place to save your life. I protected you when I could've easily not. Would you bet your life on the fact that they'd do the same?"

I paused, thinking through what he'd said, but eventually I shook my head. "I'd want them to tell me if the situation were reversed. It's not fair. We have to be honest with each other."

He scoffed. "Do you really believe everyone here is being honest with each other?"

I nodded, but it was halfhearted. "Whatever. It's your funeral… All I'm saying is once that secret's out, we no longer have the upper hand. We have nothing to bargain with. Nothing to ensure our survival. They might find it on their own, sure. They might find coconuts, too. But right now, we're the only two who know a direct path to water. That gives us some immunity." He paused. "Just… think about it, okay? Anyone out there could be the person who brought us here. Anyone out there could know exactly why we're here. You just don't know." With that final, solemn phrase, he turned away from me and headed forward, moments later pulling a branch back to reveal our small, boulder encampment.

I tried to force his words from my mind. They meant

nothing. I wasn't Noah. I didn't want to behave like him... But was he right somehow? Did our secret make me more powerful? I wanted to go home more than anything, but did I honestly believe someone on the island could have something to do with why we were there?

The thought sent chills down my spine. He was wrong...

He had to be.

CHAPTER ELEVEN

I don't know why I didn't tell them about the waterfall. Maybe Noah had gotten in my head about it, maybe I had my own reasons, but as we made our way back to the camp, seeing the makeshift hut Harry, Ava, and James had crafted, I didn't breathe a word about our discovery, and neither did Noah.

This only made me feel guiltier when, upon seeing me, Harry rushed toward us with his arms outstretched. When he reached me, his hands gripped my biceps. "Thank God." He looked at Noah. "You were gone a long time."

"It's far away," he said simply. "And I think what you mean is *thank you, Noah, for hand-delivering the only thing keeping us alive right now.*" He placed every coconut but two down, offering a slight bow. "To which I say, you're welcome, Your Majesty. I am but a humble servant, after all."

Harry scowled slightly but didn't reply. "You okay?" he

asked me, looking down at the oversized shirt. "Why are you wearing his shirt?"

"I'm okay…" I almost told him the truth about what had happened, but something stopped me. I hated how much I'd allowed Noah to cause me to doubt the people I wanted so desperately to trust. "He gave it to me so I wouldn't burn anymore."

Harry's expression appeared taken aback. "Oh, good. That's a good idea."

I nodded toward the shelter. "That looks great. You've been working hard."

He shrugged one shoulder, looking away from me. "It'll do for now. I'm not sure how long it'll hold up, but for a day or two at least we'll have somewhere dry to sleep."

"Here." A coconut was thrust into my face, and I followed the length of the outstretched arm that held it to meet Noah's eye. He had one coconut held up to his mouth and the other was, apparently, mine. "You should lie down."

"I'm fine," I said angrily, then cooled my tone a bit. "But thank you." I took it from him, unable to deny how thirsty I was and lifted it to my lips. I began to take a sip, then felt guilty for doing so in front of Harry, so I lowered it and held it out. "You should have this. I had some out there."

He looked at the coconut, then back at me. His answer was powerless. "I'll get my own. It's okay. There are plenty…"

"It's fine, Harry, honestly. I drank one on the way back. You must be so thirsty." He swiped the back of his hand across his dirt-streaked forehead, his dry, cracked lips confirming what I'd said.

"Thanks," he said finally, taking it from my hands and gulping it down quickly. When he was done, he rubbed his hand across his lips guiltily. "Sorry… I guess the heat got to me."

"You've been working hard," I said. "We all have. We should rest for a while, rehydrate, then make a plan for exploring more of the island."

He nodded, keeping his voice low. "Are you sure everything went okay out there? Noah was—"

"Still within listening distance," Noah called loudly from a few feet away, his coconut in the air. "And, I was a perfect gentleman, Grandpa, don't worry."

I gave a conceding nod. "It's true. He was. He took care of me when I overheated."

"You what? What happened? Are you—"

"I'm fine now." I cut off his panic. "Honestly. I just needed to rest a bit. Who would've guessed sunburn, exhaustion, and dehydration would be a bad combo?"

"Okay, you sit," Harry said. "Let me get you some more to drink."

"I'm fine, Harry," I tried to argue, but it was no use. He'd already scooped two more coconuts from the pile and had made his way toward the rock we'd been using to bust them open. I fought back against the deep pit of guilt inside my stomach as he delivered mine. If I brought up the waterfall now, they'd only wonder why I hadn't told them the second we got back, wouldn't they? How could I keep something this important from someone so determined to take care of me?

Suddenly, from behind me, I heard Ava cry out in apparent pain. I spun around quickly to see her clutching her stomach, sweat beading on her temples.

"What is it? What's wrong?"

Her expression was agonizing as she looked at me. "I don't know, I just—" Before she could finish her sentence, she doubled over, vomit spewing from her lips and onto the sand.

"Ava!" I dropped my drink and launched forward, reaching for her as she continued to be sick. At the same time, the men backed away, sounds of gagging and groaning could be heard from all around. I touched her bicep, moving a hand to her hair to pull as much of the dark curls back as I could.

When she'd stopped, she shook her head, wiping her arm across her lips. "I'm sorry. I don't know what happened... I just suddenly felt..." She stopped, her dark skin seeming to grow paler as she staggered a half step backward.

"Are you okay?" Harry asked, still several steps back from us.

"I don't know..." she said powerlessly. "I just feel...off."

"Are you going to be sick again?" he asked.

"And, if you are, aim it that way," Noah said, slurping his drink loudly.

"Here, let's just get you set down on the sand." I took her hand, my other palm on her upper back as I helped her sink down onto the warm sand beneath our feet. Once she was able to relax a bit, her expression calmed.

"Thank you. I feel better already." She swiped sweat from her brow. "I'm sorry, guys."

"You don't have to apologize," Harry said, taking a small step in our direction as I swept sand over her vomit, covering it completely. He handed me one half of his coconut and I placed it in her palms.

"He's right, you probably just overheated. It's easy enough to do. I should know," I told her. "Just keep drinking."

"But slowly," Harry instructed, now standing beside where I'd knelt down next to her. "Take small sips rather than gulps. It'll be easier on your stomach."

She did as she was told, drinking slowly and taking steady breaths in between each gulp.

"I don't think we should go anywhere today," Harry said firmly, and I glanced over my shoulder at him.

"What?"

"I know we wanted to explore some, but we need to take our time. You overheated earlier, and Ava did just now. Finding anything on this island won't matter if half of us are sick or, worse, dead. None of us are used to heat and hunger like this. We have to be careful not to overdo it. For now, we need to just rest until the sun goes down for the evening. We can use Noah's knife to carve spears. Then, maybe we try to catch some fish for dinner. Tomorrow, we'll head out early before the sun's too high."

"What if we can't afford to wait?"

"We can't afford not to," he said simply. "I'm sorry. I wanted to go too, but I won't risk either of you collapsing out there."

"I'm fine," Ava said, moving to sit up. "Honestly, I think I just drank too fast."

"And I'm fine, too," I agreed. "We have to explore

tonight, Harry. We have to. I don't think I can spend another night here not knowing what's going on."

"I agree with him," Noah said, taking us all by surprise. "If either of you collapse or get sick, we'd either have to carry you or make camp wherever we are. It makes more sense to stay here for the night and try tomorrow. Besides that"—he stretched his arms over his head and tucked them behind his neck—"I could use a nap."

"It's settled, then," Harry said, looking relieved.

"No, it's tied," Ava argued, her eyes narrowing at James. "What do you think? It all comes down to your vote."

"Alright," Noah said, bobbing his head up and down joyfully, "it's like an episode of Survivor. Let's put it to a vote."

James grumbled, his arms draped casually over his knees as he stared at the sand. "I'm starving," he said after a moment. "So if my choice is to carry you two through the forest or stay here and eat seafood oceanside tonight, I guess it isn't too difficult to decide." He shrugged, looking out toward the water. For some reason, I felt he was choosing to side with the men, rather than on the side he truly believed was right, but I saw no point in pressing the issue.

"So that's how it's going to be, huh?" Ava said, picking up on the same vibe I had. "You all outnumber us, so you make all the decisions?" I met Harry's eye, feeling betrayed. Up until that moment, I'd believed he was on our side. Had Noah been right all along? Was everyone finally accepting that it was every man for himself? I no longer felt the nagging guilt over having kept the waterfall a secret between Noah and me.

"It's not like that," Harry said softly, bending down so he was eye level with me, though he was looking at Ava. "There are no sides. There is no us or you. It's all of us. We're in this mess together, and we have to look out for each other… I'm doing this to protect you both." His eyes were serious, but not stern. I wanted to believe him, but I couldn't. I felt as if he were hiding something… As if they all were.

Finally though, I nodded, watching as James and Harry began gathering sticks for Noah to sharpen with his knife.

It was the first time I'd felt truly alone on the island, even with Ava by my side. It was the first time, too, I considered the possibility I may never leave it. That I may never see my husband, my family, my friends again. The mere thought was utterly devastating.

By NIGHTFALL, James had managed to catch three fish that we were forced to split. The meat settled in our bellies, barely making a dent in our true hunger, so we filled up on water from the coconuts and lounged around the fire. Everyone was relatively quiet, mostly lost in our own thoughts.

"What do you guys miss most of all?" Ava asked, bringing most of us to a sitting position as we tried to think of an answer.

"Chocolate cake," Harry said, scratching his belly. "I'd kill for a giant slice of chocolate cake right about now."

"Beer for me," James said, though I had doubts about whether he was old enough to drink legally.

"Sex," Noah said with a low grumble, rubbing his bicep casually. "You're all lying if you don't say sex is what you miss most." His eyes found Ava. "Those of us who've had it anyway."

She rolled her eyes but didn't say anything. No one denied the truth in his words, and I felt something warm low in my belly at the thought. He wasn't wrong.

"Well, I, for one, miss bubble baths," I said anyway, trying to change the subject.

"Yeah, because *bubble baths* are better than a nice round of bumpin' the ole uglies," Noah sneered.

"I miss my family," Ava said sincerely, interrupting the argument I'd had planned. The mood shifted at once, the lightness in the air dissipating.

"Yeah," Harry said with a long, drawn-out sigh. "Me too."

"Me three…" I trailed off, thinking of my husband. My parents. It was almost too painful to do.

We fell silent again for what felt like a long time, before Harry spoke again. "We need to find out if we all have something in common."

"Why?" Noah asked, batting his eyelashes playfully in the glow of the fire. "Are you planning on playing matchmaker?"

"No." He didn't bother to indulge Noah with a snide response back. "Because we need to figure out why we— the five of us specifically—are here."

"You mean you don't think it's random?" James asked, his eyes wide with concern.

"It might be," he conceded. "But it would be smart to narrow things down a bit."

"Like what?" I asked.

"Like... Where are we all from?" Harry asked, starting off the round of questions.

We went on like that, discussing where we were from, if we had any enemies, what resort we'd been staying at, why we were in the Keys, and more. In the end, none of us were from the same state, let alone area. None of us believed we had any enemies who could've been involved in anything like sending us to a deserted island. We'd all been on vacation except for Noah, but for different lengths of time, some of us at the end of our stay while some of us had just arrived. And while Harry and I had been staying at the same resort, Noah lived in the area and had just been at the beach for the day, Ava had been staying at her parents' beach house, and James had been staying at a motel with some friends nearby. It seemed as though we had no real connections between the five of us that could give any indication why this would be happening.

Eventually, the questions ran out and we settled back into the quiet of the night. By the time the moon was high in the sky and the last log on the fire had burned down to cinders, its orange glow growing dimmer, we made our way back to our shelter, agreeing that since Ava and I had sat up the night before, James and Harry would take first shift tonight and we'd rotate like we'd meant to before.

That's the last thing I remember before I woke up the next morning, my back stiff and painful, belly growling from hunger. When I sat up, I realized I was alone.

Instantly, the panic set in. What had happened? Where were they? Why had they left me?

I stood up, dusting my legs off and trying to decide what to do. If I screamed, I could put myself in danger. If I went the wrong direction, I could end up even farther from their trail.

Just as I was beginning to break down from panic, I heard a voice in the distance. *Noah.*

I moved toward his voice instinctively, keeping each step quiet, despite my labored, terrified breathing. As I drew nearer to his voice, I heard Ava too, and relief flooded my body.

"What do you think we should do?" she asked, her voice a high-pitched squeal.

"It could've been the ocean," Noah replied.

Harry's voice came next, as I finally caught them in my line of vision. "The ocean didn't do this. It couldn't have." As I pulled back the branch blocking my view of the shore, I saw them standing several feet away from me, spread out in a makeshift circle, each one staring down at the ground below them.

"What, then? An animal? It could've been an animal."

"No way this was an animal," Ava argued, shaking her head.

"What's going on?" I asked, shielding my eyes from the rising sun as I made my way across the beach. The group jumped practically in unison from the interruption, and all eyes fell on me.

"Thank God," Harry said, a hand to his chest.

"What's wrong?" I asked again. "What are you all looking at? Why didn't you wake me up?" I picked up the pace as I got closer to where they were standing, desperate to see what all the fuss was about.

"We tried to," Ava said, her fists pressed into her hips. "You were sleeping hard."

"Thought it was best to let you get your rest before we headed out anyway," Harry added.

"But what's going on?"

"I came out here to rinse off in the water, and I saw this," Noah said, pointing down toward what had once been our SOS signal, but was now just a scattered pile of sticks and rocks. Someone had dismantled our sign entirely.

"What the hell?" I asked, walking around the circle to look at it from every angle, though it made no sense from any direction. "What does this mean?"

Harry's face was solemn when I looked up, and I knew what he was going to say before he opened his mouth. "It means we aren't alone on the island. It means someone's watching us."

CHAPTER TWELVE

"But it could've been the water," James said, grasping at straws. "We don't know how high the tide got up last night."

"The sand is dry," Ava quipped.

"The wind, then... We don't know that this means we're being watched."

"Oh, come on—" Noah began to argue, but Harry cut him off.

"Look, it doesn't matter who or what it was. This doesn't change our plans of exploring the island today. If we're being watched somehow, we need to move. We can't make this easier on them."

"So, what are you suggesting?" James asked.

"We're going to find the highest point of the island and find out what we can see from there. Other people, houses, a town, fresh water... We need to understand what it is we're working with here, and the longer we sit still, if someone is trying to hurt us, the easier we're making it on them."

I nodded in agreement. "Harry's right. We can't stay in one place. It's not safe."

"It's settled, then," Ava said, "because I agree. We should gather the three spears from last night, the coconuts we still have left, and go." She shivered, despite the heat, and I noticed she still appeared to be feeling off.

"Fine, but I've got an appointment with a bush, so give me twenty minutes," Noah said, already walking away from us.

"Don't go far," I called, worry churning in my stomach as I kept a watchful eye on our surroundings.

"Trust me, you don't want me close."

I rolled my eyes and turned my attention to Ava. "How are you feeling this morning?" She hadn't eaten much at dinner the night before, claiming her stomach had still felt upset.

She waved off my concern quickly. "Oh, I'm fine. Just fighting off a bug of some sort. Leave it to me to get sick in the middle of all of this. In paradise, no less."

I smiled halfheartedly, unable to compare our current location to paradise, even if it would've been under different circumstances. "Have you gotten sick anymore?"

"Nope," she said, her lips tight. "Just yesterday. I'm pacing myself with the coconut water, though; I think that was the issue. Maybe I have a slight allergy or something."

"I'm glad you're feeling better," I said, looking away from her as I heard Noah cry out in the distance.

"Hey!" he shouted, drawing our attention to him. "Come here! Quick!"

Instantly, the four of us began running in the direction

his scream could be heard from. *Please be okay. Please be okay.* My internal pleas shocked even me, but after the way he'd taken care of me yesterday, albeit reluctantly, I felt I owed it to him to do the same. As we neared the tree line, I listened for him to make a noise again.

"Noah?" Harry called cautiously. "You...you okay? What's going on?"

"Never been better," his reply came from behind us. We spun around and, upon seeing him, my stomach lurched.

"Where did you get those?" James asked, his voice practically quivering.

"Why do you have them?" Ava demanded.

In his arms, he held two shotguns, a pistol, and two machetes. As ice-cold fear swept over me, I watched his grin spread.

"Things are about to get interesting..." His brow raised, sending a chill down my spine. "Aren't they?"

CHAPTER THIRTEEN

"Why do you have those, Noah? Where did they come from?" I asked again, begging him to look at me. Instead, he was admiring the weapons in his arms with great care. Was he going to kill us? Was this how it would end? I needed to avoid jumping to conclusions as I so often did, but how could I not?

When he finally looked up, it was me his eyes narrowed on. "Why don't you tell us?"

"Me?" I asked, startled by the accusation. "What are you talking about?"

"These were by the shelter, and since you were the last person in the shelter, I'd assume if anyone knew where they came from...it'd be you."

"I..." Suddenly, all eyes were on me. I felt chills line my skin as I shook my head, trying to find reason where there was none. "I don't know what you're talking about. How on earth would I have come up with those? They weren't there when I woke up." I thought back, though my memory of waking up alone was hazy at best. "At least, I don't remember them." I pressed my fingers to my temples, thinking.

"Either way, you need to put them down until we figure out where they came from," Harry said, his arms outstretched, palms facing the ground as he tried to ease Noah into putting them down.

As could be expected, Noah didn't budge.

"No, I don't think I will. I think I'll hold on to them."

"Are they even loaded?" Ava asked, staring at him skeptically.

"Want me to shoot and see?" he asked, a brow raised.

"No," Harry and James said all at once.

"We don't want to draw attention to ourselves," Harry added.

"I hate to break it to you guys, but someone already knows we're here." He gestured toward the weapons in his hands.

His sentence brought me back to reality. "He's right." The words sent chills down my spine. Someone did know we were there, and there was no room to question it any longer. "Someone knows we're here… Someone is setting us up."

"It could be one of us," Noah said, still looking at me. "Any of us."

"Unless you believe it was me, it couldn't have been any of us. You were all at the beach together, and I swear to you, the weapons weren't there when I woke up. I would've told you about them."

Noah's brow raised, but it was slight. I knew he was thinking about the waterfall I'd kept a secret, but I brushed the thought away, going on.

"That means someone waited until I was awake and away from the shelter to put the weapons down. They left them somewhere they knew we'd return. They wanted us to find them."

"Someone could be looking out for us," Ava said, her voice nearly a whisper. "Maybe they were giving us protection."

"From each other, yeah," Noah said.

"We aren't a danger to each other," Harry argued.

"Maybe we're on TV after all," James added in hopefully, but the longer he spoke, the less certain he seemed. "Maybe this is all a setup. Maybe the guns aren't loaded and the knives aren't sharp…"

Noah laid the weapons on the ground carefully, keeping just one shotgun, and placing his body between us and the weapons. Without warning, he fired a shot into the air, causing us all to jump and scream. Harry covered his head with his hands. Ava fell to the ground.

"What the hell is wrong with you?" I demanded once I'd realized we were still okay. I charged toward him angrily, my hands in fists at my sides. "Why would you do that?"

"You've already said whoever planted these knows we're here and knows where we are, so now we've also disproved the theory that the guns aren't loaded. What should we do next?" he asked, a lopsided grin on his lips.

"I don't understand you…" I said, turning away from him, my belly burning with anger. "Why can't you just take a single thing seriously? Why does everything have to be a joke?"

KIERSTEN MODGLIN

"There could be animals out here," Harry pointed out. "You could've just drawn them toward us."

"Animals who'd run toward gunfire?" Noah asked skeptically.

"At least if he did, we could get something real to eat," Ava said, her hand on her stomach as she stood finally.

"We each need a weapon," I said finally. "In case someone—a person or animal—were to attack. There are five things. That's obviously intentional." I reached for a weapon, but Noah stepped in front of them, wagging the gun. He didn't point it at me, but it was enough to send ice-cold fear through my veins.

"Ah, ah, ah," he said, waving the gun again. "Not so fast. I'm the one who found the weapons, apparently. I'm the one who gets to decide what we do with them."

"Oh, give it a rest, Noah. She's right. We need a weapon each. It's only fair," Ava said.

"Who says I want to play fair?" he asked, his brows drawing down in mock confusion.

"You can't shoot us all at once," James said, taking a step toward him aggressively. "You might be able to take one of us out, but it's four against one, man."

Noah's eyes bounced between us, his expression unchanging, but I caught the glimmer of fear in his eyes. "Are you really willing to take that chance?" he asked finally.

"Yeah, I am—" James took another step toward him, now shoulder-to-shoulder with me. His hands balled into fists at his sides.

"We don't have time for this, guys," Harry said, exasperation in his tone. "Come on. We need to get going if we want to explore, especially if we're worried about someone watching us. The best form of protection is for us to keep moving."

"I guess we could just leave him here," Ava said, crossing her arms. "If he won't share the weapons, he can keep them all and be by himself."

"Fine by me. You all go on your little jungle adventure. I'll be here working on a tan." As he said it, a darkness fell across the bright sand, and we looked up to the sky where a storm cloud had crossed in front of the sun.

"So much for your tan," Ava joked.

Suddenly, lightning shot down from the cloud, connecting with the horizon.

"There's a storm coming," Harry said ominously as the wind began to pick up. As if further confirming his words, thunder cracked overhead, loud and booming in the otherwise near-silence. I jolted, feeling tears prick my eyes.

Why? Why was this happening? Why couldn't we seem to catch a break? Why did everything seem to be working against us?

"Looks like travel plans are canceled…" Ava whispered. "Again."

"This vacation is really turning into a nightmare, isn't it? I hope they aren't expecting a tip." Noah winked and twirled the gun around again, but as James took a step toward him, he rolled his eyes. "Oh, relax, would you? You can all have your weapons. But I'm keeping this one."

"Fine by me," Ava said, stepping forward. "I'll take the pistol."

"Woah," Noah tried to stop her. "What do you know about handling a pistol?"

She pointed it in the air. "Want to find out?" She smirked. "I told you, my dad's a hunter. I've been around guns all my life. Do *you* know what you're doing with that?" She jutted a finger toward the shotgun in his arms. "How to load it? How to turn the safety on? How to clean it?"

His eyes narrowed. "Fair enough. She gets the gun." He took a half step back and allowed her to take the pistol. James made a move for the other shotgun, and Harry and I settled on the machetes. Okay by me, honestly. Guns had always made me nervous. I'd never grown up around them and had no desire to be around them now, let alone carrying one.

The wind howled, reminding us of the impending storm, and another bolt of lightning burned across the sky, this time the thunder following close behind it.

"We need to get to the shelter," Harry warned, holding his machete awkwardly.

"In the forest? Isn't that more dangerous with all the trees?" Ava asked as rain droplets began to pelt us. She shielded her eyes as we all waited to see what Harry would have to say.

"Sitting at the trunk of a tree, maybe, but under the boulder we should be safe. We should gather up the shells we had before and set them and the empty coconut shells out to catch as much water as we can, too. It won't be much, but every little bit helps."

Without needing further instruction, we jumped into action as the rain picked up even more, its roar deafening as it splattered onto the sand and trees, making it nearly impossible to see each other from just feet away. My skin ached as the rain slapped my sunburn, but I did my best to ignore it.

Harry and I split the empty, discarded coconuts while the others laid them out next to the seashells, in a somewhat neat row. They were already beginning to fill as we walked away, heading for shelter just as the storm began to rage.

We huddled under the rock, drenched and shivering as the wind howled and the lightning lit up the sky that was filled with sunshine just an hour before. We lost track of time, no longer able to count on the sun to help us determine how much of the day passed, and most of us dozed in and out of sleep, with thunder waking us up before we found any sort of true rest.

Hours later, when the rain finally slacked up, the shelter Harry and the others had worked so hard on had been completely knocked down, the branches shredded and splintering. We were windburned and sitting on muddy ground, soaked through our clothes and exhausted, despite the naps.

As we made our way out of the shelter to assess the damage, Harry gasped, and I looked around for whatever it might be that he saw.

"We'll rebuild it," I assured him as Ava and James went to check how much water we'd been able to accumulate. "We'll all work together and get it fixed. With these"—I gestured toward where we'd laid the machetes near the back of the boulder—"it'll be much easier."

"It's not that," he said, still staring blankly into space. He pointed his nose upward. "Do you smell that?"

There were lots of smells out there in the jungle. The salty air, the stench of body odor and rotting fish bones from the night before. I inhaled deeply, trying to decide what it was he was smelling at that moment.

"I don't know… What is it?"

His eyes met mine. "Smoke," he said. "And it's not coming from our fire."

"The lightning?" Noah asked from behind me, true fear on his face for the first time. Harry's grim expression neither confirmed nor denied it, but as I took another deep breath, I smelled it too.

Somewhere on the island, there was a fire. And if it grew to be too much, there'd be no escape.

CHAPTER FOURTEEN

"We have to move to higher ground," Harry said, jumping into action and scooping up our weapons. "I need to see where the smoke is coming from. If it is a fire, we need to see where it is and if it's still manageable. If we can put it out, we'll have to... Otherwise, it's going to spread like...well, wildfire." He shoved my machete into my hands and, together, we made our way toward the beach to collect James and Ava.

They were bent down next to each other, examining the coconuts, and I noticed a closeness between them I hadn't seen before. They kept their voices low, their bodies practically touching as Ava picked one up and drained it. James watched her almost hungrily, and I felt my skin crawl at the sight.

"Hey," I said, interrupting the moment. Ava jumped, sloshing a bit of the water onto the sand, and James stood abruptly. I watched her rub her arm across her mouth and stand too, a bright smile on her face.

"You guys! They're all full. Fresh water!" She gestured toward the coconuts waiting for us.

Okay, so maybe I'd misread pure happiness as attraction as they stood farther apart now, both staring at us with waning smiles.

"What's wrong?" James asked.

"There's a fire in the forest," Harry told them. "We have to get going. No more delaying it. We have to find the highest point we can access and try to get an idea of where the fire's coming from."

"Do you think other people started it? The ones who left the weapons?" Ava's tone was high with fear.

"Maybe, but it could've been the lightning, too. We just don't know. Either way"—Harry moved toward them—"everyone get a drink and fuel up for the trip. There's no way of knowing how long we'll be traveling or when we'll be able to stop again."

Needing no further coaxing, we made our way toward the coconuts and seashells, drinking the fresh rainwater in gulps. I'd never tasted anything so magnificent in all my life.

Once we'd finished the water—seconds later, mind you—Harry pointed to me. "Can we borrow your cardigan-thingy?" He gestured toward his shoulders. "I'm going to tie it up and make a makeshift pack. We can use it to carry these shells. You never know when we might need them."

"Oh, sure," I said, pulling my arms out of Noah's T-shirt long enough to shrug the sarong off my shoulders. I handed it to him, and he tied the ends together carefully, loading up the coconuts and seashells and tying it one final time. "There." He held it up, admiring his work. "It's not perfect, but it'll do."

"It's great," I said, taking it back from him and sliding my arm through the opening so it hung like a grocery sack. It was heavier than I'd been expecting, and there was no less-awkward way to carry it, so this would have to do.

"Okay then, if everyone has their weapons and their... things..." He looked around, and I knew he was thinking about what few items we had—Harry's book, our phones, my Kindle. "Our fire was put out by the storm and our shelter's gone, so we have nothing to do here. Unless anyone can think of anything before we head out, we'll get going."

With nothing to add and no reason to stay, we followed Harry's lead as he left the shore and disappeared into the forest, walking past our shelter without so much as a glance in its direction. I couldn't explain the sudden sadness that swept through me. It was just a rock with branches now scattered around it, but it had kept us safe. For our time here, it had been the closest thing we'd had to a home, and I couldn't deny the grief swelling in my stomach over never seeing it again. It seemed no one else shared my sentiments as we hurried past it and into the vast, unexplored forest.

THE AFTERNOON HEAT WAS SWELTERING; the humidity from the storm had recreated the intense feeling of opening the dryer door and being smacked in the face by the warm, wet heat.

God, I missed dryers.

I missed everything. Even small things, like opening a bag of chips on the way home from the grocery store and being stuck in traffic when your favorite song comes on. I missed the big things, of course—my husband, my mom, my bed, my friends, *air conditioning*, but it was the little things that really seemed to get to me the most. The things that snuck up on me in the quiet, unexpected moments.

We made our way through the forest, swatting away buzzing insects and mosquitoes and being smacked by branches, twigs, and thorny plants every few steps. My mouth felt drier than it had in our time on the island, and my legs burned as we trekked through the mud and over boulders.

When we finally stopped in the center of a small clearing, I realized I was panting, my chest tight with haggard breaths. Harry was staring into the distance, a hand up over his brow to shield his eyes from the sun.

"There," he said, pointing toward the sky. I looked up, following his finger. "The mountain. The cliff up there. That's where we're going."

The cliff he'd gestured toward looked thousands of feet away, and I felt my legs shaking at the mere thought of it.

"I don't smell smoke anymore," Noah said, tilting his nose upward. "Do you?"

He was looking at me, but it was Ava that answered. "I haven't smelled it in a while. Maybe we were just smelling the remnants of our fire."

"I don't think so," Harry said. "But the wind stopped

blowing too. It's possible the scent was being carried on the wind. If lightning did start a fire, the rain may have put it out and we just caught a bit of the smell."

"Well, if we're not in a hurry, can we at least take a break?" James bent over his knees. "My legs feel like whipped cream."

"I think the term you're looking for is 'jelly,'" Ava said with a giggle. "Your legs feel like jelly."

"Potato, pat*ah*to. Whipped cream tastes better." He winked.

"Are we planning to eat your legs?" Noah teased. "I'm not super into the whole Hannibal thing, and if we're eating anyone's anything, you would not be my first pick."

James rolled his eyes, not taking them off Ava for even a second. "Whatever. Either way, I don't feel like walking anymore."

"I agree," I said, nodding dramatically as my lungs burned with a sudden stitch. "I need to rest."

"It's going to be dark soon anyway," Harry agreed, though his tone was rife with disappointment. "We'll make camp here for the night and then head out as soon as the sun's up tomorrow. James, can you get a fire started?"

"Sure thing. Ava, you want to help me?"

She nodded, following him away from where we stood. I realized then I'd been right before, in my assumption that there might be something between them. Though they were the closest in age, it struck me as odd that James, the brawny but mostly silent one had taken so easily to the outspoken and fierce Ava. Still, I found myself feeling thankful they had each other, even while nursing a bit of bitterness myself to be alone.

God, sometimes I missed my husband so much it felt as if it were burning me from the inside out. *At least, if he were here,* I thought tempestuously, *without the cell service he's so reliant on, he'd be forced to focus on me.* With or without his focus, I knew with him there, I'd feel safer than I did at present.

"Good. We'll leave the pack with the coconuts here, so in case we get split up, we know where to come back to. While you are building the fire, we should look for food and more coconuts for the night. You two want to come with me?"

"I've been the coconut fetcher the past few times. What do you say I take a rest this time and keep the place safe?" Noah asked.

Harry's brow furrowed, but he'd learned Noah's quirks by then. He knew, as we all did, that he'd try to push the boundary. The trick was learning how to push back without causing him to shut down or lash out. "Fine, just give us your gun," he said, extending his hand.

"No way."

"We need a gun if we're going to hunt. So, either you come with us, or we need to borrow it."

"You're going to get it back, Noah," I added, placing the sack next to a tree and resting my hands on my hips. "Come on. Before it gets dark. Don't you want to eat something real for once?"

Groaning, he stepped forward. "Alright, fine. I'm coming."

We'd only been walking for a few minutes when I

heard the rushing of water in the distance, and I realized we must be close to the stream that led to our waterfall. Noah and Harry heard it at the same time, everyone's heads perking up at once. Noah met my eyes, a question in them, and I gave a stiff nod.

Who were we to say no at this point? Perhaps it was the dehydration getting to me again, or the desire to wash my body for the first time in...days? Weeks? How long had we even been here? It all seemed to run together anymore.

"Do you hear that?" Harry asked before we could say anything.

"It sounds like water," I said, hoping Noah would play along.

"Fresh water," he agreed. "It sounds close."

Harry made a sharp left and hurried forward. As I made a move to follow him, I heard something else. A rustling behind us. I froze, though both of the men were moving ahead without me. I spun around, looking in every direction, searching for the source of the sound. Had I imagined it?

"Hello?" I called, gripping the handle of the machete in my hand. The forest around me was silent except for the distant sounds of the stream and the men's voices carrying on ahead. They hadn't realized I wasn't keeping up with them.

As another rustling sound came from just in front of me, I took a step backward. Someone was definitely there. Just beyond the tree line. I took several steps backward, weapon outstretched, refusing to turn my back to them.

"Who's there?" I called, trying and failing to keep my

131

voice steady. I spoke loudly enough that I hoped the men would hear me and come to my aid, but soon the sounds of the voices had faded altogether, and I knew I was alone.

Shhhhshhhshh...

The rustling had grown closer. My heart leapt into my chest, and I found myself unable to take a breath. I took another step back, my entire body trembling with fear, and heard a *snap* beneath my feet. My body tensed, and I stepped off the broken branch I'd cracked just in time to hear rushing footsteps headed in my direction. As I did, I saw a flash of blonde hair just beyond the trees.

A woman. I was sure of it.

"Hello?" She'd been watching me.

The footsteps grew closer, and I felt a hand on my back. I jumped. "Are you okay?" Harry asked.

At the same time Noah said, "What are you doing?"

"There was a woman," I said, pointing toward the trees where I'd seen her only moments ago. "A woman in the bushes."

"Are you sure?"

"Was it Ava?"

"No, no... She had blonde hair. She...I didn't get a good look at her, it was just a flash. I think she was following us. She must've heard you coming and gotten scared off."

"Maybe it was just a bird," Harry said, squeezing my shoulder carefully as Noah moved forward to investigate, his gun drawn. "I'm sorry we disappeared. Why did you stop?"

"I heard something, like swishing...the trees, I guess. I could hear her moving around through the grass..."

"Why didn't you say anything?"

"You were already far enough ahead by the time I realized it, and I didn't know if I was in danger. I was worried if I screamed, I'd draw attention to myself if she didn't already have eyes on me."

Noah had been swallowed up by the forest, but I could hear him moving through the grass in the distance. The same sound I'd heard earlier. The sudden crack of a gunshot caused us to jump and birds to soar through the air.

"Noah?" I cried out, my skin cold. Harry was trembling beside me, his jaw slack.

"Noah, you there?" Neither of us moved, both frozen in place from fear. The rustling sound was back, and then he appeared, a giant grin on his face as he dragged the hairy body of a wild boar toward us.

"Dinner is served," he said, licking the sweat from his upper lip as he breathed heavily.

I took a cautious step toward him, my belly growling at the thought of food. My mouth was suddenly full of saliva, and I swallowed twice before speaking. "Did you see anyone out there? The woman?"

He bent down, lifting the boar's legs and walking in the direction he and Harry had come from. "Nah, I hate to break it to you, but you didn't see a woman out there. What you saw were birds."

The white ones that had flown up when he shot the gun. But…it wasn't possible, was it? I knew what I'd seen.

"It was a woman. I saw her hair."

"Blonde hair, right?" he asked, glancing over his shoulder. "Like the white of the birds. Pretty ones too…seagulls, maybe? I don't know. Either way, there was no woman. Or, if there was, she's long gone."

Harry ushered me away, one hand still on my shoulder, and I was pretty sure he thought I might be having dehydration-induced hallucinations, but he didn't say as much. Instead, he kept a firm grip on me, leading me away from the place where I'd stopped and toward the sound of the rushing water.

When we finally reached the source of the sound, a fast-moving stream with crystal-clear water and dark rocks throughout, Harry chuckled to himself.

"I can't believe we actually found fresh water. This is amazing." His hands dropped from my shoulders and I moved forward, leaning down over it and dipping my hands in before rinsing my face.

"Is it safe to drink?" Noah asked cautiously.

"It'll be safer once we boil it. We'll set up camp here tonight instead of the clearing. It's probably okay, with the rocks and moss to help filter it, but I don't want to take any chances. We don't have anything to help if someone gets sick."

"Someone should head back and tell Ava and James that we're eating here instead," Noah said, not offering to do so himself. I bent down, letting the water wash over my calves and arms, its crisp coolness refreshing. I hadn't realized how dry my body felt, how much I craved water in every way.

"I'll go," Harry said finally. "I need to get the sack anyway, so we can start boiling some water. Will you be okay here?"

I nodded, sinking down in the water, my teeth chattering from the chill of it, but I found myself unable to move. "I can go with you, if you want. Just give me a minute to rinse off." I brushed the water up over my shoulders, washing my face.

"I'll be fine. They're not far. Just stay right here and relax, but don't drink anything. Be careful getting it too close to your eyes, nose, or mouth." With that, he was off, disappearing through the trees, and Noah and I were left alone.

He stepped into the water, keeping a safe distance between us as the whites of the crashing rapids slapped into his calves. "Did you really think you saw a woman back there?"

"Why would I lie?"

"I don't know… It wouldn't be the first time."

"What the hell are you talking about?"

He gestured toward the water, the answer in his movements.

"You know why I didn't say anything about that."

He nodded. "I do, but I didn't honestly expect you not to."

"Well, I didn't. And now here we are, and none of it matters anymore."

"Our secret isn't our secret anymore," he said slyly, staring up at the trees. "What do you think we'll find out here? Someone? Something?" A pause. "Nothing?"

The question weighed heavily on me, and I wondered what exactly I hoped we'd find. Did I want to find people? Someone who'd put us here? Or was it easier to believe it was an accident somehow? But then…what about the note? And the SOS signal? No, there were too many signs that pointed to this not being an accident, but rather, by design. So, then, the question became, did I want to confront the person who'd brought us here or would I rather go on not knowing?

I finally settled on, "I don't want anyone to get hurt."

"What do you think they want from us?"

"They?"

"The people who brought us here. Whoever *they* are…"

I hadn't truly considered that there were multiple people involved, though I guess it was more logical than thinking one person had managed to do it all themselves. Was the blonde woman just one of many? "I don't know, honestly." The truth was, whatever scenario I managed to come up with, it just didn't make sense. "I mean, we can't be on a TV show, it's just ridiculous. But they're obviously setting us up for something."

"To kill each other," he said, sucking in a breath. "Look, we could make a pact, you and me."

"A pact?" I scoffed.

"Why not? You already know you can trust me, and I know I can trust you. We kept the secret about the water. It's perfect."

"I've already told you, Noah, I'm not going to hurt anyone." I couldn't even make myself say the word.

"I'm not saying you have to, I'm just saying… I mean, if shit hits the fan, you've got my back, and I've got yours."

"Fine, but I've also got Ava's back, and Harry's, too. I care about them."

"But if it came down to it, if you had to make a split-second decision and save one of us…" He waited for an answer, one that I couldn't give.

"I don't want to play this game," I said, standing up out of the water finally and making my way to the shore. The mud squished between my toes as I kicked out of the flip-flops I'd been wearing. "I don't know why you feel like we have to all pit ourselves against each other. Why you need an alliance. Why you need secrets. The boar you killed feeds us all. The water Harry will purify gives us all something to drink. The shelter they built kept us all safe. Can't you see we're all in this..." I stopped, refusing to make the *High School Musical* reference he was waiting for. "We can't do this alone. None of us. If any of us get off this island, we all do. When will you accept that?"

He bent down in the water, brushing it up over his bare stomach. The tops of his shoulders had started to turn pink, and I realized he still hadn't asked for his shirt back. "Probably around the same time you accept that it's just not feasible for the five of us to live on this island forever."

"I don't want to live here forever. I want to go home." Tears pricked my eyes at the truth in my words. Our time on the island had worn on me, and though I still didn't feel ready to confront whoever had done this to us, I felt exhausted by the idea of staying in a constant state of survival forever. Utter hopelessness swelled in my chest.

"Then you have to be willing to do whatever it takes. Just like the note said." His face was serious, his eyes drilling into mine.

I looked away, forcing myself to regain my composure. If I hoped to survive this, I had to get ahold of myself. "Well, if we are on a TV show, you'll be the one to end up in prison when it's all over."

He gave a dry chuckle and scooped a handful of water to run over his raven-colored hair. When he looked up, his expression was serious again, his voice softer somehow. "Do you think your husband is still looking for you?"

"I hope so." The truth was, sometimes I wondered if he'd even noticed I was gone yet. Though I knew it was implausible, there were times that I thought maybe he'd holed up in the suite, grateful for the uninterrupted time, and just forgotten all about me. I knew it was impossible by this point that he still hadn't realized I was missing, but how else could I explain why they still hadn't found us? My husband had every resource in the world available to him. If he wanted to find me, he would've...

Unless life is easier without my nagging... My constant fussing and interruptions.

If I believed that terrible thought, I'd have to believe my husband was a much crueler man than I knew him to be. But why hadn't he found us? It just didn't make sense. I couldn't deny the voice in my head saying he'd given up on me. But where did that leave us? What did that say about my marriage?

Sometimes we know the truth about the people we love; we know the truth in our bones and in the fiber of our being, but we can't admit it, not even to ourselves. Sometimes the truth lies in the quiet moments, in the first thoughts, the answer that pops into our heads before we have time to tamp down the intuition that we so often do, because it's easier than admitting the truth.

We'd rather live with the mistakes we've made, shut out the things we've learned, the way we've grown, than take on the challenge of admitting our marriage sucks, or our friend is toxic, or our relationship with our parents isn't healthy.

So, we ignore the voice, ignore the feeling in our gut that grows stronger every day, and we pretend that life is so much longer than it is and that we'll get more chances for better days. And that was what I'd done with my marriage for so long. If I was back in the real world, it was what I'd continue to do. But here, on the island with nothing to muddle my head, only silence and my thoughts, I'd been forced to reckon with what I'd known for so long.

My husband didn't love me.

Not like he should.

He tolerated me, sure.

Took care of me.

But some days I felt like little more than something to interrupt his constant flow of work.

Did I think he'd still look for me? Of course.

Did I think he'd be sad that he couldn't find me? Yes. He wasn't a monster.

Did I think losing me would reawaken something in him, make him realize how much I'd meant to him and how much he'd missed out on? It was possible. A girl could hope. But, at the moment, all my hope was being used up just to make it through the day.

"Who do you have looking for you?" I asked, realizing we'd been sitting in silence for way too long.

He shrugged, shaking his head. "My parents, probably."

"Brothers, sisters?"

"Nope, just me." He shook his hands off, swiping them

over his shorts, and made his way out of the water. "I had a brother who died when I was young."

He wasn't looking at me as he made the confession, but somehow, as he revealed something intimate about himself, it felt as though we were locked eye to eye, baring our souls to one another.

"Oh, Noah, I—"

"Do you think they have our pictures plastered on the news? Like real news, not just local?" He changed the subject, grinning then, though I saw the sadness behind it. "I'll bet we even have a Twitter hashtag. Something like *HashtagTheFiveWhoDisappeared* or *HashtagTheMissingFive*."

"The Florida Five," I joined in, picturing it in my head. Would there be national news coverage for something like this? Would they still be searching for answers? Or would they have already written us off as having drowned or ran away? Would they be digging into our internet searches or our cell phone data? Trying to pinpoint where we were?

"I'd obviously be the face of the campaign," he joked. "People everywhere will wonder how something like this could've happened to someone so handsome, intelligent, talented—"

"Humble..."

He laughed, shaking his head. "There's no room for humility in the real world. People only want you to be humble so they can make sure you don't shine." He dusted off his shoulders, standing up and pretending to shoot a basketball. "Besides, bragging comes naturally when you look this good."

"Bragging? Noah? *Never*." Ava's voice carried through

the forest as they appeared, the three of them carrying an armful of sticks, with the sack hanging off Harry's arm.

Noah feigned a laugh and held out his knife. "Come on, Annie Oakley. Daddy brought home the bacon. The least you could do is be grateful."

"The bacon, *literally*," James said, spying the hog and rubbing his stomach hungrily. "Oh, hell yes. Tonight, we eat like kings."

"Why are you giving me this?" Ava stared at the knife, but didn't take it.

"I assumed you knew how to clean it or whatever... You're the one always bragging about hunting."

Her hip cocked out to the side, and though I couldn't see her face with her back to me, I knew she was grinning. "And you don't?"

"No," he said. "I can clean a fish, but I don't know anything about *real* animals."

She snorted, taking the knife finally. "Okay, A, fish *are* real animals. And B, please don't ever call yourself *Daddy* again."

As she set to work preparing our dinner, James instructed Noah on how to help him with the fire, and Harry and I filled the coconut shells with water, placing them delicately on the stones of the fire until they boiled, which seemed to take forever.

Once dinner had been cooked, the water was cleared to drink, and the sun had set, we all settled into the evening, relaxing by the fire with full bellies and wet hair from playing and rinsing off in the water.

Harry had told us he'd wake us up bright and early, but

as none of us had any alarm clocks, he was just guessing like we'd done the morning before.

"I was thinking..." I propped myself up, my elbow in the dirt, cheek resting in my palm. "Once we get up there tomorrow, one of us should turn on our phones. Just to see if we have service."

"We didn't have it on the beach," James said skeptically. "You think we'd have it somewhere higher up?"

We all looked at Harry, who seemed caught off guard by the question. "I mean, it's always possible, I guess."

"But not probable?" I asked.

"Well, I would think if we had access to a cell tower anywhere on the island, we'd have access to it just about everywhere. I mean, maybe not in the depths of the jungle, but out in the open where everything's clear... I just wouldn't expect it to be any better. But, I don't know, guys. Believe it or not, there are things I actually don't know a lot about. I live in the city. For as long as I've had a cell phone, I've never had to worry about service." He traced his finger through the dirt. "It's worth a try, at least."

Noah lit up, giving that same lopsided grin he so often did. "Well, whaddya know, Boy Genius doesn't know everything after all."

"I never claimed to know everything," Harry said. "I just happen to know a few things." He pushed himself into a sitting position, fiddling with a blade of grass. "And those few things are probably the only reason we're all alive right now, Noah, so maybe lay off a bit."

"Easy, hoss, I'm just playing with ya."

Ava twirled a finger through one of her curls. "Relax,

Harry, Noah doesn't know how to communicate with people unless he's insulting them. Some of us never learned people skills."

"Fat load of good people skills would do me out here, Princess," he snipped.

"Some of us are making friends," she said, looking up at James, who was on his side lying just above her, her head resting on the ground in front of his stomach. Apparently, they'd made the decision to no longer hide whatever it was they had going on. The line had been drawn, and Ava and James were firmly on one side together while the rest of us, the outsiders, were alone.

Without a pact.

James ran a hand over Ava's arm and moved to stand. "I need to take a leak." He tossed the bone he'd been picking at to the ground and walked away from the group, standing near the edge of the clearing to get some privacy, but not so far that we couldn't still see him.

Suddenly, Ava clutched her stomach, shooting up and running toward the opposite side of the forest. Before she'd made it, the vomit had begun spewing out of her mouth, and I heard her coughing and gagging as the sickness overcame her. I stood, too, trying to get near her, but this time it was James who rushed to her side, his hands holding her hair back. I stared at the hog carcass, my stomach churning, as I tried to convince myself I was just imagining the ill-timed nausea.

Harry and Noah were still. By that point, we were all so used to the terrible smells of living with four strangers, none of whom had washed in days, that nothing seemed to bother us too much.

When she'd finished getting sick, Harry handed a coconut shell to James, who handed it to Ava, lifting it to her mouth gently. She sucked the liquid down.

"Why does it feel like I'm the only one getting sick around here?"

"Do you think it could've been the meat? Or the water?" Ava stopped drinking as I asked the question. "Maybe we did something wrong with cooking it?"

"It could be either," Harry said, still playing with the strand of grass in the firelight. "I guess we'll know if someone else gets sick."

My stomach lurched, and I forced the thought down. I wasn't getting sick. I was fine. I'd just watched someone else get sick, and it made me feel queasy. But the truth was, I was terrified. I'd had food poisoning once in college and spent the next day and a half in the bathroom. All I remember of that time is pain and the cold floor digging into my knees, and the agony of the emptiness I felt, unable to keep anything down. I'd thought then I was going to die, and that was in the comfort of my own home, surrounded by clean water and medicine and access to medical care if things got too bad. I couldn't imagine dealing with it here where we lacked...well, everything.

"I feel much better," Ava tried to reassure us. "Honestly, it just hit me. I'm probably dehydrated again. I haven't gotten sick since yesterday, and that was just from coconut water."

James led her back to where they'd been sitting, and they sank to the ground together. The night sky was dark and cloudy, the wind blowing just enough to keep it too cool for comfort, and we each seemed lost in our own heads.

I lay back on the grass, thinking about all that had happened and willing myself not to be sick. Not to feel sick. I heard Ava giggling about something that James had whispered in her ear, though the rest of us were not privy to the joke.

I felt eyes on me.

I looked over, expecting to see Noah staring at me, but to my surprise, he was staring into the forest, seemingly lost in his own thoughts. I looked down toward my feet, where Harry was lying. He was still playing with the grass, occasionally stoking the fire to keep it going.

Why, then, did I feel like someone was watching me? I looked toward the woods then, thinking about the woman I thought I'd seen earlier. The one Noah claimed hadn't existed. But, thinking back, I could've sworn I caught a glimpse of face. Her long, pointed nose. Fearful, blue eyes.

Or...maybe I was wrong.

Maybe they were green...

THE NEXT THING I KNEW, I was waking up, not realizing I'd even fallen asleep, and there she was. Staring at me from beyond the trees. The blonde woman I'd seen earlier.

I jolted up in a flash, rubbing the sleep from my eyes. "Who are you?" I demanded, scrambling to my feet.

As soon as I'd moved, she turned, bounding away from me with stealthy footsteps. She disappeared behind a tree, but the white of her clothing stuck out as she hurried through the dark woods.

"Wait!" I cried, sleep still clouding my thoughts. My legs were heavy, my head foggy as I raced toward her. My foot caught in a thicket of weeds, and I fell forward, smacking into the ground thanks to my still-slow-from-sleep reflexes. I groaned, pushing myself up, and cursing aloud as I realized I'd lost sight of her. Which direction had she headed?

I heard a branch crack behind me and turned around, shocked to see Harry with his machete held out. "Are you okay? What are you doing?" he demanded, lowering the weapon and helping me to my feet. He dusted me off carefully. "You scared the hell out of me. I thought you'd been taken."

"Did you see her? Did you see the woman?" I asked, still looking around and hoping to catch a glimpse of her.

"What woman?"

The hope in my chest deflated. "She was just here... The woman from earlier. She was watching us."

He looked around, spinning in circles to see every angle. "I didn't see anyone out here except you. Where did you see her?"

"She was in the clearing with us, near the trees. When I woke up, she ran away. I was trying to catch her, but I tripped..." I tried to catch my breath, still searching the woods for her. She had to be there, she just had to. "I tripped, and I..."

"Do you ever sleepwalk?" he asked carefully, placing a hand on my shoulder again.

The look I gave him must've been abrasive, even in the

moonlight, because his head jerked back and he frowned, then attempted to smooth things over. His thumb caressed my shoulder. "My daughter did. When she was young... She used to terrify my husband and me. We'd wake up, and she'd just be standing in our room." He shuddered, just from the memory.

"I didn't know you had a daughter."

"Daisy," he said. "She's twelve now. Grew out of the sleepwalking years ago." His voice cracked as he said her name, and when he looked away, I knew he was pretending not to wipe his eye.

"I wasn't sleepwalking," I said firmly. "I know what I saw."

He didn't look convinced, but refrained from arguing anyway. Instead, he put his arm around my shoulder completely. "We need to get back. Before the others wake up and wander off searching for us. If the woman was here, she's long gone now." He looked to the sky. "It'll be light soon, I'll bet. You and I can stay awake until then, in case she comes back."

I nodded, though I didn't want to leave, and let my feet carry me back to the pseudo-safety of our fire.

"Daisy must miss you," I said, wondering why he hadn't mentioned her before.

"They probably don't even know I'm gone yet," he said, his tone harsh.

"What do you mean?"

He sighed. We'd reached the clearing where the others were still sleeping soundly, and he sat down beside me, keeping his voice low.

"It's not my proudest moment, but when I left, Drew

and I were in a fight. I told him I needed some space, that I was going to visit my parents for a few weeks." He shrugged. "For all I know, that was the last thing I said to either of them. I called Daisy the day before we came here, but she didn't answer. Drew was supposed to have her call me when she got home from practice, but she didn't before I got on the boat."

He shook his head dramatically. "This isn't like me. I'm a planner. I plan everything. I plan our outfits, our meals…and I just…got on the damn boat. Just on a whim. *What could go wrong, right?*" He gave a dry, sarcastic laugh. "The one time I take a risk, and this is what it gets me."

"It's not your fault, Harry. You know that."

"Then whose fault is it?" he demanded. "Because it sure as hell feels like mine. It was so hard for us to adopt her. We used our entire life savings, spent months waiting, and now, because I had to throw a temper tantrum *over a canceled vacation nonetheless,* all of that amounts to nothing. She'll grow up without me because I was selfish."

He was crying then, no longer trying to hide it. I sat in silence, in horror, at not knowing how to console him. Despite feeling so close to him because of all we'd gone through, he was still mostly a stranger.

"You weren't selfish. You were human. People are allowed to feel disappointment, anger… It's normal. But, in the face of all the uncertainty and darkness, you are the reason we're still here. You said it yourself today, everything you've known about keeping us alive, all the books you must've read to get that knowledge—you're the reason we're alive, Harry. I don't doubt that for a second—"

"You're trying to make me feel better, and I appreciate it, but you guys would've been fine without me—"

"I would've never guessed we could use coconuts to boil water. I thought for sure they'd burn up. And I definitely thought moving water was safe to drink. None of us had any idea how to build a shelter. The list goes on, and on top of that, you were the one keeping calm when we arrived. You were the one who knew what to do, what to gather, what to assemble... You saved us all." I watched him try to temper his growing smile, then added, "What happened to us... The people who brought us here are the only ones to blame. You have nothing to feel guilty about. And we're all going home, okay? We're going to find our way off the island and get out of here."

"You really think so?" he asked, stifling a yawn.

I looked up toward where I knew the mountain was, despite being unable to see it in the darkness. "I know so. You're going to see Daisy again."

He swiped his finger under his eye. "I'm sorry I had a meltdown. I've just been trying so hard not to think about them, and the dam broke."

"You don't have to apologize to me," I said, willing him to look at me. "I think meltdowns are absolutely warranted right now."

He chuckled, sniffling. "Do you have kids?"

"No. It's just me and my husband." Was it inconsiderate to say I hadn't wanted any when he'd had to work so hard to have a child of his own?

He was quiet. The wind began to rustle the trees around us, and I felt a drop of dew touch my cheek. "I'm glad they found each other." He jutted his head toward

Ava and James, cuddled together in the dirt. "No one should be alone out here."

"We aren't alone," I told him and watched as a shiver ran through his body.

"Is it selfish to wish he were here with me?" He sniffled again.

"Your husband?"

He nodded. "I mean, obviously, I'd much rather I be with him, but I just keep thinking... I would do anything to have him here right now. I'd do anything to hold him and tell him I'm sorry. To get through this together and brag about it at our twenty-fifth wedding anniversary." The laugh he released through his tears was heart-breaking.

"I know what you mean. I wish my husband were here, too." I didn't know if it was the truth, even as I said it, but it felt like the right thing to say. Of course, it would be nice to have someone I knew here. Someone I trusted. It would be nice to cuddle up with my husband, to let him make me feel safe. But did he make me feel safe anymore? It was hard to tell. It had been so long since we'd been together, alone without the constant interruptions from his phone or laptop. Did we even know who we were without the buzz of incoming emails? When was the last time we'd held eye contact for an entire conversation? Out here, I was worried our deepest flaws would be front and center.

"It's okay, you know," Harry said after a pause, "to look for comfort somewhere else. What we're going through is traumatic. We don't know if we'll ever see them again."

I looked at him, scowling, but the fact that I'd been

staring at Noah as my thoughts were with my husband hadn't gone unnoticed by either of us. "I'm just trying to get us off the island. I don't have time for comfort. And we will see them again." I emphasized the words, needing us both to believe them. "We're getting off this island, Harry. All of us."

His lips grew tight, and he said nothing else, so I sank back onto the ground, resting my hands on my chest as I breathed in and out, repeating the words over and over, trying to make myself believe them.

We're getting off this island.

We're getting off this island.

We're getting off this island.

I had no idea how wrong I was.

CHAPTER FIFTEEN

W hen I woke up again, the sun had begun to peek over the horizon, painting the sky brilliant shades of reds, blues, and purples. I sat up, taking off the shirt Noah had lent me and rinsing my body in the stream. Ava began to stir, waking James up as well, and I smiled at her when she opened her eyes.

I finished rinsing off, dabbing the water across my skin carefully, and pulled the shirt back over my head. The bikini I'd been wearing for days now had begun to chafe and rub, and I desperately wanted to take it off but had nothing to replace it with. I knew everyone was likely dealing with a similar situation.

"Morning," I said, when Ava sat up.

"Morn—" she stopped, her face full of confusion. Then, she scrambled to stand and rushed toward the tree line again, emptying the remaining contents of her stomach. The combination of the rising sun and the noise of her retching drew Noah and Harry from their sleep as well, and Harry rubbed a hand over his eye.

"Ava?" James rushed across the clearing, reaching for her. He looked at me. "Do we have any more water?"

"I don't want—" She tried to speak, but was interrupted by more sickness.

"We don't have any more anyway," Harry said, "but we can boil some."

"Is it the water making her sick?" Noah asked, his voice deep from sleep.

"It can't be," Harry told him, reassuring us all. "Not if no one else is sick, too. It has to be something else." He sat up, his body hunched over in thought. "It could be blood sugar... Are you diabetic? We already asked you that, didn't we?"

Ava dabbed her mouth, staying still for a few moments as if to make sure she wasn't going to be sick again. Then, she shook her head. "No, I'm not diabetic," she croaked out.

At Harry's question, I remembered the day we'd gotten off the boat, how weak Ava had felt then. We'd asked her the same questions... That felt like a lifetime ago.

"You said you don't have any illnesses, right? I'm not trying to pry, but if you've missed your medicine for a while, that could explain why you're the only one who's sick."

"No, nothing like that. I'm healthy," she said. "No medicine except a multivitamin I usually forget to take and melatonin to help me sleep."

"Then what could it be?" James asked, resting his forehead against her temple. "She can't travel like this."

"James, I'm fine, I—"

"No," I agreed. "He's right. Harry, we can't have her

traipsing all around the island while she's obviously sick. It could be any number of things: a parasite, dehydration, some weird tropical island sickness..."

"We have to get to the cliff," Harry argued, his tone soft and understanding. "I hear what you're saying, I really do. But it's the only way to see what's around us and figure out a way out of here. We have to go."

"Then I'll stay with her here. The rest of you can go," James said.

"We shouldn't split up," Ava cried.

"We don't have a choice. You can't travel right now. We have to get you better first. I'd never forgive myself if something happened to you. I'll stay here with you, protect you, and they can come back and tell us what they've found."

We all looked around, no one able to determine whether this was just a bad idea or a terrible one. Finally, Noah sighed, placing his hands on his knees and standing up.

"Well, that's fine. Leave the real work for the adults, you two." He clucked his tongue, stretching his arms over his head with a loud groan.

"You need to keep her hydrated," Harry told James begrudgingly, obviously not crazy about the idea of splitting up. "Boil the water for several minutes and then let it cool before you give it to her. Wait right here. Don't leave this area unless it's an emergency. We'll use the machetes to cut marks in the trees directing you to us. If you have to leave for any reason, follow that trail toward us."

"Will do," James agreed, his face solemn. I think we all felt like it might be the last time we saw each other.

Harry turned to me. "We should find some coconuts to take with us when we travel. Want to help me look?"

With that, we made our way toward the outskirts of the clearing while James comforted Ava, helping to ease her down next to the fire before he began filling the empty coconut halves.

Half an hour later, with coconuts and weapons loaded up, Noah, Harry, and I said our goodbyes and headed out into the woods, pointed toward the cliff in the rising, early morning sunlight.

We made our way through the tangled, strange woods in silence, as talking seemed to only make our throats drier. We spoke only when we needed to warn each other of fallen branches that may trip our step, or once, when we crossed paths with a snake slithering across the branch of a tree.

We stopped whenever anyone got too tired, which was often, and caught our breath, drinking from the coconuts sparingly.

As the cliff began to come into view, I felt a strange sense of urgency fill me. When Noah asked if anyone needed to stop for a break when we found the latest clearing, I was the first to decline, and Harry followed my lead. I just wanted to get there. This was the closest we'd been to figuring everything out, and I just wanted it to be over. I just wanted to understand what was happening, what was going on.

As we neared the bottom of the cliff, we stopped briefly, catching our breath. It was several stories high, the bottom framed with boulders of every size, and it jutted out away from the earth, straight on top, and nearly a forty-five-degree angle of a ledge where we could stand. It was covered in moss and ivy, the stone a dark gray that reminded me of pavement and made me crave home.

Once we started climbing, we'd have no shade from the blazing sun that was growing higher in the sky by the minute. Noah's shoulders and chest were already red and blistering, Harry's arms and face, too.

"Let's leave the coconuts down here, and I'll wear my sarong, that way you can have your shirt back." I started to pull it over my head.

"No, we might need those up there, especially in the sun."

"We could carry them," I offered.

"I don't need my shirt back, if that's what you're worried about. I'm going to burn anyway. May as well get it over with."

"Okay, if you're sure."

Whether or not he was, he didn't say. Instead, he placed his foot on a small boulder, hoisting himself up and turning around to take my hand. I did the same for Harry, and we continued the pattern, finding our footing one by one and then helping the others to find theirs.

Finally, when my muscles burned, my body trembling so hard I was sure I was going to collapse at any moment, when the sun felt as if it had baked my skin, we reached the top of the cliff. I collapsed on the warm rock with a loud groan before I'd taken the time to look over my surroundings. I was too tired. I didn't even want to think about how much harder the trip down may be.

"We're so high up," Noah said, standing just in front of me, his hands resting on his hips. His chest glistened with sweat, rising and falling with heavy breaths. "What are you doing?" he asked, looking past me.

I looked up, my head rubbing painfully against the rock, to where Harry was standing near the edge of the cliff.

"Harry?"

He put a hand up over his eyes, looking out over the forest. "There," he said, pointing straight ahead.

"What?" Noah said, moving toward him.

I turned over, standing up and making my way over.

"Holy shit, is that what I think it is?" I stared at the odd shape at the base of the mountain several miles away, the space that had been cleared, the strange rust-colored space that had replaced rock. I watched as the smoke billowed out of the top of it, an odd mix of terror and hope filling my stomach.

"Yeah," Harry answered. "Yeah, I think so. I'm pretty sure it's a house."

CHAPTER SIXTEEN

"What do you think it means? Do you think that's where the woman lives?" I asked. As far as we could see, though we couldn't completely see the far side of the island, the entire jungle appeared uninhabited aside from the house. From where we were standing, we could see a vague outline of the beach—our beach—and the rest of what we could see was nothing but trees and mountains.

It appeared there had never been any type of civilization here, no ports, no villages. It was just us and whoever lived in the house. But whether or not they would help us wasn't clear. My emotions kept flipping between outright terror and cautious optimism.

"I don't know," Harry said, still trying to look for a sign of anything else. "Someone obviously lives there."

"We have to go there," Noah said, his jaw tight. "We need to go and see if we can confront them."

"That isn't smart," Harry disagreed. "We don't know

who it is. How many people there are. Whether they're armed. We have to use our heads here."

I shook my head, needing it to make sense. If someone else was on the island, which we had all but confirmed, I couldn't just sit around and wait to learn whether they were going to harm us. I couldn't stay on the island a moment longer if I didn't have to. Despite all that, I knew Harry was right. He was always right. "For all we know, it's just a random woman who lives on the island and is as scared of us as we are of her. She was there last night, and she didn't try to hurt us. She just ran away. And she may have left us weapons. If she were planning to hurt us, why would she have armed us?" I struggled to find a sensible reason.

"Then how do you explain the note?" he asked. "You're forgetting that people brought us here and dumped us on an abandoned island with nothing to eat or drink and no explanation, and then they left a note that said we should kill each other in order to get off the island. What part of that makes you think these people are friendly?"

"Because they haven't hurt us," I said, grasping at straws. "And they could've. If they have weapons like what they brought us, why haven't they hurt us yet?"

"Maybe this is all a test. Maybe they want to see who's good and who's bad?" Noah offered, though even he didn't look like he believed it.

"A test for what, though? And why this group of people? We've already ruled out any of us being connected before. It all just seems so random..." Harry paused. "Look, I'm not saying we aren't going to go to the house, I'm just saying we have to be smart about it. If we march up to the door and knock on it today, without knowing what or who is behind it, we're setting ourselves up to be ambushed."

"So what are you suggesting instead?" I asked. He was being logical. I knew he was right, but it didn't make it sting any less. I wanted answers, and I wanted them right then.

"We need to get back to the clearing and tell the others what we've found. Then, we can start making our way toward the house, set up a camp nearby, and keep an eye on them. Sooner or later, someone's going to come out of the house. If it's just the woman and she's unarmed, we can confront her. If it's an army of people with military gear, on the other hand, maybe we take a breath and come up with a game plan from there."

Noah swiped sweat from his forehead, breathing out heavily. "Okay, fine. Let's do that. We just need to get down from here and out of the sun. Can I have a drink?"

I reached for a coconut from the sack and handed it over, spying my cell phone still in the pocket of the sarong.

"Hang on, I just want to try something." I pulled the phone out and pressed the button to turn it on. Noah slurped down some of the water before passing it to Harry to finish the rest. They watched carefully as my phone lit up, immediately warning us of a low battery. Honestly, I was sort of surprised it turned on at all after days in the blazing heat, sand in all its crevices, and no time on a charger.

I went to my call log, selecting my husband's name with my thumb, and closing my eyes to send up a silent prayer that it might work. What would I tell him? That we were still here. That he shouldn't give up looking. What had happened. I'd spill it all in seconds, crying and trembling as I heard his soothing voice, his promise that he'd never give up. That he'd search night and day until he found me.

The vision was so clear in my mind, for a second, I almost believed it was real.

Instead, a beep sounded, and when I opened my eyes, my heart fell.

No Signal

The alert was displayed on the screen, crushing any amount of hope I may have had.

"No signal," I read to them, breathless as new tears found my eyes. I hadn't realized how much hope I'd pinned on being able to reach him. As if it would solve all my problems. I just wanted to feel something familiar. I wanted to hear his voice and let him hear mine. I needed to know he hadn't given up hope. I needed him to give me a reason not to.

"We're on an island in the middle of nowhere," Noah said coldly, though I suspected he was trying to cover his own disappointment as he wouldn't meet my eye. "Of course there's no cell phone signal. Haven't you ever been on a cruise?"

I shoved the phone back into its pocket and turned away from him. Harry put a hand on my arm gently, trying to comfort me.

"It was worth a shot."

I nodded, unable to speak. The lump that had formed in my belly upon our arrival had begun to swell into a black hole of hopelessness. With each passing day, a bit more of my remaining hope disappeared.

"We should go," Noah said, leading us toward the edge of the cliff and turning around slowly, easing his foot toward the rock below. I slung the sack over my shoulder like a crossbody purse, making it easier to carry than it had been on the way up, and followed his lead.

As I eased myself down, pressing it onto the rock below. I felt it slip too quickly, losing my footing, and let out a scream as I imagined the fall to my death. Noah's hand was under my foot in a moment, carefully guiding it to a new rock.

"Easy," he said before releasing me.

I tried to catch my breath and slow my trembling before trying to move down to the next rock. As I moved, I accidentally looked out over the forest, realizing how far up we were and how ill-equipped we were to be making a journey like this. On the way up, I'd been so determined to make it I'd hardly noticed, but on the way down, it was all I could see. We weren't mountain climbers. Truth be told, I didn't even really like heights. Yet, here we were, climbing this mountain in the blazing sun, half dehydrated.

Okay, so mountain was a bit of an exaggeration, I guessed, but it didn't stop the fear from crashing into me like waves. For some reason, I hadn't thought about how dangerous the climb was until I'd nearly fallen.

"Don't look down," came the warning from above. When I looked up, Harry's dark eyes met mine, his smile kind. "You're okay, just don't look down. Pay attention to where your hands and feet land. We're in no hurry. Stare at the rock in front of you and nothing else. You're fine."

I nodded, following his advice and staring at the rock in front of me, easing my foot down to the next rock carefully. My fingers had begun to burn, both from the temperature of the rock and from the utter exhaustion of carrying my weight up and down the rock.

I tried to ignore the tremble as I saw Harry lowering himself onto the rock above me.

"Not too far now," Noah said from below, and I refused to look down to make sure.

I knew I had to be getting near the bottom as we started to become level with the trees, rather than towering over them. At seeing that, my nerves calmed some. It was just like climbing the trees in my backyard as a kid. I'd survived that with little more than a few scrapes and scars, so I could do this. I was smarter now. Stronger.

My foot slipped again, and I felt myself losing my grip on the rock above. I cried out, my heart pounding in my chest, my ears, and somehow even my vision as I fought to regain my grip. Tears welled in my eyes instantly, and I whimpered, my foot floating through the air, tapping and tapping for the rock I'd slipped off from.

What happened next came in a flash.

As I tried to recall it, it seemed to happen in a millisecond, all at once. I felt Noah's hand reaching for my toes. Heard him expel a heavy breath as he said, "Hold on—"

Harry, from above, looked down in a panic, his foot flailing to find a spot to land. My scream had distracted him, and he was now looking at me. "Are you ok—" His hand slipped, or maybe his foot… It all happened so fast, I couldn't be sure of which it was. He screamed, both hands clawing to regain control.

I remembered the look on his face as he stared down at me, his eyes wide with fear. Then in the next second, his body was off the rock, his scream filling the air. In a flash, he fell sideways, clawing and clamoring to regain his footing, to take hold of something, anything, as he tumbled down the side of a cliff. I felt Noah's hand leave my foot, felt my own body reaching for my friend as he fell, and then I remembered nothing.

Nothing except the crunch as Harry's body connected with the ground below.

CHAPTER SEVENTEEN

M y own fear didn't seem to matter anymore as I rushed down the side of the cliff. For the most part, I didn't remember how I got down. I only remembered the moment my feet touched the ground, just seconds behind Noah's, as we rushed toward where Harry's body lay.

He wasn't dead. It was my first thought. I watched his chest rise and fall with haggard, worn breaths. He'd landed straight down, as if he were just sleeping, and there was no blood. His glasses were strewn across the forest floor, several feet from him, but aside from that, without knowing what had happened, you could've easily assumed he'd just stopped in for a cat nap rather than having fallen more than thirty feet.

"*Harry,*" I cried, my hands shaking as I hovered them over his body. His eyes fluttered open and closed, but he gave no real indication that he had heard me.

He groaned.

"Don't touch him," Noah warned, bending down on his knees next to me. "You could make it worse."

"*Harry,*" I cried, snot and tears pouring down my face. I shoved my hair back out of my eyes, but it was no use. It fell back into my eyes as I hovered over him. "Please wake up. Please."

"He's not bleeding," Noah said, but his tone wasn't hopeful. In fact, it almost sounded worse. "Harry, can you hear us?"

Again, his eyes fluttered, and he expelled a ragged breath, but he didn't move. I ran a hand gently over his legs, then his arms, feeling for anything out of place. "What do we do?" I demanded of Noah, though I knew from the blank look in his eyes that he had no idea.

"I...I don't...I don't know. Harry would know," he said, his voice cracking at the mention of his name.

I choked back a sob, rubbing my palms over my eyes. "We have to get him back to the camp. Can we carry him together?"

"If his back's broken, that could hurt him more," Noah said, shaking his head feverishly. "We have to leave him here."

"We can't just *leave* him here. We have to go and get Ava and James. We need their help. We have to carry him to that house. Whether they're good or bad, we have to take our chances. It's Harry's only hope. We can't give up. We have to do something."

He chewed his bottom lip, pressing his fingers to his temple. "We need to make something flat to carry him. Maybe we could find a hollowed-out log or something. Wait here, I'm going to go look." With that, he was off in a flash. I should've asked where he was going or when he planned to be back, but I could think of nothing else.

"*Harry,*" I cried, letting my head rest on the dirt next to him. "Why aren't you waking up? Please, please, Harry." I clutched his hand, wiping my eyes with the back of my arm. "It's all my fault... This is all my fault. This wasn't supposed to happen. We can't make it without you." I sobbed, my cries echoing throughout the forest.

Suddenly, I felt his grip tighten on my hand. I looked up, seeing that his eyes were open. He was staring at me strangely, his eyes glassy.

"*Harry?*"

He coughed, his body convulsing, and I saw the blood. A small drop trailed just under his nose, the remnants of the splatter that had come out onto his shirt. When he opened his mouth, his teeth were painted crimson.

My body hurt watching it happen, the grief gripping at my organs with its cold, spindly fingers. I held his hand, using the other to dab up the blood with his shirt. As I lifted the bottom of his shirt up, my body went cold. His stomach, once creamy white, was quickly turning a deep shade of purple, like ink dots spilling onto a canvas.

No. No. No. No.

I shook my head, wanting to dry the blood, to stop the bleeding, but unable to reach the wound. He was bleeding internally, nearly gone already if the blank stare was any indication. I couldn't let him go like that. I couldn't let him die. We needed him. His family needed him. Daisy needed him.

"What do I do, Harry? What do I do? You're the only one who would know; Noah's right. You probably know the herb to give to stop the bleeding or the right position to lay you in…" I choked back sobs, talking because there was nothing else I could do. "You can't leave us like this. You can't leave Daisy. Do you hear me? You have to stay with me. You have to fight. You have to fight for us. For her."

I tried to catch my breath, my lungs burning from lack of oxygen. *What did you do?* I screamed into the forest, no longer caring if anyone heard me. "Why did you do this? He didn't deserve this. We didn't deserve this." I wailed a painful, furious cry into the air, then let my face fall to the ground, breathing in the dirt and grass beneath me. I couldn't force myself to get up. I couldn't move. I never wanted to move again.

I felt his fingers move slightly, twisting themselves through my hair, and I looked up. His eyes were still in a far-off place, his gaze pointed toward the sky. Tears blurred my vision as I watched a small smile form on his lips.

As he released a breath, almost a shudder, his words were a whisper. I knew in an instant they would be his last. "Daisy…be…safe." His head flopped sideways, blood dripping to the ground from his nose and mouth, and he never took another breath.

No. No. No.

When I lifted his shirt again, his entire torso was nearly black. I didn't know what was broken or what I should've done differently, but it all hurt just the same. Everything felt lost. Rage built up in my chest, a swelling bubble of heat ready to combust.

I pounded my fists on the ground, releasing a guttural

scream as my tears mixed with the dirt until it had become mud beneath my face. It wasn't fair. It shouldn't have happened.

One minute, he was alive and fine, and the next, he was just gone.

No warning, no goodbye, and I was the only person there to hear his last words. It should've been Daisy. No, there shouldn't have been any last words. He should've been home with his family. We all should've, instead of dying here alone on this island.

I looked up, slowly lifting my hands to his eyes and closing the lids.

"I'm so sorry," I whispered, the guilt over what I'd done overwhelming me. If I hadn't lost my footing, he wouldn't have been distracted. He wouldn't have fallen to his death. If I'd been more careful, he'd still be alive. I'd have to live with that truth for the rest of my life, however short it may be.

If we ever made it off the island, I'd have to tell that truth to his family. To his daughter. I'd have to tell her that his final thoughts were with her. I'd have to watch her face crumple as she sobbed into her only remaining father's chest.

I'd have to do it all and know that somehow, on some level, it was all my fault.

I sat up on my knees, my head hung low as I sobbed, letting the emotion overtake me. What was the point of any of it? If we were all going to die—and without Harry, we surely were—what was the point of fighting it anymore? We'd be better off spending the rest of our lives playing in the ocean until the heat or hunger took us out than trying to find a way back home.

It was obvious now that was never going to happen.

"I'm so sorry," I whispered again, closing my eyes. My head was heavy, chest tight. Nothing made sense. Everything hurt, every thought shattered me from the inside. He was a stranger, yet he was a friend. I barely knew him, and yet, I loved him.

He didn't deserve this.

I let myself collapse next to him, staring into the distance where his glasses lay as my vision blurred with tears and anger.

He didn't deserve this.

Where was Noah? When would he come back?

He didn't deserve this.

I closed my eyes and faded into the darkness, hoping by some miracle, I'd wake up and find out this had all been a dream.

CHAPTER EIGHTEEN

When I awoke, dusk had begun to settle, but I was still alone. Noah hadn't returned.

At realizing that, I sat up quickly, my body stiff from the ground. I let go of Harry's hand, placing it gently on his stomach and standing up. Why hadn't Noah come back? Had he abandoned me? It was going to be dark soon, and I had no idea which way home was, nor enough time to get there. I also had no idea how to build a fire.

I looked toward the sack on the ground, kicking it gently. There were three coconuts left and I had our two machetes, but Noah had taken the gun with him.

I was alone in the woods with no one to help me bury Harry and no one to help me survive the night.

I turned to walk away from Harry, though I desperately didn't want to leave him alone, and grabbed the two machetes from the ground. I couldn't carry two efficiently, but the idea of leaving one there for someone else to find was terrifying. I took a step toward the woods and heard a *crunch*.

No.

His glasses.

I stepped back, my skin crawling with repulsion. How could I have forgotten they were there? I bent down, trying to make out the frames in the shadows, and picked them up. They'd twisted, one side turned upward and its lens completely shattered. I cursed under my breath, tears filling my eyes once again as the pain of his loss was suddenly front and center again. I turned the frame correctly, folding the glasses and placing them in the pocket of his shirt. He couldn't be buried without them, and I knew that was what would come next. After I managed to find Noah.

If I managed to find Noah.

I turned away from Harry's body as a bird flew overhead, its body casting a shadow over mine. As I neared the edge of the woods, I saw the white shape of a body sitting on a rock. For a second, I thought it must be the woman, but then I saw the dark of his hair, buried in his hands.

"Noah?" I called, rushing forward. I moved quickly. He wasn't moving. Had he been hurt? What was he doing?

As I neared him, I realized his shoulders were shaking with sobs.

"Noah, what is it? What's going on?"

He looked up at me, his eyes shadowy and brimming with tears. He shook his head.

"I can't do it," he barely managed to choke out.

"Can't do what?"

"I can't do it. I can't see him like that. I can't watch him die. He's going to die…"

Finally starting to understand what was happening, I

bent down onto my knees, placing a hand on his thigh. "Noah, he's...he's already gone." I meant it to sound gentler, but it came out matter-of-fact. "I'm sorry. I didn't realize the two of you were so close." Honestly, it completely confused me. I'd never seen them do anything other than fight.

He rubbed his eyes forcefully. "We weren't." He sniffled, shaking his head. "I hate this shit, man."

"I know, it's hard..." I patted his leg carefully, still confused.

"My brother died when I was six. Freak accident. I saw it happen..." He shuddered, giving in to the tears again. "I can't watch people die. I'm sorry. I didn't want to leave you to do it alone. I just couldn't be there..."

"I..." The confession made me breathless. He'd never intended to get anything to help Harry. He'd already known it was too bad to save him. He'd walked away so he didn't have to watch him die. "Oh, Noah... I'm so sorry."

His face scrunched uncomfortably, fresh tears glimmering in the moonlight. "I shouldn't have left you alone. I was a coward—"

"You weren't—"

"I was—"

I grasped his face between my palms, forcing him to look at me. "*You weren't.*" I paused, staring at him with what I hoped was a kind-but-forceful gaze. "You did what you had to do to protect yourself. You went through something traumatic, something most people can't even begin to understand, and this brought back memories. It makes sense, Noah. You didn't do anything wrong."

He stared at me, silent for a moment, his eyes darting back and forth between mine. Then, without warning, he shoved forward, his lips colliding with mine so hard I immediately tasted blood. I recoiled, pushing him away from me.

"What are you doing?" I demanded, standing up as I dragged my hand across my mouth in horror.

"Oh, shit. Oh, god. I shouldn't have... I wasn't thinking. I just—"

"You weren't thinking," I repeated. "I have a husband, Noah. Our friend just died. You can't just... You can't just do that."

He hung his head, and I realized I was rubbing salt in an already torn open wound. "I wasn't thinking. I just acted."

It wasn't an apology. I wasn't sure what it was, but it wasn't that. It should've been an apology. I was a married woman, and he knew that. "I know we're all in a weird headspace right now. Just...you can't kiss me, Noah."

"Understood," he said, giving a firm nod. He stood from the rock, rubbing his palms over his arms quickly, as if he were cold. He wiped a stray tear from his cheek, his tone cooler, but not unfriendly. "What are we doing tonight? We can't see the trees we marked in the dark. We're going to have to make camp."

"We have to bury him," I said. "Before anything else. He deserves to be laid to rest the right way."

"I don't disagree, it's just... How will we manage that?"

"We'll use our hands if we have to," I said, the very thought of leaving him without a burial making me sick. "We can't just leave him."

For a moment, I thought he was going to argue, but instead, he offered a small, sad smile. "Harry could use coconuts for just about everything. If he were here, I'll bet he'd suggest using them to help us dig."

In a morbid way, it felt as if we'd come full circle. Harry had taught us how to survive on the island using only what was readily available, and now we'd use what we'd learned from him to pay our respects.

We worked in silence, both of us sniffling and wiping away our tears as we dug. The process was long and grueling. My forearms burned, my fingernails had chipped and broken to the point that most of them were bleeding. The moonlight cast shadows across our faces so we had a form of privacy, though we were completely together in this.

When we'd dug a grave as big and deep as we could manage, our bodies and hair caked with mud and both of us completely and utterly exhausted, we stood there, the reality of what we were about to do sinking in.

"He deserved better than an unmarked grave in a random jungle in the middle of nowhere." The words came out angry, bitter, and without being able to make out Noah's features in the moonlight, I couldn't tell whether that was what he was feeling too.

"It seems like that's all any of us are going to get."

"Don't talk like that," I said with a sharp inhale, though I couldn't deny that I'd thought the same thing.

"Come on. You know as well as I do, if Captain Mega-Brain can't make it in a place like this, the rest of us don't stand a chance."

"Harry's…" I could hardly bring myself to say the

word. "Death...was a terrible accident, but it was only an accident. We can still survive this. You have to believe that."

I watched his fists move to his hips. "Why do I have to?"

"Because..." I had no real answer. "Because if you don't, what's the point?" I'd felt all the same things earlier, but now, hearing Noah say them, I felt powerless and angry that he'd given up so easily. We had to keep fighting. We had to never give up. If we didn't, Harry would've died in vain. His death had to mean something, it had to propel us forward, give us a reason to keep going.

"I guess the point is that there is no point. We're trapped on this stupid island with no idea when or if we'll ever be rescued, no resources or idea what we're doing to even attempt to survive—"

My voice rose with anger as I cut him off. "Harry taught us—"

"What?" he screamed, his voice echoing throughout the forest. "He taught us what? How to boil water in coconuts and how to build some makeshift shelter that the slightest storm will destroy? Can we really live like this for years? For the rest of our lives? Do we even want to?"

"What are you saying, Noah?" Anger and hopelessness had begun waging war inside of me, each emotion fighting for my attention. *How dare he believe we are all going to die?*—but also—*we are all likely going to die.*

"I'm saying we're fucked. Don't you get that?" He launched forward, grabbing two handfuls of dirt and throwing them to the side with a loud growl. "How are we supposed to fight this? We don't know where we are, we don't know what we're up against, we don't know anything."

"You're wrong. We don't know where we are or why we're here, but we do know something. We know that someone else is on this island. Harry died helping us to get that information. So, stop. Stop with the *poor pitiful us* talk. You're allowed to be mad. You're allowed to be sad. But you're not allowed to give up. You're not allowed to feel defeated. Harry died, and we're still here. We have to keep going, if not for ourselves, for him. For your brother. For Harry's daughter. We keep going because they didn't get to. Because as long as we're breathing, we still have something to fight for. You don't get to give up right now. You have no right to do that. None of us do."

"I don't get you sometimes, Ace," he sneered. "Let's just get this over with."

With that, he climbed out of the shallow grave, and I followed his lead. Fresh tears filled my eyes as we stood over Harry's body. I had no idea what, if any, religion he followed. I'd never been religious myself, but I knew there were certain things done certain ways. Whatever we did, I didn't want to be disrespectful.

Noah placed his hands under Harry's shoulders, lifting him carefully and waiting for me to lift his feet. Together, we moved slowly, lowering his body into the grave. I touched his hand again, one last time, knowing I'd be the last person to touch him, the last person to see his face.

"I'm so sorry," I whispered, kneeling down beside him. "I'm so sorry this happened to you, but I promise to tell Daisy how brave you were. I promise to tell her how you saved our lives and...how proud of her you were." Silent tears cascaded down my cheeks as I held his cool hand. "Thank you for teaching us. For taking care of us and keeping us calm. I don't know how we'll do this without you, but I promise we will. We'll keep going."

To my surprise, Noah knelt down across from me on Harry's opposite side. He didn't touch him, didn't say anything, but he tucked his chin to his chest, listening to my words with reverence.

"I know we hadn't known you for long," I went on, "but you were one of my best friends. I trusted you with my life... I'll always be grateful for everything you did for me. For all of us." I dusted my tears away, squeezing his hand gently. "I promise you won't be forgotten. People will know about you. Everyone will know."

As far as eulogies went, it may have been the worst ever. I didn't know anything about him, really. I didn't have a cute story about his life growing up. I didn't know his favorite restaurant or the name of his childhood pet. I couldn't speak to his life and all the good I was sure he'd done. I could only honor him the way I knew how, with my utmost respect, with the words I wished he was still there to hear.

"That was nice," Noah said, interrupting the silence. "Really nice." There was nothing insincere in his tone.

I sniffled. "Thanks." Standing up, I grabbed a handful of dirt and sprinkled it on his body. Noah did the same. We repeated it over and over, until his body was mostly covered—at least as far as we could tell in the darkness. Then, we pulled the rest of the dirt in on him, patting it down gently until the loose dirt had all been placed on the grave. I lay down next to it, putting my arm over the lump of earth. "We have to put something here. Mark his grave somehow. So when we need to come back, when we get found, we'll be able to find his grave again."

"We'll mark it in the morning before we leave," he promised. "For now, I need to get a fire started... And let's both hope like hell I know how."

"I'll help you find wood."

He held his hand up to stop me from standing. "You're exhausted. I'm not going anywhere. I'll find enough wood to get us through the night without leaving you. Just rest."

"Are you sure?"

I yawned as he nodded and began gathering up sticks and brush along the forest floor. I knew he must've been just as exhausted as I felt, but it didn't stop him from working. I lay my head on the mound of dirt again, cool tears trailing down my cheeks and mixing with the soil. I closed my eyes, saying another goodbye to my friend in my mind.

WARMTH HIT me suddenly and my eyes popped open. The fire was going, its flames lighting up the dark night.

"I fell asleep?" I asked, attempting to blink the blurriness from my vision. How had I fallen asleep so easily? I stifled a yawn, answering my own question. Grief was heavy, exhausting. Add that to all I'd been through that day, let alone the days leading up to it, and it was all I could do to keep my eyes open.

Noah was sitting next to the fire, his arms wrapped

around his folded knees. He nodded, the left side of his mouth rising slightly. "You snore."

"I do," I said, too tired to deny it.

"Me too," he said simply. "Grit my teeth, too."

"We'd be a fun pair for a sleepover, hm?" I said dryly. My chest hurt, I assumed from digging for so long, but also from the pain of it all. It still didn't feel completely real.

He was silent for a moment, not meeting my eye. Then, he inhaled sharply. "You were a good friend to him."

"I barely knew him…"

"It didn't matter. Going through what we have together…none of us are strangers anymore."

It felt true enough, but my throat was too dry to respond. I looked around. "Where are the coconuts?"

He pulled one from the sack I hadn't seen sitting next to him and smacked it down onto one of the rocks near the fire. We were all beginning to be experts at just the right amount of force it took to crack them open.

He handed it to me, licking a bit of juice from the side of his hand. I gulped the sweet nectar down until the coconut was empty. It felt as if it had been years since I'd had anything to drink. It felt as if it had been years since we'd left the clearing this morning. I looked to my left, at the grave I was still half resting on.

"How are we going to tell the others?" I asked, feeling sick at just the thought of it.

"I don't even want to think about it," he said, his upper lip curled in repulsion, yet I was sure it was the only thing he'd been thinking about. "It's tomorrow's problem.

Tonight, I just want to stare at this fire and not think about anything at all."

I sat up straighter, cracking the coconut the rest of the way open and picking at the meat mindlessly. "Can I...can I ask what happened to your brother?" He didn't look at me, but I watched his jaw tense. "You don't have to tell me if that's too personal—"

"We were in the car with my mom. It was Theo's fourth birthday. We'd pulled into the driveway, and he unbuckled his seat... I didn't think anything of it; he did it all the time. Mom didn't see him in time. He was holding on to the door... I remember Dad standing on the porch. Theo was banging on the window waving at him... Somehow he grabbed hold of the handle, and the door opened. He fell face-first... Mom reached for him, but it all happened so fast. He was crushed by the tire before she had time to stop." The visions of the story swept over me as he replayed them, each moment of the scene that must've played out, the guilt his mother must live with, the pain of his father watching it unfold from feet away, powerless to do anything.

"That's terrible..." I managed to squeak out. His face was solemn, despite blinking through tears that trailed down his cheeks. He didn't bother wiping them away, and I wondered how many times he must've had to relive the event aloud. "I'm so sorry, Noah. I didn't mean to pry."

"It's hard to talk about him." His Adam's apple bobbed up and down with a hard swallow. Finally, he looked over, meeting my eyes. "But it's good to talk about him, too. My parents...they...they couldn't talk about him. Still can't. My mom couldn't walk past his pictures for years without falling apart. It's…I don't know if it ever won't be raw. For any of us."

I stood up without volition, making my way toward him and wrapping an arm around his back. He stiffened slightly under my touch but didn't shrug me off or push me away. Instead, he went back to watching the fire.

"I'm still coming to grips with the fact that I'll probably never see them again. And, I think what terrifies me the most about that, is knowing that they'll have to go through losing their only other son. I don't think they'll survive it."

"They aren't going to lose you," I promised, the words eerily similar to what I'd said to Harry the night before. I forced the thought away. "We're going to find our way home."

"I know you want to believe that, but I just don't see how."

I fought back bitter tears. "I just have to believe it. I can't give up. Not yet…"

"Have you ever lost anyone?" he asked, turning his face toward me. "Anyone you were close to?"

I shook my head, almost regrettably. "No, not really. Both sets of my great-grandparents died when I was really young, but I don't remember them all that much. Just pictures and stuff. And there've been a few of my classmates who've died since we graduated. Nothing like what you've experienced… I'm sorry."

"You're sorry you haven't lost anyone?" he asked with a small grin.

"I'm sorry you have."

He jutted his chin toward Harry's grave. "Well, now we both have."

"Yeah, I guess you're right." It didn't feel equal, not really, but was there a way to measure grief? To decide who felt more pain? My pain felt significant in that moment. I couldn't imagine—and didn't want to—how Noah must've felt the day he lost his brother, and so many days after that. The pain was unbearable to even think about.

"I don't want to be," he said, his eyes lingering on mine for a second too long. I looked down, my face burning with embarrassing heat. I needed to move away from him. We were too close. Why had I moved to be near him after what had happened in the woods? "Don't worry. I'm not going to kiss you." It was as if he'd read my mind. I guess I hadn't done a great job of hiding it.

"I wasn't thinking that..."

"Yeah, you were." His determined stare was an obvious dare to get me to look at him, but I couldn't. He'd see only shame there, because the truth was, I had enjoyed the kiss. I'd be lying if I said I hadn't thought of doing the same thing since he'd saved my life in the jungle on that second day. But what did it matter? I had a husband. Feelings like what I was having were not allowed.

"Harry said he thought you had a thing for me," I admitted, tucking a piece of hair behind my ear and staring at the fire with unyielding concentration.

"Harry wasn't wrong."

I looked at him then, unable to resist the pull of his gaze any longer when plagued by the truth in his words. "I never knew..." I lied.

"Yes, you did. But it didn't matter before, when I thought you were married and we were going home."

"I am married," I said firmly, "and we are going home."

His eyes softened, and he cocked his head to the side slightly. "You are married, but we may not be going home. And sooner or later, we all have to come to grips with that." He looked away then, patting his leg. "Look, I'm not going to force you to do anything you don't want to do. If you want to stay loyal to your husband for the rest of time, more power to you, but all I'm saying is there's a very real chance we aren't making it off this island. There's a very real chance we could all die tomorrow. Or next week. Or the week after. James and Ava got that. They're taking advantage of every moment they have on this island… They're having fun—"

"I wouldn't call any of what we're doing fun—"

"They're having the most fun they can, then," he said. "And I don't see why we can't do the same."

"So, because we're the only other two on the island, I should sleep with you?"

He scoffed. "No, you should sleep with me because we're on a deserted island, with no guarantee of tomorrow, and you're wildly attracted to me."

I furrowed my brow, pressing my lips together. "I'm not wildly attracted to you." My body physically revolted against the lie. I felt my core tighten, my words sounding strange and foreign, but he just laughed dryly and lay back on the ground, his hands under his head.

"Whatever you say, Buttercup. Sooner or later, you'll come around. I just hope I'm still living to see the day."

"We should get some rest," I said, shutting down the

subject. I lay down beside him, mere inches between our bodies, but I'd made sure they weren't touching in the slightest. I could hear his breathing, feel the warmth from his skin, the warmth from the fire by our feet. I closed my eyes, listening to the sounds of the forest, the crackling of the fire, and the rhythmic music of our breaths syncing together, slowing.

Then, sleep found me, and I let it take me away from the pain and worry. At least for a few hours.

CHAPTER NINETEEN

Nice work. One down, three to go until one of you leaves the island for good.

The note had been laid across Harry's grave, held down by a small rock. When we awoke the next morning, the sun had risen high in the sky. It was the latest we'd ever slept in on the island. The thought made me feel sick because I realized that meant we were beginning to grow accustomed to our surroundings enough to find deep, restful sleep.

Now we were making our way back toward camp, the note hidden in Noah's pocket, but its words still echoing in my head. It confirmed what we all thought, that whatever game or experiment we'd found ourselves involved in, for any one of us to leave, the others had to be dead.

I didn't know if the 'nice work' was referring to us surviving, or the fact that Harry had died. We walked side by side this time, traveling as one force, rather than three separate individuals as we had on our way to the cliff. We passed the trees we'd marked, the weight of both machetes in my hands weighing on me.

We passed the bit of mud where Harry's shoe had slid on our way here. Neither of us pointed it out as we walked past, but I saw us both clock it. I knew we were thinking of our friend, hoping to remember everything we could about our time together.

I also knew we were bracing ourselves for the harsh reality of having to deliver the news to Ava and James. Ava, in particular, had been as close to Harry as I was. The news would be a shock to her, and she was already in such a frail condition. I only hoped that rest had done her well, and that we'd find her healthy and prepared for what was coming.

Not that any of us could truly prepare.

As we neared the campsite, I heard the trickling of water and the lilts of their voices.

"That's what it means," Ava was saying, panic in her tone.

"It can't."

"It does."

They were arguing, I realized, their heated tones carrying across the forest.

"It has to be a trick, then," James was saying. "You'll see. They'll be back any minute—"

"And if they aren't? What if they don't come back? What if they were part of it all and—"

A branch snapped under Noah's shoe, and their voices stopped suddenly.

"Who's there?" I heard James cry out, and I thought instantly of the guns they both had access to.

"We come in peace," Noah called out, teasing them with his hands in the air as we rounded the corner and came into view. They were standing near the water, their eyes wide with fear. When they saw us, relief flooded their expressions. Then, practically at once, the worry was back.

Here goes nothing.

"Harry?" Ava asked, a certain kind of knowing in her expression that broke my heart. I opened my mouth to speak but lost my nerve. She spotted the moment it happened and shook her head. "No…"

"He fell off the cliff," Noah said. "Slipped when we were climbing down."

James took a protective step in front of Ava, as if he could somehow shield her from the heartbreak itself. "How bad is it?"

"He's gone," Noah told them, tears flooding my vision once again as we relived the pain. Ava's eyes were locked on mine, and I watched tears begin to fill her almond eyes. "It was quick… He was gone within a few minutes."

"I don't understand…" James's eyes darted between the two of us. "What happened? His neck broke? Did he land on his head? Why didn't you come get us?"

"It was internal bleeding," I said. "There was nothing any of us could've done. It happened so quickly." My eyes fell to where Harry's book lay on the ground, next to the fire, and my chest filled with a new, fresh ache.

James sniffled, rubbing his hand under his nose aggressively as the other hand gripped a crying Ava's waist. "Where is he now?"

"We buried him," Noah said. "By the cliff."

"We marked it. In case we want to go back… Or for when we're found, so they can take his body."

Ava and James were quiet. He pulled her around to face him, her cheek pressed into his chest as he rubbed a hand across her face. "Shhh…" He tried to console her as she broke out into sobs.

"We did everything we could," I said, trying to quiet my own tears. "He, um, he had a daughter, Daisy. He wants us to tell her he was sorry. And that he loved her."

"Why are you telling us this?" James demanded.

"In case something happens to me," I said. "I shouldn't be the only one who knows." They seemed to be contemplating something, their faces holding more than just sorrow. "I'm sorry you couldn't be there. We can take you there, if you want to say your goodbyes."

"Yeah, maybe," James said softly, his cheek pressed against the top of Ava's head. Noah and I unloaded our weapons and the sack with the remaining coconut in it and approached the water to rinse off.

At seeing us move near them, James and Ava stepped apart. Ava swiped her tears away quickly. "How are you feeling, Ava? Are you still unwell?"

She shook her head, looking at James cautiously. When she smiled, it appeared forced. "I think I just needed a while to rest."

"I'm so glad." She took a half step back from me, and I took note, keeping my distance. What was going on? Why did everything feel so cool between us? What had changed? "Everything okay?"

They exchanged a glance, and James reached into his pocket. "We got this note this morning."

189

"Note?"

"About Harry…" My blood went cold as I saw him unfold the small orange slip of paper.

"Nice work," he read aloud, reading the words that were exactly the same as the one we'd received. I looked to where Noah stood, watching him pull our note from his pocket.

"We got the same one."

"What do you think it means?" James asked.

"Exactly what it says," Noah said frankly. "Until there's only one of us left, whoever's keeping us on this island, isn't letting us go."

Ava's eyes narrowed slightly, and I saw her gaze flick up toward James, though he hadn't noticed.

"But we think we may have found something."

Their brows shot up. "What do you mean?" he asked. "You saw something in the woods?"

"We saw a house. Built into a cliff a few miles from here. There was smoke coming from some sort of chimney on top of it."

"So that was what we smelled after the storm?" Ava asked.

"Harry thought so," I told her.

"Then we should go," James said quickly, and I found myself mimicking the words I'd fought so hard against the day before.

"We have to be smart about it. We're going to travel nearby, but we can't barge in. Not yet. Harry wanted us to watch them, to get information about who lives there and what we're up against, before we make any decisions about how to move forward."

"And what makes you think they don't already know we know where they are? What makes you think they aren't watching us right now? That's the second—third technically, if you count both of ours—note that they left for us. They know exactly where we are and what's happening to us," James argued.

"He's right," Noah said. I sucked in a sharp breath, shocked to hear him say so. "I get what Harry was worried about, but especially after these new notes, we know these people are watching us. We know they're playing some sort of sick game. We know where they are... Waiting around for someone else to die just doesn't make sense."

"I agree with you, but Harry—"

"Harry isn't here anymore," James said, his tone firm. "What he said, what he believed, it doesn't matter anymore. *We* make the decisions now. We can vote like normal and go from there."

I jerked my head back in horror, aghast that he could say such a thing. "How can you say that? Look, you can ask Noah, I agree with you. I was arguing the same thing with Harry yesterday—"

"So you should be glad your opinion won out." The thought made me sick. James's face was stony, unmoving.

"Harry was our friend. He's the only reason the four of us are still alive out here. I think the least we can do is respect his last wish and listen to the advice he gave us."

"You're outnumbered," Ava said, "because I'm siding with James now. We should go. There's no sense waiting any longer."

I looked at Noah, hoping he'd side with me, but he

simply shrugged. "They're right. You knew they were right yesterday. It was why you argued. We have to find out what's going on." A flicker of sadness filled his dark eyes. "Get you back to your husband."

"I just—"

"Look, I'm not arguing," James said. "It's three against one. If you want to stay here by yourself, be my guest. Noah will show us where the house is. We're getting off this island, no matter the cost. I'm not waiting a second longer. Are you coming or not?"

Indignation and fury seethed through me, and while I wanted to scream and throw a tantrum, I forced myself to remain calm. "Yes," I spit out. "Yes, I'm coming. We've been walking for hours. Could we just have a break to rest and cool off? We can leave in a few hours. We'd make it by evening."

"You can take five minutes while we find some coconuts, get our shoes on, and load up the weapons." Something had definitely shifted between us. James had never looked at me so coolly, almost angrily. I tried to catch Ava's eyes, hoping to make her see reason, but she wouldn't look at me. "But we're leaving straight away."

When they walked away, disappearing near the tree line, I looked at Noah, shuffling toward him in the shallow water.

"Don't try to change my mind. It won't work. I agreed with you yesterday. I agree with them now."

"I'm not trying to change your mind." I knelt down, brushing cool water up over my shins and calves, aware that Ava and James were likely somewhere not too far away, listening to whatever we might be saying. I lowered my voice to barely above a whisper, sure that over the sounds of the water, they wouldn't be able to hear me then. "Do you think something is up with them?" I asked, not looking at him.

"Definitely," he said, copying my movements. "Something's changed."

"What do you think it could be?"

"I don't know, but...you need to stay close to me." I furrowed my brow. "I'm not saying this to...whatever. This isn't me trying to hit on you. They have two guns. We have one. We have to be cautious... Play it smart until we find out what's happen—"

"What are you two talking about?" James's voice boomed, stepping out from the tree line, the shotgun slung over his shoulder. His smile was almost antagonistic.

"Nothing," I said, standing up. "Just trying to cool off."

He waited, as if he expected us to say more.

"We ready?" Noah asked, clasping his hands in front of him.

"Let's go," James said as Ava reappeared from the forest too, the pistol held firmly in her palm. I swallowed, a chill running over me as I picked up both machetes.

"Let's go." I hoped they hadn't heard the tremble in my voice.

CHAPTER TWENTY

I t was late afternoon before we arrived at the cliff house. We'd come across a dirt path that led straight to the door, and I had to wonder how often the path was traveled. There was no grass growing up through the dirt, so I had to believe it was at least frequented occasionally.

The T-shirt I was wearing had been drenched through with sweat, its dingy cotton clinging to my body with a vengeance. Ava kept a distance from me, so different than before, and James seemed to play the buffer, holding her hand and keeping her close, but occasionally casting a glance back toward Noah and me to make sure we hadn't wandered off.

Something had changed—between them, and between us. Perhaps it was just the loss of Harry. Maybe he had been the glue holding us all together. Maybe we were all just trying to recover, trying to hang on however we could.

But that wasn't it. There was more, at least.

I felt it in my bones. Ava wasn't herself. The bubbly

girl I'd gotten to know, who I'd cared about, who I'd considered a friend…

I looked to Noah, wondering if he felt the tension as strongly as I did. If he still believed it would be us versus them. I didn't want it to be. When he'd said it, I thought he was being ridiculous, but now, I just didn't know.

Up close, the door was larger than I'd expected. It was made of a solid, rusty metal with a wheel in the center that looked as if it might not have been turned in decades. I wondered, briefly, if we'd been wrong. The smoke wasn't going anymore, and the door could've led to anything. There was no guarantee it was even inhabitable, let alone actually housed someone.

But I hadn't imagined the woman. Of that, I was sure. She was real, and she was somewhere on the island. Maybe just steps from me.

"What do we do now?" I asked, waiting for James to tell us his master plan.

He looked around, shielding his eyes from the afternoon sun. He wiped the sweat from his brow and dried his hand on the side of his shorts. When he moved toward the door, his hands outstretched, I gasped. He connected with the wheel, attempting to turn it.

"Wait—" I tried to stop him, but it was too late. He shoved it with a heavy groan, but the wheel didn't budge.

He grunted, stepping away and dusting his hands, the palms now painted burnt orange from the rust. "It's locked anyway." He sniffled, dusting his hands again. "Here, you knock on the door, and we'll all be ready," he said, staring at me.

"Wha—"

"Whoa, hey, no," Noah said quickly, interrupting my own protest. "Like hell are we letting her knock on the door."

If we were back home, I would've said I didn't need him to *let* me do anything, *thankyouverymuch*, but for once, I was thankful for him speaking for me.

"She's the only one who doesn't have a gun." James lifted his gun, pointing it at the door. "Whenever they answer, we'll have our guns on them."

"Whoever is in there, they gave us these guns, James. Do you honestly believe they gave us their entire supply of weapons? That they don't have just as many, *if not more*? This place is elaborate. It's well hidden. They're watching us somehow… There's no way whoever lives here isn't protected."

"We'll just have to take our chances. This is the only way in." He tipped his gun toward the door again. "Come on, we're wasting time."

"What are we going to say when they answer?" I asked, begging him to see reason. "We can't just barge in. Please think this through."

"They haven't hurt us yet, okay? If they wanted to kill us, they would've done it already. They have to be willing to see reason. They have to agree to a sit down and…a discussion." He was thinking on his feet, something I didn't think he was particularly good at. "We can make them see reason. Negotiate."

"With what?" Noah asked, pleading with him now rather than his usual sarcastic tone. "Sticks and coconuts? We have nothing to offer them. We need to think about this before we act. We're not just sending her to knock on the door without a plan. We're here. We made it. We found it. What's next?" He looked at Ava, then at me. "Anyone have any ideas?"

"Ahhh, we don't have time for this," James groaned, rushing toward the door with his hand outstretched. His fist connected with the heavy metal with a loud *thwomp, thwomp, thwomp.*

"What the fuck, man?" Noah asked as James darted backward, never turning away from the door, his gun held awkwardly but at the ready nonetheless.

Everyone brought their weapons up, and I dropped one of the machetes, trying to dry my sweaty palms so I wouldn't lose the one that remained. My heart thundered in my chest, making my ears hot and my vision tunnel.

This was it.

We were going to meet the woman.

We were going to find out why we were there.

Seconds passed, feeling like hours, and we waited, our weapons unwavering. I watched the wheel on the door for the slightest movement, knowing that when it began to turn, I'd need to be at my best. Prepared to duck or run or hide at a moment's notice.

Noah shifted a half step, so he was in front of me only slightly. The movement was barely noticeable, but I felt warmth fill me as he did it. I knew then that even if I'd never agreed to our pact, it was in place. Noah would protect me, and I would do the same for him.

No matter what.

What we'd gone through, all of us, but particularly the two of us, had cemented the deal, even without my intention.

After another long, drawn-out pause, James's weapon dropped slightly. He took a step toward the door, preparing to knock again. All at once, the door opened, only slightly, and I watched something small and silver scurry across the forest floor before it shut again with a loud *thud*.

A mouse?

A can.

As it registered, foggy, pressurized air began spewing out into the air with a steady *pstttttttttttt.*

"What the—"

"Get back!"

"Run!"

Our response was immediate and identical, the four of us darting for safety. I heard the creak of the door being opened again just as shots rang out, and I braced myself for the blow. This couldn't be how it ended. It just couldn't.

"Get down!" a man shouted, and I fell to the ground at his command, my face pressed into the dirt as I panted, trying to make sense of what was happening. "Hands flat on the ground. Don't touch your weapons. No sudden moves."

I couldn't see anything for the fog from the can. It hadn't burned like I'd expected, so it wasn't tear gas, but it was still potent enough to fill the small area with a dense fog so thick I could hardly see where my machete landed, several feet in front of me. I looked to my left, at Ava, and my right, at Noah. We were all in similar positions, faces crushed to the ground, waiting for what would come.

"Now, I want you all to listen to me, and listen well…"

This was a new man. I tried to place their accents. They weren't Southern. Midwestern, maybe? Then again, I supposed they could've been faking it. They sounded older than I was, but not by much, and confident. In control.

"You shouldn't have come here," he went on. "You don't belong here."

Did he mean we didn't belong on the island? Or here, at their door? I opened my mouth, wanting to explain.

"You need to go back to the beach," the other said, shutting me up before I'd begun. "You got the notes. You know the rules. You have your weapons... You have your orders. Get it done."

Noah met my eyes, our cheeks still resting on the ground, and I had the sudden urge to reach out and touch his hand, but I knew I couldn't. No sudden moves.

"Why are you doing this to us?" James asked, his tone high-pitched and fearful. "Who are you people?"

"No one you need to worry about," came the first man's reply. "Now, we're going to go back inside. Only one of you can leave, that's the rule. So, if you want to ever get off this island, ever see your families again..." He cleared his throat. "You'll do what we say. And if you ever come back here again, none of you will leave. Not ever."

We stayed silent as their words sank in for all of us. When I heard their footsteps descending, James called out, "What if we all agree on one of us to leave? What if the rest of us will stay? We don't have to die, but we have to stay."

"Don't try to negotiate with us. That's not how it works. We make the rules. Was that James? Man the fuck up, *James*," came the sour, aggressive response. "You've got the gun, so use it. Don't get distracted by—" The man's voice cut out, and I heard a grumble.

The other man took over. "It's against the rules. Don't try to play us. We're watching you. We'll know if you try to trick us, and then none of you are going to get off this island. Ever." He made a *hmph* sound and added, "Now, once you hear the door close, you're to count to thirty, then stand up, gather your weapons, and make your way back to the beach. Do not return here." There was no room for negotiation. I heard the wheel creak and the door squeal as it opened, and then I heard the thud that told us we were alone.

Or, at least the most alone we'd ever been or ever would be on this island with the strangers watching us.

I let out a heavy breath, tears I'd been holding in flooding my eyes. I let my body relax, my limbs flat and limp on the ground. Noah reached out, clutching my hand carefully. On my other side, I heard Ava crying and James trying to console her, despite the tremble in his own voice.

"I'm so sorry," he told her softly.

Noah stood, tugging me to my feet. "We should go," he said, leaving no room for argument as he pulled me away from the house.

"We can't just leave," James tried to argue.

"We've shown you where the house is." Noah didn't bother looking back. "If you want to stay here, be my guest. We're going back to the beach." He gripped my hand tighter, pulling me in front of him, his hands resting on either side of my waist. He was protecting me once again, but I didn't need it. Eventually, I heard James's and Ava's footsteps following behind.

The trip hadn't given us any answers, but had managed to steal away any remaining hope we'd held on to. I couldn't help thinking of my promise to Harry, that I'd someday tell Daisy about his bravery. I knew then I'd almost certainly never see that promise through.

CHAPTER TWENTY-ONE

"Maybe we could build a raft." The idea came weeks after Harry had died. I couldn't be sure of the exact time because I'd given up trying to keep track of it. The sun rose, we hunted and gathered, boiled fresh water, and slept.

We'd crafted three shelters since our last one, none that came anywhere near as sturdy as Harry's had, and none that had survived more than a few nights. Eventually, we just gave up, choosing to sleep unsheltered and take cover under the boulder whenever a storm got too bad.

By that point, we'd all developed deep tans, no longer burned by the sun even on its hottest day. We had bumps and scars and bruises from our time in the wilderness. We knew how to crack a coconut, clean a boar, catch a fish, and start a fire. We'd become experts on which coconut might hold the most juice, spotting fish darting beneath the ocean's surface, and which wild animal made which sounds.

We knew our surroundings, the small amount of ground we'd allowed ourselves to turn into a home. We were surviving, taking on roles and tasks, and finding our way in our new normal.

But nothing was okay. James and Ava hadn't stopped being cold to us, even if they slipped up occasionally and made a joke or laughed at one of ours, even if they passed us the food in the evening without a stony gaze or handed us a coconut without a locked jaw. Nothing was the same, and I suspected nothing ever would be again.

They disappeared constantly, telling us that Ava's stomach was upset again, though it was rare that I actually saw her get sick. They said certain foods, especially on hot days, seem to upset her, but from where I was sitting, it seemed more like they needed excuses to sneak off together.

Noah kept me close to him, and I no longer refused to oblige him. He was the closest thing I had to a friend with Harry gone, and that was a commodity I couldn't deny I needed.

Once every few days, the four of us would make our way to Harry's grave, placing fresh flowers on the mound of dirt that had begun to sprout fresh grass. It was probably the only thing we did together where I could forget about the tension and let the sadness take over, let my grief over our friend be the only thing I felt.

"We have plenty of logs. We could find a way to tie them together. Something big enough for one or two people to float on," James said, when no one responded to his comment about building a raft.

"And let me guess who those lucky two would be," Noah said dryly.

"The girls could go, if you don't trust me to send help back for you," he said, his brows furrowed.

"Do logs float?" Ava asked, wide-eyed. "Like...really float?"

"There'd be no way to steer. The tide would end up pushing you right back up to shore," Noah said.

"You don't know that. If it could get out far enough, maybe we could catch the attention of a boat, and—"

"It doesn't matter. You know the rules. We can't do that. We shouldn't even be talking about this," I snarled, keeping my voice low. In the weeks since that day, there'd been no talk of escape. We'd followed the rules of the mysterious men behind the mysterious door. Why was he suddenly interested in disrupting the safety we seemed to have?

For a while, no one said anything. I picked at the meat in my hands—fish, again. It had been days since we'd managed to catch a boar or goat, and I was growing tired of fish. I stared at the fire. Next to it, we'd built a stack of our now-useless items: our phones, my Kindle, and Harry's novel, which none of us could bear to open. The pile was almost a shrine to who we'd once been.

James threw the remainder of his food down with force, a huffed breath released at my expense. "You're really just okay with this? After all this time? None of you are going to try and find us a way out of here?"

"There is no way out," I said, sighing as I leaned back a bit. "Don't you get that, James? This is it. This is our life—"

"Easy—" Noah began, but I cut him off.

"No. You were right, Noah. You told me that I needed to accept it, but I couldn't. I wanted to believe we'd find a way. There's always a way, I thought. But there's not a way out of this. There wasn't for Harry, and there's not for us." Ava scoffed, drawing the group's attention to her. "Do you have something you'd like to say?" I demanded, the heat contributing to my frustration.

She rolled her eyes, taking a sip of her coconut water and refusing to answer.

"Do you?" I asked again. "Because I would really like to know what exactly it is that I've done to piss you both off so badly. If you want to build a raft, build a damn raft, but count me out."

"Yeah, you'd like that, wouldn't you?" Ava asked, finally looking at me. It felt as if it was the first time we were making meaningful eye contact in so long.

"I'd like what?"

"Drop it, Ava," James warned, putting a hand on her knee.

"No. Please." I held out a hand to stop him from talking, my tone clipped. "I'd like to hear it. What is it you think I'd like?"

She appeared to be contemplating whether or not to say whatever was clearly on her mind, her nostrils flaring, eyes darting between mine. "If we build a raft and get caught, and they kill us…then the two of you are left to decide what to do next. It would make it easy on you, wouldn't it? You wouldn't have to take us out like you did Ha—"

"Ava!" James cried, cutting her off, but I'd heard enough to know what she was going to say.

I stared at her, my eyes wide, jaw slack. Every ounce of anger had deflated from my body, replaced only with utter devastation. "Do you think that we…" I could hardly say the words. "That we killed Harry?"

She didn't answer, but she didn't deny it, a challenge in her eyes. The silence was a blow. I felt the weight of it in my chest, crushing my lungs as I inhaled deeply.

Beside me, Noah scrambled to his feet, stepping toward her. "How the fuck can you say that? You know how much Harry meant to her…"

I wanted to stop him, to calm him down, but I wanted to know the answer, too.

James stood up, facing off with him. "Ease up, bro. She didn't even say anything."

"She didn't *not* say anything," he said, looking James up and down aggressively. "Is that what you think, too? Is that what you've both been whispering about during all the times you sneak away?"

"It's not like that—"

Ava stood up, touching James's arm gently and narrowing her gaze at Noah. "We don't owe you an explanation for the way we feel."

"And how exactly do you feel?" I asked, still feeling as if the wind had been knocked out of me. I couldn't bring myself to stand up. "That's what changed, isn't it? When we came back, you were different… It's because you think we did this on purpose." It wasn't a question, but as she broke eye contact, she confirmed it.

"We weren't with you," James said. "And we got the

note that said 'nice work.' When we found out Harry died, well…"

"We don't know what happened while you were out there," Ava finished for him when he seemed unable to do so himself. "What we know is that you left with our friend, and you came back without him in a place where we're all meant to kill each other. All we have is your word that you didn't get Harry out of your way, and that you're not planning to do the same to us."

I clutched my chest, shaking my head at her in shock. "Do you honestly believe I'm capable of that? After all we've been through?"

"Why didn't you come get us?" James asked, his tone soft. More out of curiosity than anything. "Why wouldn't you have come and gotten us when it happened? Why bury him without us?"

"Because…it all happened so fast. We didn't mean to…" I tried to find the words to relive the night I'd spent so much time trying to forget.

"What would you have had us do?" Noah demanded. "Carry his body miles across the jungle or leave it there and hope animals hadn't gotten to it before we could make it here and back?" He huffed a breath. "We'd just watched our friend die. We were in shock and just trying to deal with it the best we could. He fell. It was an accident. If you don't believe us, just leave. Build your raft and leave. See what happens. Believe me, if we'd meant to kill you, you'd be dead by now."

"Noah," I said, shocked by the last sentiment. I shot up, grabbing hold of his arm and trying to ease the tension. "Ava," I begged her to meet my eye. When she finally did, I went on, "Harry was my friend. Losing him..."

Tears sprang to my eyes without warning. I placed my hand on my chest. "It broke me. I can't...I can't explain to you how it happened. How quickly, how devastating... We wanted to bring him back. We wanted to save him. But we couldn't. We did the best we could while we were still processing what had happened. We would... We'd never hurt you."

I glanced at James. "Either of you. We're in this together. We've always been in this together. I care about you both, and nothing could change that. If you can't trust us, if you don't believe me, there's nothing I can do. I don't know how I'd feel if the situation were reversed. But what I can tell you is that I'd do anything to protect you. Harry's death was a horrible accident and nothing else."

I brushed away a stray tear and turned away from her. I felt as if I were going to pass out, my head throbbing. I needed to get away before I said or did something I regretted.

"Where are you going?" Noah asked, glancing over his shoulder.

"I need to walk," I said. Then I added, "I'll stay close." I knew he'd worry otherwise, and I desperately needed my alone time. I hoped he wouldn't follow me.

CHAPTER TWENTY-TWO

"*Psssst.*"

I opened my eyes, looking up at the dark, starry sky with hazy vision. The sand was hard and itchy against my back, and when I rolled over, it fell from my hair in a gentle cascade. I looked around, sure I'd heard the noise.

In the distance, I saw Ava's and James's bodies curled together next to the fire, two dark lumps in the sand only recognizable by the bump of a bun atop Ava's head that she'd managed to fashion with a particularly strong weed we'd found. Farther down the shore and closer to me, but still not close, Noah lay, his arms and legs outstretched like a starfish, as he always slept. I furrowed my brow, looking behind me. Had I dreamed the noise?

"*Pssssst.*" It came again, more real this time, making me jump. I looked toward the edge of the trees, my throat growing dry as I saw the flash of white. The blonde hair, blowing in the wind next to the trees. She was watching me. She was waving me in her direction.

I looked at Noah instinctively, weighing my options. Should I go? Should I yell? Should I run?

"Psssst," she called again, waving her hand ferociously between us. "Come here," she whispered. "Hurry."

I took a deep breath, taking a cautious step toward her. It felt like the best and worst idea all at once. She was alone and didn't appear to be armed, and I'd seen her twice now, without her trying to hurt us.

"Who are you?" I asked when I got close enough to talk, but not close enough for her to grab me, should she try. I kept Noah's feet in my peripheral vision, the rest of his body and the entirety of Ava's and James's blocked by the trees.

"What are you doing out here?"

"I'm a friend," she said quickly, her voice too low as she glanced behind her, almost like she was afraid someone was watching us. "I don't have much time. I came to warn you..."

"Warn me—"

"You can't build a raft," she said quickly, cutting me off.

My blood went cold. "What are you talking about? How do you know about that?"

"I heard you talking today."

"But how? Where do you live? How did you even get on this island?"

She glanced behind her again. "*They* brought me here."

"They? They who? The men in the cliff house? Who are they?"

"I don't have time to explain. If they find me here, they'll kill us both. Just..." Behind her, I heard a branch crack. She jumped, her body tensing. "Just don't get on the raft. They know about the plan. They know everything."

"How do they know? Are they watching us? How are they finding out so much? What do they want from us?"

Her eyes widened, and she shook her head. "I'm sorry... I can't—" Another branch snapped. This time, it sounded closer. She took a step backward, and I moved forward.

"Wait! Please don't go. Please help us."

"I can't," she said, lowering her voice even more. "Just...don't build the raft. They'll kill anyone who tries to escape. Be careful. And please, don't tell anyone I was here..."

"But what—"

"I have to go. I'm sorry. Don't tell anyone you saw me." She jutted her head toward the water, toward my friends. "You can't trust them."

"Who?"

"Anyone," she said firmly. She turned from me then, without another word, and I felt my heart sinking as I watched her hurry away, the bright white of her hair, skin, and clothes disappearing into the dark abyss of the woods.

"Please! Wait!" I called in a hushed tone, but it was no use. She was gone, and I was alone again, with nothing more than her ominous warning to guide me. I felt a shiver run over me and backed away from the woods, suddenly feeling like I was being watched. What had she heard in the woods? Who was coming for us? Why had they brought her here? Why had they brought *us* here? What did she know?

I walked back toward the ocean, watching the waves attack the shore like angry claws, pulling in bits of sand and shells with every touch. It was peaceful at night, dark and steady, a roar so defined I could hear it even when I was back near the falls. I could hear it in my sleep.

I'd been to the beach so many times back home, but never at night, and never in such an uninhabited place. It was different here.

I sank onto the sand next to Noah, watching him stir a bit at my disturbance, but he didn't wake. Among the many things we'd learned on the island, sleeping through every noise and bump in the night was one of the most important. Between the animal noises, the cracks and snaps of the trees, the thuds of coconuts falling, and the roar of the ocean, we were surrounded by a constant stream of noise unlike what we were used to in our lives back home.

I glanced behind me, checking the tree line to make sure no one was making their way toward me. The woman's appearance had shaken me, but not enough to follow her. I wouldn't go into the woods at night alone, and her warning about not trusting anyone had left me on edge. I wished I knew who she meant.

Surely not Noah. Ava, perhaps. Her coldness today had shaken me. But I truly believed she was scared, not malicious. And James, as doting toward Ava as he was, was kind at heart. I had never returned to our circle, and they hadn't pressed the issue, but once, when I glanced over at them from my place on the sand, he'd met my eye, a small, apologetic smile on his lips. He wasn't evil; he was in love. I couldn't believe any of them intended me harm.

But then what else could she have meant? I wrapped my arms around myself as the wind howled, cooling my skin. Noah stirred again, and I scooted down so I was lying beside him, keeping our bodies a safe distance apart. I couldn't bear the thought of disturbing him. I didn't want to talk. There was no way I could without saying something about my encounter with the woman.

Noah and I had a pact—protect each other above all others. Did that include telling him about this? I'd keep him from participating in any escape plans, and I had to hope that would be enough.

I checked the tree line again, knowing there'd be no more sleeping tonight. I was too paranoid, too sure someone was just beyond the tree line with an eye on me. I looked over at Noah, then at Ava and James, and for half a second, I could swear I saw Ava's head lifted off the sand, her face turned toward me, as if she were watching me.

How long had she been like that?

I blinked again, and her head was back down. Had I imagined that?

CHAPTER TWENTY-THREE

To my great relief, the next day there was no further mention of the raft. The fight, but not the pain of it, seemed all but forgotten as we sat around the fire and ate a few of the berries Ava had picked for breakfast. It seemed as if another storm would be blowing in soon—the air felt heavier, smelled different than usual, and the tide was stronger.

"I'm going to the falls," James said almost abruptly, interrupting the silence and my thoughts as he stood up and adjusted his shorts. "I need a shower. You coming?"

Ava nodded, tossing a few of the berries from her hand back into the pile, and together they headed toward the forest without so much as a goodbye to us. When they'd been gone a while, Noah dropped the rest of his breakfast and dusted off his hands.

"You okay?" It was the first we'd really spoken since the argument the evening before. At my wish, he'd left me to myself as I tried to process everything, so it felt strange to be talking about it now.

"I'm okay." I pressed my lips together, hoping he believed me. I didn't want to think Noah was working against me; I had to trust that he wasn't. I needed to have faith in his loyalty to me as much as I needed water. He was all I had, and the solitude would kill me before his betrayal.

"Don't let them get to you. We're all just freaked out..." He slid closer to me, keeping his head down, voice low.

"We've been freaked out. All of us. But we'd never accuse them of being murderers," I argued, anger bubbling in my belly at the reminder.

He shrugged, not responding right away, and plucked a berry from the pile again before popping it into his mouth. "We might. You don't know what we'd do if the situation were reversed."

I glowered at him.

"Look, I'm not saying it's right. It's ridiculous, but...we left with three people and came back with two. I'm just not surprised they have their suspicions about it."

"And you're okay with that? With them thinking we possibly killed our friend?"

"Of course I'm not okay with it," he said simply. "But" —he stood up, stretching his arms above his head and looking toward the ocean—"I'm also not okay with being on this island, or not having access to shampoo or tooth-paste for weeks. It is what it is." He held out his hand to me, and I took it, allowing him to pull me to my feet.

"So what are you suggesting we do about it? Just ignore it? Just let them believe it?"

"Well, I'm suggesting we let them believe what they will, which is what they'd do anyway, and we spend the day in the ocean." He tilted his head toward the water. "What do you say?"

"Our friends think we're murderers, and you're suggesting we go for a swim?" I stared at him in disbelief.

"Do you think there'll be a better time?" He scoffed. "Come on. We've been on this island for weeks now, months maybe, and we never get to enjoy it. Live a little." He winked at me, my insides coming alive with electricity at the gesture.

I glanced out at the ocean, its waves beckoning me toward it. "Fine," I said, trying to force down a smile. "Okay."

"Yeah?" His boy-like grin was contagious. "Alright! Come on." He took off toward the water at breakneck speed, looking back in a form of challenge. "Race me!"

I pulled the T-shirt over my head, dropping it onto the ground and charging after him, unable to keep myself from laughing as he hit the water and nearly tripped trying to slow himself down.

I made it to him seconds later, grabbing a handful of water and tossing it at him playfully. His expression lit up with a playful grin.

"You're going to get it!" he shouted, smacking the water toward me aggressively as I squealed.

We were avoiding reality. It wasn't that we had forgotten about Harry or the betrayal we felt from our friends, but for the moment, it was nice to pretend that we could. To splash and play and laugh in the sun as if we were just a normal couple on a normal vacation.

Thinking of that made me think of my husband, of how we'd been in the beginning of our marriage, when vacations were still a thing we enjoyed together. Long before his many promotions; long before he'd forgotten he was supposed to love me too. As much as his career if not more.

My heart sank. I'd begun to accept the fact that I'd never see him again, that there was no escape from the island, and that I wasn't willing to hurt anyone even if it did mean I could escape, but I still couldn't let down my wall for Noah.

I was a married woman, even if my husband was on another continent, and I couldn't force the guilt away for the way Noah made me feel.

Alive.

Seen.

Beautiful.

But he wasn't an option. I knew that, and yet I seemed to be in a constant state of war with myself over it. Despite the issues in my marriage and the distance between my husband and me—both physical and figurative—I still felt committed to our marriage. Maybe it was foolish, but I still loved him. So why couldn't I forget my growing feelings for Noah? I knew I had to.

But in that moment, as he scooped me up from behind and spun us around until we both collapsed in the water, a heaping mess of laughter and happiness, it was nice to forget. Nice to pretend.

When we stood, he brushed a piece of hair from my eyes, his eyes lingering on mine for a second too long before he looked away.

"I was thinking of going to the falls later today. When James is done... Would you want to come?" There was a hint of something in his question, but I couldn't place my finger on what. We'd gone to the falls together countless times now, as we'd all agreed no one should be allowed to go alone. So why did he seem nervous asking?

"Sure," I said, touching his arm gently. "Everything okay?"

When he looked at me again, there was a familiar heat in his expression. A heat that had all but disappeared since the night he kissed me. He opened his mouth, as if he were going to say something, then closed it again. Finally, he splashed me. "I just need a bath. And, since I'm down-wind from you, I can confidently say you do, too."

I groaned, rolling my eyes at him, and turned to run away with a loud laugh. I was thankful that the conversation had gone back to playful. It was where I was comfortable with it. *Playful* was what I needed our relationship to be, though I knew that wasn't fair to him.

HOURS LATER, Ava and James still hadn't returned, and Noah and I lay on the sand, our bodies drying in the midday sun.

"What did you do? Before all of this? What did you do for work? You never told me..."

It was crazy how much we knew about each other, and yet how much we still didn't know. I knew the way he slept, the sound of his snores, the expression on his face when he was scared, the different ways he moved when we hunted, the fact that he preferred fish to boar, and that when he hit the water in the falls, he would always dive as if he were a mermaid, then pop up and ask if I saw that—each time, as if it were something brand new. I knew about his brother's death and his estranged relationship with his parents.

I didn't know his favorite food, his age, his career, what clothing he wore when he wasn't dressed in red swim trunks, or what he liked to do for fun. Was he into sports? What shows made him laugh? Was he a reader or a gamer? Did he go for a jog every morning or smoke pot in the afternoons?

We were simultaneously each other's closest confidant and complete strangers.

"I was…a realtor. In what feels like a past life." I smiled, almost bitterly, thinking of my life then. The stupid things I complained about. The luxuries I took for granted. "When my husband and I got married, I went down to part time, though. And eventually, I left it."

"You didn't enjoy it anymore?" His hands rested on his stomach, and he looked at me each time he spoke, before looking back toward the sky as he waited for an answer.

"No, I did… Honestly, I don't know why I quit. It became too much of a hassle, I guess. I was working so much, and my husband was, too. We never saw each other, and it just felt like someone should make the sacrifice."

"And that someone was you?"

I pursed my lips. "He never asked me to." It was the truth, but it didn't feel like it. The question never officially came up, though he'd all but hinted at it in the months leading up to my decision. "His company provides our health insurance, he has a 401(k). It just made more sense for me to leave. I'd been meaning to find something a bit more stable, but I just never got around to it, I guess." I sighed. "What about you? What did you do?"

He laughed dryly. "I was a professional diver. Remember?"

His words shocked me, taking me back to our conversation on the boat so long ago. I gasped. "Oh my god. That feels like forever ago... I'm sorry I didn't remember."

It was my turn to look his way. He shrugged. "No biggie."

I moved my hand to his arm. "No, Noah... I should've remembered. I've just had a lot..." A laugh escaped my throat at the ridiculousness of my statement. "On my mind."

"Yeah," he said, laughing too. "Being a hostage on a deserted island will do that to you."

When the laughter stopped, we were both looking at each other, our heads turned and cheeks resting on the sand. My hand was still on his arm, and I felt him move it slowly, sliding his hand up until our palms met. There was a question in his eyes, and I couldn't answer it. I looked away as my pulse sped up, my face burning hot. I laced my fingers through his, giving him the answer I both hated and loved all at once.

"So," he changed the subject, but kept our hands pressed together, "do you think our Twitter campaign is still going on?"

I snorted, grateful for the release of tension, and shook my head. "Are you kidding? With a face like that? They're probably just ramping up production on our Netflix special."

"They'd better get Darren Criss to portray me."

"I was thinking Manny Jacinto," I teased.

He scowled. "Are you kidding? I'm totally a Darren."

"Okay, whatever you say..." I grinned at him again, feeling looser already. It was easy with Noah, even here on this island. I'd misread his wall in the beginning for coldness, but in truth, I'd never met anyone warmer or kinder. I could do it, I thought. I could survive on the island with him. If this was how the rest of my life looked, though I wouldn't be happy about the lack of modern conveniences and the fact that strange people were watching us apparently, I wouldn't have too many complaints. As far as being a hostage went, a girl could do worse.

"Do you think we should be worried about them?" His brows shot up, nodding his head in the direction of the jungle.

"Because they've been gone a while or because they might kill us?" I was only half joking, and his expression told me he knew that.

"Both, I guess... They've been gone most of the day now. You don't think they're hurt, do you?"

I hadn't thought about it, honestly. Any moment that Ava and James weren't glaring at me with their accusing eyes was A-OK with me. "I just assumed they were avoiding us like usual."

He hesitated, then sighed. "You're probably right."

"Honestly, I'd just rather not see them. It's so awkward..."

He squeezed my hand gently, his thumb caressing my knuckles. "We didn't do anything wrong. You know that.

If someone's going to feel awkward, let it be them. They're the ones who made the situation what it is."

"Do you think things will ever feel normal again? That it'll blow over?"

"Normal as in the way it was?" His brows bounced up. "Nah, probably not. But we'll find a new normal, just like we did here."

"When did you become so wise?" I asked, chuckling to myself. "When we met on the boat, I thought you were just some dumb kid."

He placed his hand to his chest as if I'd stabbed him with my words, feigning pain. "*Kid*, ugh. I'll bet I'm older than you think."

"Twenty-three, tops," I challenged.

His laugh was immediate and dry. "I've got socks older than twenty-three."

My brow furrowed more. "You can't be older than thirty."

He held up two fingers. "Thirty-two...maybe thirty-three by now. My birthday is in August, and I've lost track of the days."

"My birthday's in August, too," I said, shocked. "The seventh."

"My fellow Leo, I knew I liked you." He laughed. "I'm the fifteenth. Happy late or early birthday."

I grinned at the sentiment. How strange was it to truly not know how old we were? I guess it didn't matter anymore. "Happy late or early birthday to you."

He was quiet for a moment, then asked, "Is that why you're reluctant with me, because you thought I was younger than you?"

"You are younger than me," I told him. "And no. I mean, in part, maybe, and in part because we're just trying to survive and finding romance isn't at the top of my to-do list, but mostly because of Ned."

"Your husband?"

I nodded.

"Do you miss him a lot?"

"Some days," I told him. "Always, really... But some days it's almost impossible to go on."

"That's how it was when Theo died. It doesn't get easier. You just get used to—" He froze, his eyes wide. "I didn't mean that it's as if your husband had died, I just—"

"It's fine," I assured him. "In a way, I guess it is like that. The grief I mean. The acceptance that I may never see him again." I suddenly felt guilty for holding Noah's hand, but I couldn't bear to pull away. In some strange way, it was as if he were grounding me, keeping me on the island so I wouldn't float away with my grief.

"Have you? Accepted it, I mean?" Though I knew he had selfish motivations for asking, he seemed genuinely curious. There was nothing pushy in his tone.

"More today than yesterday, but less than tomorrow."

His thumb began caressing my knuckles again. "If you love him, you shouldn't give up."

I was silent, because the thought of answering brought tears to my eyes. The thought of never seeing Ned again was debilitating, but the truth was...the thought of never seeing Noah again hurt just as much.

I didn't know the time to make that choice was quickly approaching.

CHAPTER TWENTY-FOUR

When evening fell and James and Ava still hadn't returned, we could no longer deny that something strange was afoot.

As the sun began to sink into the horizon, we headed out into the forest, weapons in hand, listening quietly for the slightest sound. Noah led the way with me close behind.

We traveled the same path as usual, hardly having to watch our step as we'd already memorized where the root that stuck up an inch too high was, where the plant with the thorns hid, and where the ditch you could nearly miss if you weren't paying attention was. We knew our path backward and forward, which meant every bit of our energy could be focused on seeking out our friends.

As we grew closer to the falls, I thought I heard Ava's whimpers. My blood ran cold, and I knew from the ashen, wide-eyed expression on Noah's face that he'd heard it, too. We quickened our pace, hurrying forward. Something was wrong. Something was wrong. Something was—

Naked?

James and Ava were far from in turmoil, their bare bodies pressed together on the shore next to the falls. Ava cried out in ecstasy, her hands gripping James's back. He let out a moan of pleasure, pressing his lips to hers feverishly.

For a moment, we stood there frozen, the shock of what we were seeing smacking me so suddenly I couldn't do anything but stare. All at once, the heat of embarrassment burned my face, and I backtracked quickly, just as Noah did, pressing ourselves against a wide tree a few feet away. My eyes were wide, my hand over my mouth as I watched him process what we'd seen.

He snickered, pressing his forehead to mine, my back against the tree as our bodies melted together, each of us trying our best to hide our stifled laughter. It wasn't as if we didn't know—or at least suspect—that Ava and James had been sneaking off to have sex, but seeing it like that, seeing our friends in the throes of passion was embarrassing and hilarious all at once.

He took my hand, pulling me away from there quickly, and as we made it back to the beach, we both burst out laughing with giggles so demanding and necessary my insides burned.

"At least someone's enjoying themselves around here," he said through his laughter, tears in his eyes.

"Maybe a little too much. I think we're on our own for dinner."

"The way they were going at it, we may be on our own for life."

"Do you think they've been doing it all day?"

"If so, they've got no excuse to be crabby when they come back."

"You don't think they saw us, do you?" I asked, the thought sobering. As much as I enjoyed poking fun at catching them in the act, the idea that they'd caught us catching them was mortifying.

"Nah, they were pretty focused," he said, shaking his head as the laughter finally subsided.

"I'd be terrified someone would catch me. They're braver than I am." I placed my hands over my nose and mouth, trying to shake the image from my head.

"Eh, who cares? It's not like they could check into the Holiday Inn. We're all adults... Animals out in the wild." He winked at me, then looked away. "Anyway, we should really think about dinner. What will it be tonight? Berries or fish, my dear?" He adopted a fake accent and bowed forward, as if he were a waiter. "I might be able to have the chef whip you up a fresh pineapple or two."

My stomach growled at the thought. "Pineapple sounds lovely, kind sir."

He stood, holding out his arm for me to loop mine through. I did the same, suddenly very aware of our touch and the close proximity of our bodies. I had to stop it, get the thought out of my head, and move on.

Noah had to continue being Noah, and I had to continue being me—*married* me. An hour later, we returned with two pineapples from the plants we'd discovered a few days—weeks?—before. They didn't grow many, which made the fruit a commodity that up until this point we reserved for special occasions.

When we reached the fire, I was surprised to see Ava and James there, deep in conversation. James saw us first, his back straightening as he saw the pineapples in our hands.

"You only brought two?" he asked, his lips downturned.

"These were the only two that looked ripe," Noah lied. "And we didn't know if you'd be back for dinner."

"When have we ever not come back for dinner?" he asked.

"When have you ever disappeared into the jungle for an entire day without telling us where you were going?" came Noah's quick retort.

"Appreciate you checking up on us for that, by the way."

"We did check up on you," Noah said, and I was amazed that he could keep a straight face. "By the falls. You were fine."

Ava's face blanched. "You what?"

"Yeah, so next time, tell us where you're going and when you'll be back. We need to know if we need to come looking for you." He sat down across from them, and I followed his lead, watching as he pulled out his knife to begin peeling and slicing the pineapple. "And yes, we'll share these with you." He shoved a chunk of pineapple toward them both with a mock, exaggerated smile. "What are friends for?"

"We're sorry," Ava said, her words catching me off guard. When I met her eye, she appeared completely genuine. "We're sorry for disappearing all day, and I'm sorry for what I said to you this morning. I was upset and…and scared, and… You've been nothing but kind to me, both of you, but especially you, Katy. I know you'd never hurt Harry. I just spoke without thinking. When we got that note and you returned without him, it was just scary. None of us know what's going on or who's with whom… It just took us a while to get our heads on straight. I'm really sorry."

She was crying suddenly, and I felt terrible for the anger and resentment I'd felt toward her.

"You don't have to apologize—"

"Yes. Yes, I do." She was gripping James's hand tightly, white halos around his knuckles from the pressure. "It wasn't right. I was dealing with my own stuff, and—"

"Ava, you're fine. You're forgiven. We're all dealing with our own stuff, and this island doesn't help. It's all stressful and scary, and honestly, I'd be shocked if you were handling it well. I can't imagine what you must've thought getting that note and seeing us come back without him. But what I told you was true. I loved Harry. I mourned his loss. He was a great friend to me. To all of us."

She nodded, taking a small bite of her pineapple as Noah resumed passing slices around.

"I just miss him," she said, wiping her tears. "And I miss my family."

"We all do," Noah said, the only words he'd spoken since her apology. I couldn't quite get a read on how he was feeling.

She rested her head on James's shoulder, and he kissed

it gently, his own eyes filled with tears. My own vision blurred with fresh tears as he pushed the sack that usually held coconuts, but had quickly become our carry-all, toward us. "We brought berries too. Some fresh ones since the ones from this morning had started rotting."

"Thanks," I said, pulling it closer to me. As I reached for a handful, I saw Ava eyeing me with too much enthusiasm. I froze, and her expression fell. Then, when she realized I was watching her, she looked away quickly.

Was I being paranoid?

I'd just condemned her for accusing me of a nearly identical crime. Could I really be so hypocritical now?

I put the berries down without saying a word and finished off my pineapple, waiting until Noah had sliced and divided every last bit. When I could no longer avoid it, I pushed the berries away from me.

Ava watched me intently. "You're not going to eat any?"

"I'm full," I said, shaking my head. "But thanks. They look delicious."

"More for me," Noah said, reaching for them. Ava and James both watched as he grabbed a handful, their eyes locked on the berries as they were lifted toward his mouth.

"Wait!" I grabbed his arm instinctually, stopping him, but once I had, all three of them stared at me as if I'd suddenly turned blue.

"What's gotten into you?" he asked.

"I...I just... Sorry, I think these might be different than before." I found the words, deciding on them as they came out.

"Different how?" he asked, staring at them strangely. He put them down.

I studied them. "Did you get them from a different plant? They look brighter somehow."

James and Ava exchanged a worried look. "We picked them from the same place," James said quickly. "Would it make you feel better if I ate some, too?"

I hesitated. "It's probably silly. I'm sorry."

"Yeah, I thought we were okay again," Ava said.

"We are," I told her, still not reaching for the berries. I wanted to eat them, to trust her, just to keep the peace, but James wasn't reaching for one. It would've been simple enough for them to disprove the theory, so why weren't they? Because they were offended by the accusation, or because I was right?

Noah nudged the basket forward more. "Go on, then. Make us look like idiots."

James appeared unsure, casting a quick glance to Ava before reaching forward and taking a handful. I waited with bated breath as he put them to his mouth.

"Stop!" Ava cried, wincing with her eyes squeezed shut. James tossed them from his hand as if they were poisonous to the touch, not just taste.

Noah leapt up, grabbing hold of his gun and pointing it at them both. "What the fuck is going on?" I was just behind him, reaching for the machete beside my feet. Was this really happening? Were we going to have to fight them? I felt sick suddenly, my throat dry, knees weak.

Ava reached for her own gun as quickly as Noah had, bouncing between pointing it at each of us. James didn't reach for his gun, but instead stood between the three of us, his arms outstretched. "Wait, hold on, hold on... It's not what you think."

"It's not what we think? I think your girlfriend just tried to poison us."

"It wasn't her idea," he said, shaking his head. "It was mine, and only because we didn't have a choice. If you're going to shoot someone"—he turned his back toward her, facing us with his hands in the air—"shoot me. But let her go."

"What are you talking about?" I demanded.

"No one was planning to hurt anyone until you pulled this. That little apology was all a show, wasn't it? Well, brav-fucking-o, give her the Oscar, ladies and gentlemen," Noah said through gritted teeth.

"What do you mean, James? What did you mean you didn't have a choice? I don't understand."

"That's because you can't understand these people, Katy. Don't you get that? Ole Dahmer and her goon here were going to take us out and sail away on their raft to live happily ever after."

"It wasn't like that," Ava said, tears choking her voice.

"Then what is going on—"

"*I'm pregnant,*" Ava shouted, her voice echoing across the beach. Our weapons dropped in an instant, and James turned to her, his arms cradling her shoulders. "I'm pregnant," she said again, this time a whisper.

I tried to do the math in my head, none of it making sense. "I don't understand..." I trailed off, piecing together the sickness and the whispered conversations, Ava's sudden aversion to most meats and why we'd had to find other fruits to try, why she took naps in the afternoons most days lately and why James had doted on her even more than usual over the past week or two. "You're pregnant? Are you sure? How could you know?"

"I was pregnant when I got here," she said softly. "I'd just found out. My boyfriend and I…we wanted to keep it. It was why I wanted to transfer to the same college he was going to, which was what I was arguing with my parents about, why I went off on the boat in the first place."

"I don't understand." My guard was still up. Could I trust her? "Why wouldn't you tell us that?"

"I don't know," she said with a shrug. "At first, I just thought we'd be here for a few hours, maybe a day, and someone would come back for us. Then it wouldn't matter. And then, I didn't want you all to treat me like I was weak or couldn't help. I told Harry on our second night here. He was kind to me. It was a huge part of the reason we'd gotten so close. Then the morning sickness came and Harry was so busy being the leader, I had to confide in someone else. I was scared, and I—"

"You could've come to me," I told her. "I would've been there for you."

"I thought you might've judged me. Like my mom did…"

"Ava, I…" I trailed off, still trying to process all I was being told. "I'm sorry for whatever happened with your parents, but you need to tell us these things so we can be prepared."

"Prepared for what?" James asked, suddenly angry. "For her to give birth here? Without access to medical care for her or the baby? How can you ask her to do that?"

Suddenly, it hit me. All of it. I understood what they

were trying to do and why. "You were trying to get her home."

He nodded, taking her hand. "It was the hardest decision we've ever had to make."

"We've looked for every way out of it we can," Ava said, tears streaming down her cheeks. "I just can't give birth here. I can't do it. Please understand…"

"Well, you aren't killing us. Not without a fight," Noah said, moving his shoulder in front of mine.

"This is what they want," I said. "Don't you guys see that? This is all they want. They want us to fight. To choose. But we can't. If we do, they win."

"And if we don't?" James asked. "Look, I don't want to die any more than anyone else, but can we really just live our lives out here? Eventually, we're all going to die. Whether it's an accident like Harry's or an animal attack, or we just end up killing each other, someone will be the last one standing. But we have a chance right now, to choose to do the right thing. To save a life. Two lives, really."

"At the expense of ours," Noah argued.

"You were going to take the choice away from us. I don't understand why you couldn't just come to us. We would've figured something out."

"Something like what?" Ava asked. "We didn't know if we could trust you at that point. Harry's death was still fresh, and we had no idea who else was on the island."

"But you could've told us any time up until this point." I gestured toward the berries. "Poisoning us, though? This wasn't the way, Ava. We trusted you." James met my eye. "Both of you."

"So, what now?" Noah asked. "You're obviously going to try to kill us again, even if we let you live now." I saw his hand tighten around the gun again, watched him raise it slightly.

"You aren't going to touch her," James growled. "We stopped it from happening. She stopped me."

"Because she knew you'd die first and we'd realize what had happened, and then she'd be outnumbered," he spat. They were nose to nose, both seething with anger.

"Listen! Wait. I think I have an idea." I pulled Noah back, forcing the men to step apart as they waited for me to elaborate. I wasn't sure it was the best idea, but I had to think of something before someone ended up hurt. "Look, there's this woman."

"Not this again," Noah groaned.

"She's real," I said firmly.

"Who's real?" Ava asked.

"The woman I saw in the woods. She…she lives here, on the island."

"Where? In the cliff house?" James asked.

"I don't know… I don't think so. She said…she said they brought her here."

"They?" Ava asked.

"The people in the cliff house, I think. She said they're dangerous and that she was a friend."

"Of ours or theirs?"

"When did you talk to her?"

The questions flew at me as I tried to make sense of the memory, recall what she'd said. "Last night." I flashed an apologetic look at Noah. "I'm sorry I didn't tell you. She said I couldn't."

"I don't understand... What did she want?" he asked, looking distraught that I hadn't told him. I knew it was a betrayal that would take a while to recover from, but this was important.

"We didn't talk for long. She's been following us for a while. I keep seeing her. She said that they brought her here and that we shouldn't try to leave. She said they'd kill us if we did."

Ava whimpered.

"I think she's like us. Maybe she managed to build a shelter somewhere. If we could find her, I mean, she's survived here this long, and she was dressed in nice, clean clothes. She obviously isn't living in the wild. If we can find her, maybe she can help us figure out a way to help Ava. And the baby."

"So she told you where she lives? Or where to find her? Did she say she'd come back?" James asked, hope in his eyes.

"No," I said plainly. "She ran away before I could find out too much. But she must be somewhere close because she's overheard some of our conversations, about the raft in particular. I think she must be running from them, too. She said they're always watching." A chill ran down my spine as I recalled the warning. "So we have to be careful."

"So what? We're supposed to search the whole island?" James asked skeptically. "That could take months!"

"We could split up and choose sections to explore each week and—"

"Meanwhile she'll be more and more pregnant, and there'll be less chance of her surviving any sort of escape attempt. We can't wait that long. Please...please help me save her," he begged, tears in his eyes. How could he care this much for someone he'd just met? But, thinking of Harry, and of Noah too, I knew. I knew because I felt the same love for the strangers I'd spent the last month of my life with. I knew because I knew I'd do anything to save them.

But how could we trust them? There had to be another way.

"Why should we when you just tried to do this? Even after you were awful to us this morning, even when you've been cold to us for weeks... We fed you, we took care of you. We were in this together, but now we're not." Noah took a step back. "I'm sorry you're pregnant. And that you're scared, but Katy's right. This wasn't the way. You guys are on your own. There's no use pretending we're together anymore, and I'll be damned if I'm going to traipse around the island, putting myself in danger, for the person who was just about to have me killed. No, sorry, but no." He turned, storming away quickly, and I rushed to follow him.

"I'll be back," I called, looking over my shoulder to where they stood to be sure they weren't going to shoot us from afar. Maybe Noah was right. How would we ever trust them again after what they'd done? How could I turn my back on them or eat the food they prepared or sleep near them without worrying? I wasn't sure I could.

As I rushed after Noah, whose furious footsteps and long legs could move faster than mine in the shifting sand, I realized maybe he was right. Maybe this really was the end of the group as we knew it.

But then...where did that leave us?

I was fully prepared to live in peace with Noah for as long as I could, but what if they planned to make that impossible?

If only one of the groups could survive, which would it be?

CHAPTER TWENTY-FIVE

We stayed awake the entire night, watching the moon shift across the sky, casting its reflection on the water as the waves raged as angrily as our moods.

When I saw something moving across the water, I rubbed sleep from my eyes, sure I was imagining things, but it was still there.

"Do you—"

"See that," Noah confirmed, finishing my sentence as he stood up.

Someone was out in the water. *Something.*

No.

As I realized what I was seeing, I rushed forward, moving as fast as I could, but it wasn't fast enough. The world seemed to suddenly turn in slow motion, my vision tunneling, breathing shallow. "No!" I cried. "Don't do this! Please!"

Desperate and lacking judgment, the youngest members of our group had decided to go on with the raft idea anyway. Just four logs—and not even large ones—

were tied together with the sarong and long, flimsy tree branches, from what it looked like. Ava and James sat atop the logs, using thick, sturdy branches as oars.

Noah stood beside me as we both held our breath. Would it work? Would they escape, leaving us to waste away here? Would they send help? Would they find a boat and get picked up? They didn't look back at us, too busy fighting the strength of the waves as they paddled, then floated backward, then paddled and floated. They weren't making it far, and each time a wave crashed into them, I felt my stomach lurch.

Please let them make it.

I sent up the silent prayer. I harbored no ill will toward the couple, despite our differences of opinions and methods. We all just wanted to make it home alive.

They made it out past the first group of heavy and rapid waves, and I felt myself breathing easier. It might actually work. My whole body was tense as I watched them growing smaller, harder to make out on the dark horizon.

"There's a big one coming," Noah said, his voice powerless. I watched the wave rolling, saw them see it, their paddling stopping at once. "They're not going to make it."

His words sat like a weight between us as I watched the scene unfold, unable to do anything. He cupped his hands around his mouth. "Paddle this way!" he cried, but they couldn't hear us. They couldn't hear anything, I was sure, as the wave gained more traction, more height, moving toward them and picking up speed as it traveled.

Ava sat still, watching it come as James began to

paddle this way and that, each direction more hopeless than the last. I watched it crash into them, the wave splashing around them in every direction as the raft over-turned, tossing them from it. Just like that, as if they'd never been there, they were gone.

"No," I whimpered, touching my lips and holding my breath. I waited to see their heads, but Noah darted past me, diving like he so often did in the falls when he'd made it out far enough. I stood alone on the shore, crying silent tears as I saw the logs from the raft bob up to the surface finally, all separated and broken apart. I still didn't see them, but refused to give up hope as I watched Noah swim toward them. I had to believe with everything in me that he saw something I didn't.

As another large wave picked up momentum, I watched him stop. My insides were at war, half of me hoping he'd turn around, the other half hoping he'd keep going. I wanted him to save them, but I wanted him to save himself. I didn't want to be alone. I didn't want to lose him.

I felt a chill and checked behind me, feeling like I was being watched.

I was, of course. As we always were on the island.

Then, I looked back to the water, spying Noah as he swam back to me. "Noah!" I shouted as the wave grew closer. *Please no. Please don't take him from me.*

The wave hit with a force similar to what had slammed into Ava and James, and I held my breath—waiting, watching. *Please. Please. Please.*

Seconds passed, dragging on like hours, and he didn't resurface.

I couldn't do it. I couldn't lose him.

I stepped forward, letting the tide hit my ankles as I watched the ocean's undisturbed surface. If it had consumed three lives that night, it held no evidence. It scooped them up, sweeping them away as if they never existed. I fell to my knees, the crushing reality of what had happened weighing on me.

He was dead.

He'd left me.

I'd never see him again.

They were gone.

They were all—

No.

Yes.

His head was up.

His body was up.

Out of the water.

He was there.

He was okay.

He was alive.

Noah stood from the water, sopping wet and panting as he shook his head, his expression broken. "I'm...sorry. I couldn't..." He was crying, though you couldn't see it through the water already on his face. "I tried, Katy, I—"

I rushed forward, catapulting my body onto his and wrapping my arms around him. I smashed our lips together with so much joy in my heart, I thought it would explode. I felt his body tense with shock, then immediately relax, his hands on my face, my waist, my neck.

"That was really stupid," I told him when we broke apart for air.

"I know."

His lips were back on mine, the waves crashing around our feet, and if it hadn't been tragic, it would've been romantic. He gripped my waist, pushing me backward gently with cautious steps. I followed his lead, no longer caring about anything. I almost lost him. I almost never had the chance to feel this way.

I let him guide me down to the sand, let his hands explore my body, let our tears combine on our cheeks, and eventually, I let him have every piece of me. Our friends were dead, and we were broken. We'd never leave, our families would never see us, and no one would ever know what happened. This was good and this was bad, and everything in between.

My mind raced, my heart pounding in my chest. Nothing about this was okay, and yet everything about it was perfect.

It was what I needed.

It was the only thing to help.

And so, we let it happen, and our pact was sealed with our bodies, no longer just our words. We'd protect each other no matter what.

That mattered more than anything, now that we were the last two survivors.

CHAPTER TWENTY-SIX

When the sun rose the next morning, rousing me from a restless sleep, Noah was already awake, sitting next to me with a blank expression. Remembering the night's events, I shot up, staring out at the horizon.

"Anything?"

He shook his head. "I've been watching since dawn. The logs made it back"—he gestured to a few of them scattered along the shore—"but your cover up and, well... nothing else came with them." *No one else,* he meant.

The weight of it all, the reality of what had happened hit me harder than I'd been expecting it to. Harder than the night before, even. I'd been so swept up in the thought that I'd lost him, that he'd drown too, that when he'd resurfaced, nothing else mattered.

But now, several things mattered. The fact that our friends were most likely dead, drowned in an accident I should've prevented. The fact that I'd slept with Noah. The fact that we were the only two left, which could result in peace or problems.

He rested his hand on my knee, almost as if he'd read my mind, but didn't meet my eye as he said, "I don't regret it, you know. You might… I wouldn't blame you. But I don't." He swallowed, and I watched his Adam's apple bob. "I just thought you should know."

I nodded, processing.

"And…if they're gone, that doesn't change how I feel about…well, anything. I meant what I said when we made our pact. I won't hurt you."

"I know that," I assured him.

He hesitated, then released a nervous laugh. "Can you let me know where your head is? Because I'm kind of freaking out a little bit."

I knew what he wanted, but I didn't know if I could give it to him. I couldn't say all he needed to hear. I waited for the guilt over last night to hit me, but to my surprise, it didn't. Did that mean I was ready to give my husband up? To accept that my marriage was over? That I was never going home? What if Ned was still out there looking for me? What if I was wrong that he'd given up? Could I ever live with the guilt of knowing I gave up before he did? Was I willing to give up my decade-long marriage for Noah, who despite everything, was still practically a stranger? My thoughts raced as I tried to sort through them all. I had an *Island Future* and a *Home Future* waging war in my mind, with no sign of either side winning out anytime soon.

"Sorry, I'm…I'm still processing, I think. I don't want to give up on them, you know? And I don't want to give up on Ned either, despite what we did last night. I know that's not what you want to hear, and—"

"I just want to hear the truth. I don't have any expectations here."

"The truth is, I don't regret it either. And I'd never hurt you. You know that. I'm not sure where my head is, honestly. But what we did...it was good, Noah. It was what I needed to survive the storm. You're what I need to survive here." I nudged his shoulder gently, trying to lighten the mood. "You've saved me in more ways than one."

He gripped my knee tighter, a loving gesture, and I hoped that was good enough for him for the moment. "I keep thinking I'm going to see one of them swimming up, you know? Like they somehow made it. I just can't—" His voice caught, and he cleared his throat. "I hated them for what they tried to do to us, but I still feel connected to them somehow." His brow furrowed, lips drawn tight.

"I do, too," I assured him. "After all we went through together, I think that's normal. The five of us..." Two now. "What we've experienced together, we'll never be able to share that with anyone else."

"So what if we really can't go back?" he blurted out. "Ever. What if this is it? Will you be okay with it? With living here—on the island, with me—forever?"

I thought over my answer before giving it to him, choosing my words carefully. "I want to go home. I won't lie about that. But, to be honest, I don't even know what that would look like for me. It's not like I could go home now and pretend none of this happened. And I'll keep my word to you, of course. If we never get rescued, if we're stuck here forever, keeping each other safe and alive, I would be okay with that." I smirked. "There are worse places to spend eternity. Worse people to spend it with."

His half smile was forced and unnatural. "You say that now, but...what about a year from now? How are we going to make this work? I just...I think reality is beginning to set in for me, and—"

Realizing what he was saying, I felt something in my stomach tighten. "Are you not going to be okay with it?" I asked. My weapon was several feet away, and I had no desire to use it on him. Was he planning to attack me? Had last night made him realize he couldn't spend the rest of his life with me even if I was the last woman on his figurative earth?

He spun toward me in the sand, reaching for my legs. "No, hey... No, it's not that at all. We're good, Katy. This isn't about me. I'm good. I'll miss my family, my friends, my job...but I know I could be happy here. I really could. I just, I guess what I'm saying is, it's just you and me now, and I don't want to start getting attached to that idea, attached to the possibility of what life could look like for us here, for you to change your mind. And I don't want it to feel forced because we're literally the only people here."

I opened my mouth to speak, but he cut me off.

"And I'm not trying to, like, demand that you make a vow to me or anything right now. I understand you're still in love with your husband. I understand that you're still married. It's why I haven't pushed the issue since our kiss in the jungle that night. I wanted to give you space. But you obviously like me, and I care about you... I'm just trying to figure out where to set my boundary...my expectations. Because this is the rest of our lives, and I'm just not handling it well…" He trailed off, shaking his head and looking away.

"Noah, I care about you, too. And I'm not only saying that because you're the only person left for me to care about. You've been a good friend to me, even when you were pretending to be a jerk. I do love Ned. I won't lie to you about that. But I could love you, given time. And it seems like that's what we're going to have here."

"Selfishly, I want that to be enough, but I have to ask… If you were given the chance to go home, to get home to your husband, to your old life right now, would you?"

Confusion flooded my thoughts, the expression on his face growing more distraught. "Why are you asking me that, Noah?"

He sighed. "It happened before I knew you… Before our pact."

"What happened?"

"I saw a man in the woods."

"What are you talking about? What man?"

"He was older. Fifties, maybe. Bald. He approached me that first day, when I'd gone to get coconuts. He gave me the note, the one about killing each other to escape, asked me to put it down somewhere everyone would find it."

My blood ran cold. "So, you've been the one leaving notes?"

"Just the one," he said quickly. "Just that one. I have no idea who's been leaving the rest, but it wasn't me. He told me that we were part of an experiment and that someone had to kill everyone in order to escape. *Last man standing and all that…* That was what he said. I thought he was kidding at first, but then he led me to the coconuts and the falls, and told me I should keep them a secret. Said it would give me an upper hand and that I couldn't trust any of you—"

"That's what the woman told me..."

"And I didn't know you then. Any of you. So, I kept the secret. But then the closer we got, I worried that telling you would break the trust you had with me."

"Have you seen the man again?"

"No," he said, shaking his head. "Just that once. But... there was one more thing. He told me that whoever does the killing, they won't get in trouble. He said they'll be protected and..." He grimaced. "*Taken care of.*"

"What does that mean?" I asked, feeling horrified that Noah had known this all along, but also even more confused than before. What kind of sick experiment was this?

"He didn't elaborate. He shoved the note in my hand and disappeared. Said if I followed him, he'd kill me himself and save you all the trouble." He shuddered. "I believed him. About everything... Which means, if you want to go home, go back to your life..."

As realization set in about what he was offering, I began to feel sick. "Noah, come on. You know I'd never agree to anything like that."

"Just hear me out, okay? I'm not making this offering lightly. I'd never have offered before when it was the four or five of us because, well, it was just too complicated, and I worried it would make things even worse. No one would ever agree on who could be the winner—"

"Winner's a generous term for it." I scoffed.

"But now that it's just us." He licked his lips. "Look, if

you say you want to be with me, here on this island, or that you think you could want that in the future—ever—more than you want to be with your husband, then I'll let it go. But you have someone waiting for you back home."

"You have your parents and—"

"My parents are getting older. They have each other. I'm not saying I want to lose them, but you have so much more at stake here, so if you'd be happier returning, if you'd be happier back at home... There's a way to make that happen."

"By killing you?" I asked, my mouth gaped open in horror. "Noah, I could never—"

"You wouldn't have to do it."

"Why are you even talking like this?" I stood up, shaking my head and walking away from him. He jogged up behind me.

"I don't mean to upset you. I just want you to know it's an option. I wanted to be honest with you."

"It's always been an option. It's not like there was really any doubt about what was going on here, not since that first note. And especially not since going to the cliff house. We've known for a while now that any of us could've ended it... But we have a deal. A pact. And I appreciate you telling me the truth about it, but it's not like you really did anything wrong. I don't want you to die, Noah. Our friends just died, and I'm barely standing." I stopped, looking up at him. "I can't even think about this right now."

I stopped in my tracks, looking out over the ocean. "Do you..." Was I seeing things? Was I imagining it? "Do you see that?"

He followed my line of vision, squinting his eyes as if to help him see better. "Oh my god," he said, rushing forward toward the shore as I took off as well.

"Is he..." I couldn't bear to think it, let alone say it, for fear of jinxing it. *Please. Please. Please.*

In the distance, I could see James floating on a stray log that hadn't yet made its way to the shore. He had one thick arm and his head draped across the wood, his body floating lifelessly. He'd been out there all along. Waiting for us to save him. But were we too late?

Without hesitation, Noah rushed into the water, paddling out to him as fast as he could while fighting the waves as they tried to pull him back toward me. *Please. Please. Please.*

I repeated the mantra over and over in my head, bouncing up and down on my tiptoes as I watched the scene unfold. I wanted to get to him. I wanted to help him. But I also knew my swimming skills were elementary at best and, should I try to help, the likelihood was that I'd end up being more of a liability to him in the end.

So, I watched. I waited. I prayed to a god I'd long since given up on.

Please. Please. Please.

At long last, as he reached the log, he took hold of James's arm, tossing it over his shoulder and lugging him backward, moving at a snail's pace, both their heads barely above the water as they made their way toward me.

Seeing it happen, I thought of the turtles we'd often see in a pond near my grandmother's house, how they'd pop their heads up and down in the water.

But the turtles could survive it. They were meant to be

underwater for long periods of time. We were not. While I knew Noah's experience as a diver and general love for water meant he had swimmer's lungs, every time his head dipped under the water, my heart lurched.

Please. Please. Please.

I was utterly silent as I watched them grow closer, holding my breath until I could hold it no longer. As they reached a point where Noah looked like he was preparing to stand, I hurried toward them, grabbing under one of James's arms and helping Noah pull him ashore.

He was freezing cold, but I told myself it could've been because of the water. I didn't dare ask, just let Noah catch his breath as we moved him to dry sand.

Noah knelt down over him, lowering his ear to James's mouth. I watched his expression, holding my breath again.

Please. Please. Please.

He nodded, sending relief soaring through me. "He's alive," he said. His hand went to James's neck. "I can feel a pulse... He's breathing."

"Why won't he wake?" I put a hand to James's forehead, running my palm across the side of his face. "James? James? Can you hear us? Wake up." I looked at Noah. "Is he hurt?"

He looked just as confused as I felt and shook his head. "I have no idea." I began moving his legs, eyeing them for any signs of damage. I lifted his shirt carefully, fearful I'd have to relive what I had with Harry, but that appeared fine as well. As I ran my hands over him, checking him for any wounds, he seemed to stir, his eyelashes batting as his eyelids fluttered open. He looked around, obviously confused, and jolted up.

"What the—"

"Hey," Noah said, trying to keep him from sitting up. "You're okay... You're okay. Just breathe."

James looked at us with wide eyes, his body tensing as he fought us off of him. "Ava?"

Noah glanced at me, his brows raised slightly, and I broke eye contact, terrified to deliver the news. "I'm so sorry, James..."

"No," he argued, shaking his head, his water-logged features crumpling with despair. He ran a hand through his hair. "No. It can't... She can't." We let him stand, watching as he ran past us toward the water, his sobs heart-wrenching. "Please no. Please, Ava. Please don't do this to me." He fell to his knees in the crashing waves, his hands covering his eyes.

Together, Noah and I approached him. I tried to figure out what the best way to handle him would be. Should we give him his space? Let him know he's not alone? Let him know we didn't blame him and that he did all he could?

I still hadn't figured out what James's sudden reappearance meant going forward either. Would the three of us be able to live together peacefully? Would we be able to move on from all that had happened?

As the only woman on an island with two men, I felt fear bristle inside me. If anything ever happened to Noah, it would leave me alone with just James. Did I trust him enough?

Still wrestling with my wild and competing thoughts

as we approached him, I watched Noah rest a hand on his shoulder. "I'm so sorry, man. You did all you could—"

"No," he shouted, his voice loud and aggressive. "I didn't. I didn't do everything. You should've helped me. We could've saved her, but you wouldn't. You didn't care."

"Now that's not fair," I said. "We did care about Ava, but the way you went about things wasn't right. We would've figured something out, but you nee—"

"*No!*" he shouted again, standing up suddenly and running away from us toward the fire. "She'd still be here if you'd fought harder for her."

"James, wait!"

He reached the fire first, with us just behind, and bent down. I stopped short, my hands going to the air as I realized what he was doing.

"No!" I gasped loudly. He grabbed the gun from the ground, turning around and firing a shot without a second's hesitation. *BANG.*

I braced myself for the impact, my body tightening, eyes squeezed shut, but it was Noah who cried out in pain. I spun around, staring at him as deep red began to pool from his calf. He placed his hand over the wound, crimson staining his hands and the sand around his leg.

It all happened in slow motion. One moment he was looking at his leg, and the next he'd launched forward, shoving me out of the way as I heard another shot. When I opened my eyes, sitting up on the sand and scrambling toward where they were wrestling, Noah was on top of James, trying and failing to push the gun out of his hand.

"*Drop...it,*" he demanded through gritted teeth, his face red.

253

"This is all your fault. Her death is on your hands," James argued back through his tears, keeping a vice-like grip on the weapon. My heart thudded in my chest as I looked around for a way to end the fight. Where was my machete? Where was another gun?

In the distance, where we'd slept, I could see them both and my heart sank. I didn't have time to make it there and back, but Noah's life depended on me making a decision. And fast.

A gunshot rang out again, the bullet grazing some trees off to our side, and I flinched. Finally, I saw what I needed. Lying next to the fire was a pile of spears we'd crafted to catch fish. I hurried around them, grateful they weren't paying attention to me, and scooped up what looked like the sharpest spear.

I was really going to do this. I was really going to kill him.

I forced myself to feel the words, to let them weigh on my conscience as I ran back toward the men, raising the spear high over my head without allowing for any hesitation. I shoved Noah with all my weight, giving me access to James, while at the same time plummeting the spear straight into his neck. Something soft and fleshy. I knew if I hit bone before an artery, this wouldn't work. It wouldn't be strong enough. Ava had taught us that.

James's eyes lit up with horror, and I could swear, the second before the tip connected with him, I saw relief.

Maybe that's just what I wanted to believe. What I needed to believe to keep standing.

He dropped the gun, and Noah and I leapt back, staring at the horror of what I had done. I felt bile rise in my throat, spewing out of my mouth in an instant, my entire body trembling with adrenaline. James's hands flailed about, attempting to grab the spear, trying and failing to pull it loose as blood gushed out at an alarming rate.

Behind me, Noah was out of breath. He kicked the gun farther away from James with his bad leg, then collapsed onto the ground. I forced myself to calm down, squeezing my hands into fists.

I didn't have time to panic. Noah needed me. I pulled my shirt over my head, hurrying toward him and wrapping it around his calf. I applied pressure to the gunshot wound and exit wound at once.

He was paler than usual, his eyes haunted and pained.

"I don't think it hit an artery," I told him, trying not to focus on the sounds of James's gasping, dying breaths behind us. My hands wouldn't stop shaking. I'd killed someone. I'd actually killed someone. "You're going to be okay." I wanted it to be true. Needed it to be true. But I had no idea if it actually was. Harry would know, but Harry was not there. The white shirt stained red under my palms, and I pressed down harder.

His smile was faint, and I knew he was trying to seem braver than he felt. He tilted his chin toward the shirt, breathless. "Is this…your way of returning my gift?"

Tears filled my eyes as I laughed. "You saved me with it, now I'm saving you."

He placed his hands on mine, and I looked up at him, our eyes connecting in a moment of passion. "You're going to be okay," he said, sadness at the edge of his expression.

"I know. We both are. Everything's going to be okay. We just have to get this wound healed up, and you'll be set." I needed him to believe me, but I could see that he didn't.

He gently nudged my hand back from the wound, letting the shirt fall away. Despite my best efforts, the bleeding hadn't slowed. I tried to wrap the shirt back around his leg but he shook his head, stopping me. "Go back to your husband, Katy. Go back home and have a beautiful life. Just...think about me occasionally." He tried to offer a playful smile, but I saw through it.

"What are you talking about?" I shook my head, fighting with him to put the shirt back over the wound. "This is not a fatal wound. The bullet went through your leg. We just have to stop the bleeding, and then it'll heal. Don't talk like that..."

He pushed my hand away again, his face serious. "Even if you get it to stop bleeding, we have no antibiotic supplies, no gauze, no way to sterilize our hands or bandages. Back in the real world, I'd probably be fine. But we aren't in the real world, and I'm not going to make you watch me die a slow, miserable death of blood poisoning or infection. We aren't amputating my leg out here; this isn't *Lost*." He ran a hand over my hair, tucking it behind my ear. "We had a good run, kiddo. I couldn't have asked for a better place, or a better person, to spend my last days with."

Tears poured out of my eyes, my body trembling with grief. "This isn't what I want, Noah. I want you. I want this. You can't die. You can't leave me. Please."

He sniffled, his smile patronizing. "I wouldn't if I had a

choice." He scoffed. "I'd never leave you if I had a choice. But I won't let you watch me die. Not like this." He gestured toward his leg. "I'm sorry. I'm not giving you the choice here. Just..." He looked down. "Can I give you a kiss to remember me?"

I leaned forward, pressing my lips to his as my tears fell against his cheeks. My chest was tight with anguish. I didn't feel capable of withstanding any more loss. How could anyone handle this much pain?

"I don't want to lose you."

He rubbed his nose against mine gently, pressing our foreheads together. "I'm supposed to say something cheesy about how I'll always be in your heart or something, aren't I?"

I laughed through my tears, and when I pulled away, he placed his hand to his mouth, tossing a handful of berries inside of it. "Wait! Not right now! You have to give me time. We need to talk about this... To think it over. You can't just—"

He was already chewing. "If I think about it or talk about it anymore, if I spend one more second with you, I'll change my mind." He swallowed, tossing in another handful and chewing it just as quickly. His eyes filled with new tears, and I wrapped my arms around him, holding him against me as I sobbed.

"I'll never forget you," I swore to him. "Never."

"You'd better not." He kissed my forehead again, pushing me away from him carefully and attempting to stand up.

"Where are you going?" I asked.

"For a swim," he said. "One last time... It's, well, before

I met you, it was my favorite place to be. My favorite thing to do. I want to be in the water when I go." I swallowed, trying to slow my tears. I needed to say so much to him. I needed to hold him. I needed him to hold me.

"Hey," he said, placing a finger under my chin, "you did it. You won. You get to go home now and eat sushi and drink wine and take bubble baths and…probably pay way too much for therapy about all of this." He gave a dry laugh. "You're going to be okay now."

"I would've chosen to stay here with you a thousand times over this."

"I know," he said, "and I would've been selfish and let you. But now…now neither of us have to choose. I think I love you, Katy."

It was the first time he'd ever said those words. "I probably shouldn't say that, but it's my only chance and I want to say it before I die." He hesitated. "Just don't say it back. It's way too early for that… You wouldn't want me to think you're a stage-five clinger or anything."

I snorted through my tears, drying my eyes with the back of my hand as he turned to walk away, touching my shoulder with what I knew would be our last time looking into each other's eyes.

"Do me a favor, okay?" he called when he neared the water, unable to turn around and look at me. I heard the tears he was choking back. "Angelo and Analyn Valencia—my parents. Would you check in on them?"

"I will." I watched as, at my word, he walked far enough out that he could dive and jumped in, popping up to smile at me one last time. From the distance, we couldn't see each other's tears, but there was no doubt they were there. I thought then of all the times he'd jumped into the spring near the falls to pop up and ask if I saw him. "I see you," I whispered, collapsing on the shore as I cried softly, watching him swim out until I couldn't see him anymore. "I think I love you, too."

I SAT on the shore as the sun rose high in the sky, my skin scalding hot under its midday glow. I felt numb and broken all at once. Nothing and everything. I cursed the circumstances, the terrible people who had brought us there, and the fact that I hadn't grabbed onto Noah and loved him as hard as I could and as much as I could while I still had him.

It took me several seconds too long to recognize the noise behind me as footsteps headed toward me, and I spun around, shocked to see the woman standing there, her white clothes and blonde hair blowing in the breeze.

"Hello," she said simply, her hands clasped in front of her. Her smile was small, her bright, green eyes still and calm. In the daylight, I realized she looked to be close to my age and stunning. Her clothes were clean, like I remembered, but these were different than what she'd worn before. How had she managed to find clean clothes?

I scrambled to my feet. "What are you doing here?"

"I came to send you home," she said softly. "Your time here on the island is done." I took in her features—sharp nose, thin lips, the small cleft in her chin—studying her as I tried to make sense of the words.

"What do you mean?"

"You're the last person alive on the island," she said, matter-of-factly. "You won, Katy. Well done."

"I don't understand. You're...you're with them? The men? I thought you were a hostage, too."

She let air out through her nose in a sort of condescending giggle. "No, I'm not a hostage, and neither are you. Not anymore. You're free to go as soon as you'd like. There's a boat waiting for you on the other side of the island. You'll be returned to your port and given one hundred thousand dollars to buy your...*discretion*"—she flashed an evil grin—"about your activities here."

"One hundred thousand..." I tried to catch my breath. "I don't understand. Why are we here? That's it? They just die and I go home, and we all just return to our lives?"

"Exactly," she said simply.

"But why? What are you experimenting on? Why would you do this to us?"

"I don't want you to concern yourself with that," she said. "All you need to know is that your time here is done."

"But who are you? Why are you here? Why am I here?"

There was a pause, and I thought she was going to refuse to answer, but eventually she said, "My name is Ms. Sheridan. And you're here because I picked you."

CHAPTER TWENTY-SEVEN

BEFORE

As with every time before, as we headed out for our vacation, we kept the plan simple.

Each couple boarded the plane separately, each of us taking different flights from different airports to different destinations. There could be no connecting us to one another.

Once we'd arrived in sunny Southwest Florida, we'd rent a car, call an Uber, bike, kayak, or travel by whatever means necessary to our meeting spot.

It was never the same, not the same town or the same type of resort. We'd choose who got to claim first—usually by drawing straws—and decide on an area where we'd choose our picks. There was no preparation for who we'd choose. We each got to spend just a few hours watching them and had to make the decision with our gut more than anything. What the others didn't realize, even Barrett, was that, as a con woman, my gut was often all I had.

By this point, we'd all developed our strategies, and

our game was stronger than ever. I knew this round would be better than ever before. We chose the Keys this time, stopping into nearby bars, restaurants, and resorts to make our selections.

Eve and Kyle picked the man with thick glasses we'd watched for two hours doing nothing but reading books and playing trivia at a tiki bar. He was smart, they'd reasoned, and could get himself further with his knowledge than any form of brute strength.

Amber and Matt had chosen the young girl, beautiful and edgy with her deep almond eyes, ebony skin, and charming smile. They were copying the strategy that had almost won it for me last time, choosing a girl the boys would fall in love with and do anything to protect. Their mistake was choosing someone too young to see reason, someone impulsive.

Of course, Roman chose the youngest man, James, with thick biceps and an angry look we'd seen on full display when he'd nearly gotten into a fight outside of a beachside motel. He was someone anyone with no experience of how our game worked would choose. Someone whose stubbornness and rage would end up getting him killed. It was the third time he'd made the same mistake. Honestly, Roman would never learn strategy. Or maybe he was just hoping his strategy would eventually pay off.

Josie and Dan found their pick—a Southeast Asian man we'd watched playing volleyball for hours on end with a group of players, who'd brushed off anyone who came near him to chat in a passive-aggressive way. They believed he wouldn't make any connections, that he'd keep a clear head and eyes on the goal. Dan was determined to win this year. Besides Roman, they were the only ones who hadn't claimed a victory yet.

And, of course, Barrett and I found our pick, the best of all, at a resort in Key West. She was beautiful and lonely, a deadly combination, and I'd watched her spending most of her time reading books, which I hoped would mean she'd know nearly as much as the trivia man. On top of that, she was older than the youngest girl, meaning she'd have her wits about her. She'd be able to reason, to use her better judgment, and think critically in life-threatening situations.

The next morning, once we'd selected our champions, Roman had some of his staff prepare the boats and the nine of us boarded his private jet, setting off for our island, where we would relax and wait for them to arrive. And sure enough, by the evening, the boat had delivered the five of them to us and the game had begun.

The first day was always fun for me, watching from our television screens as the cameras we had planted around the island showed them struggling to make sense of what had happened. Then, once Dan had delivered the note to their camp, they'd realize what was going on.

They're always reluctant to get the challenge going, so we were used to waiting some time before the first round ended with the death of a pick, the loss of one of the teams. This group, though, they'd been stubborn. The game had lasted over a month longer than the last, making it our longest game yet.

I'd had my doubts about Katy for a bit, wondering if I'd judged her incorrectly, but in the end, the strategy had won out. Dan and Josie's pick, Noah, had fallen hard for her and sacrificed himself. So, while my pick hadn't exactly stormed her way to victory, my gut instinct, to pick someone others would want to protect, had delivered us to the winner's seat and made us four million dollars richer.

That's right, four million dollars. Five if you counted the money we'd put in as well.

The first challenge had happened five years ago, when I was still just Barrett's mistress. He'd loved me, of course, more than anything, but his wife made it impossible for him to leave. Doing so would've cost him everything, his company, his fortune... I couldn't let that happen.

I wrote him a note, the one he still has, the one that he says started it all. That made him feel like he could have true happiness with me.

I can kill your wife for you.

So when he'd first invited me to his island, my initial inclination was to say no—spiders, snakes, and sharks are the top of my *hell no* list, but when he insisted it was time for me to meet his friends, I began to formulate the plan. A week later, we'd spent an evening with his group of friends on their island, him buttering them up for their secrecy about me, and them badgering me about what I did for a living and what sort of car I drove, so I gave them a half-truth.

"I'm an analyst," I told them. In truth, I spent my days analyzing people. Figuring out how to dupe them. And my endeavors had made me rich. Granted, not filthy rich, like Barrett Laguna. Not private jet rich. Not *buy an island online with your four best friends because you're drunk and it's funny* rich. But rich enough, if there was such a thing.

So I spent the night finding the weak spots in the group, figuring out who to coax, where to push, when to let off the gas.

By the end of the night, I knew Roman had an ex-boss he'd like to teach a lesson to. I knew Amber's best friend had slept with her husband years ago and she'd never forgiven her. I knew Kyle had an employee who'd lost him nearly a billion in a deal gone wrong. I knew there was a client threatening to sue Josie for so much, her practice might go under. And, of course, I knew Barrett had a wife who desperately needed to be taken out of the picture.

So, with a push here and a prod there, I'd goaded them into imagining how funny it would be to put all five of our enemies into a room and watch them fight to the death.

"Gina would die if she couldn't have her oat milk latte by nine a.m.," Amber said.

"Darren's fat ass would die without air conditioning," Kyle joked.

I let the conversation carry for a bit before adding the final element, the thing I knew it would need to work. I enticed them with the one thing no one in that room could say no to: money.

"We could make it interesting," I'd said calmly, slowly, as if it didn't matter to me much at all. "We'd each put in a million. Winner takes all."

There'd been uneasy laughter from each of them, and a general sense of impossibility.

"But wouldn't it be nice," one of them had said. I forget now who it was. I didn't say much else. I'd dropped the bomb, created the niggle in their brains, and I'd walk away. If I was any good at what I did—spoiler alert: I was *damn* good—we'd be laying the plan into motion within a year.

The next month, Barrett got the call. They wanted to know if we could actually make it work. If I was serious.

I told them I was. Deadly so.

Six months, and a million dollar loss later, my husband's wife was dead, and I'd just stumbled into my biggest win yet.

I took on many different names in my profession, Ms. Sheridan, Ms. Danes, Erica Spelling, Noelle Barton, Ms. Smith... The list went on. But my favorite name, the one I'd take the most pride in for the rest of my life, was the one I'd taken on a year after that day, when I became Mrs. Jessica Laguna—part-time con woman, full-time love of his life.

The next summer, they were ready to do it again. Strangers, this time. Roman needed to prove to Kyle he wasn't going to lose to him so easily. And so, the tradition was born.

Win or lose, I never cared. As a con artist, I'd pulled off the biggest con of all already. I'd gotten the man and his fortune. The rest was just icing on the cake.

CHAPTER TWENTY-EIGHT

PRESENT DAY

Ms. Sheridan had me follow her across the shore, walking several feet in front of me, her arms swinging at her sides as if this were just another sunny day in her life, and not the worst of mine.

As we made our way around the island, losing sight of our campsite and the only home I'd known for what felt like so long, I began to see the end of a boat. This was different from the one that had brought me here, and I briefly felt fear, rather than the relief I'd been expecting.

I didn't think I'd ever be able to set foot on a boat again after this.

"Will you be riding back with me?" I called ahead.

"Oh, no. I have other ways of going home. No, you'll be taken back with some of our employees." She slowed her stride slightly as we grew closer, and I saw her glance back at me. "And don't worry about the bodies. Our employees will clean them up, and no one will ever know you were involved in any of this."

I shuddered at the way she'd phrased that. "I didn't mean to do it... I didn't have a choice."

"Oh, sweetie," she said, sickly sweet, though we were the same age and she didn't need to use pet names for me, "I know that. Of course, I do. I'm not faulting you for what happened. I'm just glad you survived."

She stopped when the boat had come into full view. "And"—her voice was lower now—"just between us, I know you wouldn't, but I want to make sure you understand you can never tell anyone what happened over here. Not about the people you were with or that this place even exists. If your family, your friends, or anyone else asks where you were or what happened, you're to tell them you were lost at sea after a storm and that a ship found you, alone, and returned you home. If they ask too many questions, deflect. Tell them you don't have any memory of what happened. Tell them the crew that returned you didn't speak English and sailed away after they dropped you back off at the resort. Whatever you do, you must refuse to tell anyone the truth. The crew will have you ride home below deck so you can't tell which direction you came from, just in case you were to have any funny ideas." She smiled. "But I don't think that'll be an issue, will it? You're a smart girl."

There was something empty behind her eyes. Cold. It chilled me more than anything else that had happened. Whatever was going on here, I wanted no part of it.

"I won't say anything."

"Good. I'd just hate for you to get into trouble. You understand. And, when you arrive, you'll be given the hundred thousand in cash for all your troubles. Just don't spend it all in one place." I felt sick to my stomach watching her smile and laugh as if everything could be solved with money. As if heartbreak had a price tag.

"What about the police? The news stations? Won't someone want to know how I got back to shore?"

She waved off the concern. "Oh, we're friends with some very powerful people. We've taken care of it and made sure no one even knows you were gone. And those who do won't be able to get anywhere with their theories." She winked. "Come on now, we've got to get you on your way. I'm sure you're dying to get home. No pun intended." Her smile spread too wide, her teeth too white behind pale, pink lips. "I know I am."

"Why did you help me?" I asked, it being the question I couldn't stop thinking about.

"Because, my dear, I wanted you to win." She said it so simply, as if that made any sense to me, but before I could ask anything else, she gestured behind me. "I'm sorry, you'll have to go now. We really do have to keep on a schedule. I have a flight to catch."

I looked away, stepping onto the small boat that would take me to the larger one that would take me home. A man helped me on board without a word. Did he know what was going on? Was he in on it, too?

The engine started up, and he steered me toward the larger boat. Once I was on board, he shuffled me toward the lower deck, and I glanced toward the island one last time with tears in my eyes.

I will never forget you, I vowed silently to the friends I was leaving behind and the place that would shape the rest of my life.

The man nudged me forward gently without a word, and I went where he guided me, walking into a dark room with no windows. He departed from the room and shut the door behind him. I heard the engine rev up and closed my eyes, resting against a nearby wall. I'd be on the boat for hours ahead, just like the ride in had taken, but this journey would be made completely alone.

I thought back to the boat ride in, unable to keep my mind from drifting there, and saw Noah's face, the way he'd smiled at me the first day, remembered the way he and Ava had danced together, the way James had chatted and laughed with the bartender, and Harry had sat alone with his book, drinking beer and staring out on the horizon. How would I ever explain to Ned the way these people had shaped me? What they meant to me now?

The time passed slowly, the boat's rocking making me seasick, the near-silence deafening after a month or more with the ocean's roar as a constant source of noise. But eventually, I heard the engine shut off, heard the sounds of people all around, and I saw the light peek through the crack of the door.

The noise was louder then. Music. Voices. We'd reached our port. I heard a DJ talking on a microphone, children laughing as they played, and seagulls cawing overhead.

The man led me toward the edge of the boat, where I could disembark via a metal ramp. He handed me a backpack when I reached the dock and climbed back on board without a word. Within seconds, the boat was pulling away, and I was alone.

Alone, yet surrounded by thousands of people.

Every noise was loud and frightening, and I kept worrying that everyone I passed would recognize me or begin to ask questions. How was I supposed to go back to normal after this?

I made my way toward the bar with the loud DJ and approached the counter. It took the bartender a while to notice me and, when he did, he didn't attempt to hide his grimace. "Can I help you?"

"Do you have a phone I could borrow?" He looked me up and down, and I knew what I must look like. Hairy, dingy, and dirty, with blood still caked under my fingernails, unwashed hair, and a bathing suit bleached by the sun and permanently filthy. If I were in his position, I may not have wanted to help either.

"Nah," he said, pointing in the opposite direction than I'd come from. "Check with the hotel."

I nodded, slinking away from him and turning around when someone caught my arm. I spun around, my body on fire as I prepared to fight.

The older woman released me, her smile kind, and she held out her phone. "Do you need to call someone? I'm sorry, I overheard…"

"Really?" I asked, shocked by the generosity. "Thank you." I took the phone from her, dialing Ned's phone number, thankful it was one of the only ones I had memorized.

"I was once where you are," she said, slipping me a twenty-dollar bill and a card that said **Jesus loves you!** "You've gotta get off the drugs, honey. That's no life for a pretty girl like you."

I smiled politely, thankful that she only took me for an

addict and not a murderer, and placed the phone to my ear. "Thank you," I repeated as the phone began to ring.

I heard the line click, heard his heavy breath, heard him say, "Hello?"

My heart skipped a beat, tears filling my eyes as I sank to a squatting position, the weight of everything I'd been through crashing into me. "Ned? It's...it's me."

CHAPTER TWENTY-NINE

The woman booked me a hotel room, making me swear I wouldn't use it to get high, and left me to my devices. I was numb as I took my shower, letting the water wash over me. I scrubbed the blood from my fingernails and tossed out the dry-rotting bikini, only then remembering that our phones, my Kindle, and Harry's book were somewhere on the island. I supposed the employees would clean that up, too.

Without any clothes to wear, I wrapped up in the sheet from the bed, sitting on the edge of the mattress and staring at the clock. Ned's flight would've already landed, and he'd be on his way to me.

I dreaded seeing him, as bad as that sounded. Only because I still hadn't made sense of my feelings or how I would explain it all to him. I looked at the backpack on the floor. I hadn't been able to open it yet. The money didn't matter to me. We were okay, we didn't need it, and it in no way accounted for the cost of their lives.

The very idea of them buying my silence was sickening.

But if she'd meant what she'd said, about their powerful friends, I had to be careful about my path forward. A knock sounded at the door and I stood, my body tense.

I walked across the room in a trance and swung it open. Ned stood before me, tears already in his eyes. He gasped and looked down at his phone.

"When you texted me the room number from that phone number... I was worried it was a prank. I was worried this was all a prank. I...didn't think you'd actually be here."

We fell into each other's arms, shutting the door as he came into the room. I gripped him as tight as I could, sobs ricocheting through my chest with ferocity. His strong arms held me, his chest shaking against mine as he wept.

When we broke apart, he put his hands on either side of my head, brushing my hair out of my face. "My god, where were you? What happened? I never thought I'd see you again, Katy... My Katy Kat..."

"I was taken..." I said, starting at the beginning and relaying the whole story. I left nothing out, though I glazed over my feelings for Noah and our night together as I saw the pain in Ned's eyes. I just needed to get it out. All of it. I couldn't hold the weight of it alone anymore.

When I'd told him everything, we sat in silence, him processing all that I'd told him as I did the same. "How long was I gone?" I asked finally.

"A little over two months," he said, his voice powerless.

"When you left, I called the police, but they weren't help-ful. They kept saying that there were no leads. Nothing. No one had seen a thing. I called you and called you and called you, and… I'm so sorry I wasn't there. I'm so sorry I didn't protect you." He kissed my forehead, his touch tender as he pulled me in for another hug.

"You never gave up on me?" I squeaked, desperately needing to know the answer to that question.

"I hired a private investigator a month in when I'd heard nothing. I thought, well *he thought,* and he half convinced me that you'd run off with someone else. We'd been fighting, and I wasn't doing enough… I thought you'd left me."

I rested my head on his shoulder, breathing in the scent of him. "I never thought I'd see you again."

"I thought I'd lost you." He kissed my forehead again, then my lips, and his kiss felt wrong. I pulled away, but he didn't seem to mind. Instead, he wrapped me in his arms and lay down across the bed, the two of us bundled under the sheets as I felt my breathing slow, my heart calm.

"I don't know how I'm going to handle this," I told him. "I'm falling apart."

"You don't have to deal with it alone. I'm here for you."

"I'm sorry about Noah," I said, though I wasn't sure what I was apologizing for. Sleeping with him or falling for him. Maybe both.

"Shh." He rubbed my arm gently. "We don't have to worry about that right now. Let's just be here. Rest. We'll deal with everything else once we're home. Just rest."

At his command, I closed my eyes, great relief washing

over me as I realized how tired I felt, how close to sleep I was. The bed felt wrong—too soft, too comfortable—as I drifted to sleep. Somehow, even there, I could hear the crashing ocean waves ringing in my ears.

CHAPTER THIRTY

ONE YEAR LATER

I carried my daughter across the living room as my phone buzzed, picking it up and staring at the phone number on the screen. My pulse quickened, breathing slowed.

Over the last year, I'd never given up on finding the people who'd done this to me. The woman and the two men from the cliff house who had ruined my life. I'd used part of the money they'd given me to hire a professional sketch artist and had them craft a drawing of the woman, every bit of her features down to the freckle next to her eyebrow. I'd memorized them for a reason.

Ned had begged me to give it up. The private investigator had found nothing. The police had all but called me crazy, stating that there were no missing persons reports for anyone matching the descriptions I'd given them for Noah, Harry, James, and Ava. The woman had been right. When all else failed, I'd posted the woman's sketch online, hoping someone somewhere might have a lead.

KIERSTEN MODGLIN

That was three months ago, just after giving birth to our daughter. Ned had never mentioned the fact that her hair color didn't match either of ours, or that her features didn't match our own. He loved her just the same, but still, I'd vowed to get revenge on the people who ended her father's life. I owed him that much.

Still, in three months, we'd received no real leads. Until that morning when a detective from Georgia had reached out and asked me to call him back. I'd missed him when I did, but the number on the screen was him again.

I set Cara down, sliding my thumb across the screen and placing the phone to my ear.

"Hello?"

"Hi, is this Mrs. Katy Corbeil?"

I nodded slowly, then realized he couldn't see my nod and replied. "Yes."

"This is Detective Armbruster with the Chatham County Police Department. I'm calling about a photo you posted online. Is now a good time to chat?"

"Yes," I squeaked out again.

"I've been leading an investigation into a woman I believe is conning people out of large sums of money around this area. One of the men who was duped by this woman, she got him for a deposit on a wedding, pretending to be a famous event planner... He saw your picture on social media and forwarded it to me. He believes this is the woman who did it. I wondered if I might be able to come to wherever you are so I could ask you some questions about her."

"Sure," I said, hardly managing to breathe, let alone

speak. He asked where I'd be able to meet, and I told him the name of a restaurant in downtown Nashville, somewhere busy and crowded, where there'd be witnesses if something were to happen.

I'd become more cautious thanks to the island. I now knew of the dangers all around me, even in places where I should've felt safe.

We hung up the phone, and I picked my daughter back up, kissing her soft, black hair and making my way into the kitchen with a racing mind.

"We're one step closer, sweetheart," I promised her.

She stared up at me, her eyes wide and innocent, so unaware of the darkness that existed just outside our doors.

That evening, when Ned came home, he kissed my head and patted Cara's tiny hand before answering a phone call and darting up to the office, one finger in the air. I sighed, placing his plate in the microwave to keep it warm as I began to feed Cara her dinner.

Once we'd both finished eating, Ned's voice still droning on from the office upstairs, I laid Cara down in her play yard and carried his plate up the stairs.

"No, we're going to have to come in at least under ten percent, or we're toast," he told whoever was on the phone. "No way. Evans would have our asses." He chuckled. "You got that right."

I pushed open the door, knocking cautiously as I did it and held up his plate. *Thank you,* he mouthed, making room on his desk for food by scooting some manila folders over and laying a stack of papers on top of them.

I stood waiting, knowing he was expecting me to leave. He glanced up at me, his brows up as if to say *what?* and I smiled, waiting patiently for him to hang up. He sighed, spinning around in his chair and putting his other hand to the phone. "Listen, Travis, let me call you back in just a sec." He paused. "Yep. You too, buddy." He laid his phone on his desk. "Sorry, sweetheart. Busy day." I watched as he rubbed his palms together, looking over his plate. "This looks delicious."

"Thank you. Listen, we need to talk." I eased myself into the chair in the corner of his office.

His face grew ashen, obviously caught off guard. He shot up. "Is something wrong? Is it Cara?"

I raised my hands chest-level, trying to fend off his worry. "It's not Cara. Everything's fine. It's just…I heard from a detective today."

He let out a heavy breath. "Okay…and?"

"They think they may have found her. The woman from the island."

He was up again. "They did? Do they have her in custody? Where is she?"

"They don't have her in custody. They just want me to meet with a detective and answer some questions. I'm meeting him tomorrow for lunch. I was hoping you could come."

"Yeah, of course," he said without a moment's hesitation. "But I don't understand. Is it one of the detectives we've already spoken to? Do they have more questions?"

"No, it's about a different case. Someone recognized my photo online. They think she may be a con woman."

He furrowed his brow. "Are you sure it isn't just

someone pranking you again? I mean, how many
messages have you gotten saying something similar from
someone with a username like hairymashedpotates42?"

I groaned. "This was a phone call with an actual detective. And when I returned his call, it was to an actual police station."

"Yeah, but how easy would that be to fake, you know?"
He sat down on the edge of his desk, watching me carefully. "Honey, you know I want you to find out the truth
about what happened. I know you want justice for your
friends and for what you went through, but it's time to
take a break. It's time to heal and move on. We've been
doing this for more than a year."

"But this time is different! This time—"

"Yeah, and last time was too!" His tone was exasperated. I'd exhausted him, and I didn't know how to stop.
"What's so different this time than any of the other
times?"

"None of them were real!" I shouted. "But this one
might be. Don't you get that? Don't you get why I can't let
this go?"

He hesitated. "No," came the final answer. "Truth be
told, no I don't. When you were gone, it destroyed me. I
thought I'd never see you again. I prayed for you to come
home. Come back to me. And here you are. You came
back. That's all I wanted. I don't understand why you can't
just accept how lucky you are and move on—"

"Because they're dead—"

"And justice won't bring them back!" he bellowed, then
instantly lowered his voice. "I'm sorry. I'm sorry. I don't
want to yell at you, but this crusade you're on is going to

get you killed. If these people are as powerful as you say they are, you can't keep doing this. I went along with it in the beginning because I thought it was what you needed, but I have to draw the line somewhere." His heavy breaths warned of his frustration. "I know that this is important to you, but I can't believe these people would stick their necks out for you, Katy. They're practically strangers to you. And I know you loved the one, and god knows I've tried to be understanding about it, but how much longer are you going to make me compete with a dead man?"

Tears stung my eyes at his harsh words, the even harsher reality. I sniffled, standing up and turning to walk out of his office.

"Katy, wait!" He realized he'd gone a step too far and reached out for me, but I shrugged him off.

"I just need a minute." I pulled open the door and shut it, letting myself back out into the dark hallway. I pressed my back against the wall, trying to catch my breath as his words replayed in my head.

He didn't understand. He'd never understand. No one would.

No one except the people who'd lived through it with me, and they were gone. I half expected him to chase after me, but after a painful minute of silence, I heard his voice again.

"Travis, hey, sorry, I had to take care of something. Do you still have that report pulled up?"

Exhaustion, frustration, and heartbreak reeled through me, and I closed my eyes, thinking the thought that had haunted me for over a year now every time Ned let me down. *Noah would've never done that.*

I knew he was right. That he was competing with a man who had no place in the competition, but I was powerless to control the way I felt. Cara cried out from the living room, and I dried my tears quickly, walking back to her and pretending everything was okay.

CHAPTER THIRTY-ONE

The next day, I met with the detective. Ned sat by my side, still and stony, listening as I recounted my time on the island for what felt like the hundredth time. As always, I blamed James's death on an accident, where he'd fallen onto the spear during a fight. But other than that, everything stayed totally truthful. Ned held Cara, bouncing her when she got particularly fussy and holding my hand whenever I began to cry.

The detective asked me questions about the woman's name—*Ms. Sheridan was all I knew*—her role in what had happened—*I didn't know exactly, but it felt like she was their leader*—and what kind of boat they'd picked me up with and brought me home in. I knew nothing about boats, so he had me describe both boats to him the best that I could, and I did. He told me that, if my person and the woman he was looking for were the same, he would keep me posted on any updates.

We were done within a half hour, him prying information out of me and giving me basically none. We walked to my Toyota Camry and Ned buckled Cara into her car seat before kissing my lips stiffly and heading for his own.

"I'll see you at dinner," he called with a wave over his head, already on his phone before I could answer.

I started the car, the emotions fresh and raw all over again as I sat there trying to compose myself. Had Ned not noticed the tears in my eyes when he walked away? Or did he just not care anymore? Had my grief reached the limit he'd set for me? Some days, as he ignored more and more of my pain, that was how it felt.

Two weeks went by without a word, and I assumed that would be the end of it. But then the phone rang, and I recognized the number.

"Hello?" I said before I'd even gotten the phone to my ear.

"We've found the island, Katy," he said, and I could hear the grin in his voice from there.

Adrenaline coursed through me, cold chills lining my arms. I reached for the arm of the sofa, sitting down before I collapsed.

"We found the island," he repeated. "We've found them all."

"Are...are you sure?" It felt too good to be true. How was it possible?

"I think so. I need you to fly out with me to confirm it's the place, but I'm almost positive. I'm still waiting on a warrant, but once we get it, we'll have clearance to go.

How does that sound? I know it'll be tough for you to revisit a place with such terrible memories…"

"How…how did you find it?" I asked through my tears.

"Well, it wasn't easy. I contacted every bar, hotel, or restaurant nearby where you'd said you were dropped off. All of the ones in that specific area either didn't have surveillance footage at all or didn't have any going back that far, but we finally found one a few miles up the coast that did. On the tapes, we saw a boat that matched the description you gave sailing in around the time you were dropped off. It was a long shot, but we took a chance and looked up who it belonged to—a Mr. Roman Bloom. We began looking into him and found out he has—get this— an *island* deeded to him off the coast of Florida. I did a bit more digging and discovered that Mr. Bloom is not the sole owner, but that he's co-owner with four other people, one of them being a Mr. Barrett Laguna. Barrett Laguna's first wife disappeared almost five years to the day from the time you disappeared. She was never found. His second wife, however, a Mrs. Jessica Laguna, is completely absent from social media, but I did manage to pull up a picture of their wedding from Barrett's Face-book. She matches the sketch you had made almost perfectly."

The room was spinning and Cara was beginning to fuss, but I couldn't breathe.

"Katy? Are you there? Did you hear all of that?"

"I'm here… I just…wow. I can't believe it."

"Believe it," he said. "We're going to get justice for your friends. And for everyone else these people have wronged. And it's all because of you."

I smiled through my tears, feeling my heart fill with the first bit of true hope and joy I'd been able to feel in so long.

"So, what's next?" I asked, sniffling. "What do we do?"

"We wait. I need you to stay by the phone until I get the warrant to search the island, and then I'll call you with the location for the chopper. Your husband is more than welcome to come with you. You'll be under police protection the entire time, totally safe, but I understand this won't be easy and I want you to have whatever support you need."

"Thank you."

"Okay, sit tight, Katy. I'll be in touch soon." With that, the call ended and I stared at the screen in complete and utter disbelief.

I hadn't given up, and it had worked.

I was going back.

Please. Please. Please.

CHAPTER THIRTY-TWO

A week later, I was in a police helicopter, Detective Armbruster on one side and Ned on the other.

He'd filled me in on the plan. That detectives were tracking down the four co-owners of the island to bring them in for questioning. He told me how the warrant had given them permission to search every bit of the island, that they'd bring in cadaver dogs and search every square inch, not just for my friends, but for anything else nefarious that might be there.

He told me how the man who'd found me, a Tom from Savannah, Georgia, was going to be identifying Jessica as the woman who'd stolen from him and, if I could identify her as well, they believed she could have charges brought against her for both crimes, if not more.

But first, all they needed was for me to confirm that this island was *the* island. I gripped Ned's hand tightly, my stomach in knots as we flew over the ocean. I tried not to look down, tried not to think about the last time I'd made this journey—albeit by sea, not air.

When I laid eyes on the island, seeing the aerial view for the first time, I gasped. I saw the falls from there, the cliff where Harry had died. I saw the top of the cliff house, an entire side of it previously unknown to me, that hadn't been built into the cliff and looked like an actual house. On the far side, there were four small boat slips with matching boats in them, and farther down, there was a landing strip for what must've been a private plane or jet, though neither was there.

There had been so much on the island that we had no idea about, confined to our small campsite on the beach.

If we'd explored more, could we have found the plane or the boats? Could we have escaped or radioed for help? The questions haunted me. Why didn't we try harder?

The helicopter began to descend, ready to land on a clear patch of beach as it threw sand up everywhere, creating a funnel cloud of sugary-white. I heard the engine cut off, and we waited for the two others to land before our door was thrown open. The detective climbed out first, holding out his hand for me to come with him. I did, Ned following closely behind me.

I tried to hold back the tears, my upper lip curling as I walked along the sand. I nodded, telling him this was it without the words I couldn't seem to muster. Police were swarming now. I saw another helicopter flying across the island, headed for the house. We walked along the sandy shores, and I saw that James's body had indeed been removed, all signs of its existence wiped clear. Our campsite was gone, too. All traces of the home we'd built had been removed.

"House is clear," I heard a voice say over a radio. I

needed to take them to Harry's grave. To tell them where James's body had been when we left. There was so much I needed to do, but all I wanted was to stare at the water, to feel the sand between my toes, to have a final goodbye to my friends and—

I stopped short, my breath catching.

Please. Please. Please.

I tried to make sense of what I was seeing. The detective had seen it, too. *Him*, too. A flash of skin beyond the trees. The detective reached for his gun, but I shook my head.

"No," I said, my voice barely a whisper. Time stood still as I watched him emerge from beyond the trees, brilliant dark hair, bare tanned chest. He walked with a limp, but the wound had healed.

He made it. Somehow, some way, he actually made it.

He squinted, his hand over his eyes, and I watched the recognition flood his face. I looked back at my husband, an uncertain yet somehow knowing look in his eyes, then forward at the man I believed had given his life for me. Noah looked dumbstruck for a moment, then crossed his arms over his chest, a smug grin growing on his face. I saw the tears glinting in his eyes even from where I stood.

"Do you know him?" Detective Armbruster asked, his gun still at the ready.

"I do," I whispered, tears filling my own eyes. "It's Noah… He's alive."

I didn't know how it was possible. In fact, I was sure it was impossible. But it was true. All that mattered was that it was true.

Now, as I look back on that day, I know that Harry

had been wrong about one thing during our stay. The berries he'd told Ava were poison hadn't been, or at least hadn't been enough to kill Noah. I now know the story of how he floated back to the shore after our captors' plane had taken off, how, by some miracle, his wound healed and he managed to make a shelter near the waterfall. How he'd waited a year for someone, anyone, to find him. I know that he spent every day thinking of me. Loving me. Expecting and hoping I'd return for him someday. Or, at the very least, hoping I'd have a good life because of him.

But back then, that day, I didn't know any of that. Except that I had a choice to make, and I was ready to make it. It was the same choice that Noah had given me in nearly that same spot a year ago. *Him or me?* This time, I didn't have to think. I didn't have to weigh my options. Finally, I knew what I wanted. I looked back toward Ned just once, an apology in my eyes.

And then, barreling toward Noah as fast as my legs would carry me in the burning hot sand, I chose.

ENJOYED THE MISSING?

If you enjoyed this story, please consider leaving me a quick review. It doesn't have to be long—just a few words will do. Who knows? Your review might be the thing that encourages a future reader to take a chance on my work!
To leave a review, please visit:
mybook.to/MissingKModglin

Let everyone know how much you loved
The Missing on Goodreads:
https://bit.ly/3uC0gIw

DON'T MISS THE NEXT RELEASE FROM KIERSTEN MODGLIN

Thank you so much for reading this story. I'd love to invite you to sign up for my mailing list and text alerts so we can be sure you don't miss my next release.

Sign up for my mailing list here:
http://eepurl.com/dhiRRv
Sign up for my text alerts here:
www.kierstenmodglinauthor.com/textalerts.html

ACKNOWLEDGMENTS

If I were stuck on an island, it would be this group of loving, brilliant, and patient individuals I would want stuck there with me. (Sorry, not sorry, friends!) I owe them all my thanks.

First and foremost, to my amazing husband and beautiful little girl—thank you for loving me and believing in me every step of the way. No one sees the ins and outs of this process like you two and I'm so grateful to have you by my side as we navigate this twisted, amazing journey.

To my friend, Emerald O'Brien—thank you for being my biggest cheerleader and sounding board. I don't know what publishing a book looked like before you came into my life and I never want to go back to those days. I'm forever thankful for your insights, encouragement, and unwavering support.

To my immensely talented editor, Sarah West—I'm always grateful to have you on my team, but with this book in particular, you were nothing short of a godsend. Thank you for working so hard to improve every story I bring you and for never batting an eye at my wild schedule.

To the proofreading team at My Brother's Editor—I'm so grateful to work with your powerhouse team! Thank you for polishing each book until it shines and for always giving me that final boost of encouragement before it reaches readers.

To my #KMod Squad—*yep, I'm taking all of y'all on the island, deal with it*. Seriously though, I'm so humbled and honored by your support every single day. Thank you for cheering on each new release, for loving my characters and their stories as much as I do, for the reviews, the tags on social media, the recommendations to friends, the emails, the comments, and for being the best fans in the world.

To my agent, Carly Watters—thank you for being a champion for my books and for me. Thank you for believing in their potential and helping me to reach new heights and achieve my dreams.

To Katy Corbeil and Jessica Laguna—readers who won a chance to be written as characters in this book. Thank you for trusting me. I had so much fun writing you both into this world and I hope you loved your characters!

Last but certainly not least, to you—thank you for reading this story. I spent many long nights creating this world, these characters, and their suspenseful and, at times, heartbreaking story. During those long writing sessions, I'd often think about what my readers would feel during certain parts or about certain characters. What they'd take away from certain moments. Who they'd hate.

Who they'd love. If they'd feel anger, hurt, or betrayal right along with these characters. I thought of you, Dear Reader, and what your journey would be with Katy and the others. No matter how you ended up feeling— whether you loved or hated it—I offer you my sincerest thanks for supporting my art and my career. If you look close enough at each of my stories, there's always a lesson that can be found. I think with this one, the lesson was this: I, like Noah's Lola, believe we are stronger together. I'm so thankful you decided to take this trip with me.

ABOUT THE AUTHOR

Kiersten Modglin is an Amazon Top 30 bestselling author of award-winning psychological suspense novels and a member of International Thriller Writers. Kiersten lives in Nashville, Tennessee with her husband, daughter, and their two Boston Terriers: Cedric and Georgie. She is best known for her unpredictable suspense and her readers have dubbed her 'The Queen of Twists.' A Netflix addict, Shonda Rhimes super-fan, psychology fanatic, and indoor enthusiast, Kiersten enjoys rainy days spent with her nose in a book.

Sign up for Kiersten's newsletter here:
http://eepurl.com/b3cNFP
Sign up for text alerts from Kiersten here:
www.kierstenmodglinauthor.com/textalerts.html

www.kierstenmodglinauthor.com
www.facebook.com/kierstenmodglinauthor
www.facebook.com/groups/kmodsquad

ALSO BY KIERSTEN MODGLIN

STANDALONE NOVELS

Becoming Mrs. Abbott

The List

The Missing Piece

Playing Jenna

The Beginning After

The Better Choice

The Good Neighbors

The Lucky Ones

I Said Yes

The Mother-in-Law

The Dream Job

The Liar's Wife

My Husband's Secret

The Perfect Getaway

The Arrangement

The Roommate

Just Married

THE MESSES SERIES

The Cleaner (The Messes, #1)

The Healer (The Messes, #2)

The Liar (The Messes, #3)

The Prisoner (The Messes, #4)

NOVELLAS

The Long Route: A Lover's Landing Novella

The Stranger in the Woods: A Crimson Falls Novella

THE LOCKE INDUSTRIES SERIES

The Nanny's Secret

Made in the USA
Coppell, TX
06 July 2021

58478183R00184